"I AM _____ **O "**

"I hol_____
Apollo _____ d
the Lord of the Sun. Phoebus Apollo."

"Great Diana," began Virgil, raising his head, "where is your divine brother and why should two humble mortals be needed to find him?"

"My brother acted against the will of great Jupiter. He illumined men's minds, permitting them to unbind some small portion of the force that causes the sun to burn."

"Nuclear power!" I exclaimed.

"He has been heavily punished by being made mortal. And he has no memory of being a god. In every age, he dies a tragic death."

"In every age? What do you mean?" I asked.

"He is living and dying throughout what you call time. You must begin at the beginning and try to find him. At night, when I reign, I will carry your spirits back through time and you will seek out my brother. If you can cause him to recover his divine nature, Apollo will again command the light. If you fail, Phoebus Apollo cannot resume control of the power that your people play with as a child may play with the mane of a sleeping lion. And the lion will awake. On the day dedicated to me he will devour the child."

Diana left us then and we just sat there for a time. Finally, I said to Virgil, "Just to be sure I got it right, what she said was that if we don't find her brother the human race is going to be destroyed by nuclear power."

"That's what she said."

"On the day dedicated to her. When's that?"

"The ides of August. August thirteenth. Six days from now. . . ."

MICHAEL LAHEY
QUEST FOR APOLLO

DAW BOOKS, INC.
DONALD A. WOLLHEIM, PUBLISHER

1633 Broadway, New York, NY 10019

First Printing, August 1989

1 2 3 4 5 6 7 8 9

PRINTED IN THE U.S.A.

To Patsy,
who thought I could.

I
▪

I think it takes some doing to get lost in the woods in Tuscany. There are paths and huts and old fences—people coming and going for three thousand years at least. You have to be pretty stupid, and that figured, because I had a dumb reason for being there. My whole situation called for some deep thought, but I could have stayed in my *pensione* in Florence, or gone down by the banks of the Arno on a nice park bench. Now night was falling, I was going in circles and that damn stray dog was getting closer. He'd been howling for half an hour, just like a wolf, but of course there are no wolves in the Tuscan woods. Probably some big old German shepherd, abandoned by someone who couldn't keep him and didn't have the heart to have him put away. Could be worse than a wolf.

"Help! Is anyone there?"

You're in Italy, jerk.

"Aiuto! C'e' qualcuno?"

Not a sound. If anything, the trees seemed to draw more closely and darkly around me, and my shouting had silenced the birds and even seemed to silence the leaves. I had time to turn very slowly all the way around, peering as far as I could in every direction through the bushes and branches, before I heard the howling again—this time very close. I got out my knife. How did Jack London do it? He thrust his forearm into the wolf's jaws . . . I put the knife back into its sheath in order to pull off my sweater—I was going to wrap it around my forearm. Just when I had it up around my eyes and ears, someone tapped me on the back. I spun around.

A soft but rich English voice said, "Did you call for help?"

I took up where I had left off with my sweater, and when I finally got it off I saw that the voice belonged to a smartly-dressed man of medium height and undefinable age—anywhere from fifty to eighty. Fifty, because his skin was healthy looking and his eyes were clear and bright. Eighty, because his curly hair was thin and snow-white, and there was a general brittleness about him.

"Yes, I was calling for help," I said.

"You seem to have managed on your own."

I stared at him. He was definitely referring to the sweater. British humor.

"Yes. Well, no, really I'm a bit lost, and there was that wolf . . ."

"You're lost! And you heard a she-wolf!" The old fellow was obviously quite pleased.

"I don't know what kind of wolf . . ." I began to say, still looking around uncomfortably.

"A she-wolf, a she-wolf," the man insisted. "She drives people here. But don't worry, she doesn't really exist."

"I heard a she-wolf that doesn't really exist."

"She exists . . . allegorically. In you, essentially. Do you know what that means?"

"Yes. I mean, I know what allegory means."

"That's encouraging. And how old are you?"

When strangers ask personal questions it's because they're taking a survey or trying to sell you something or worse, but this time my shields didn't go up; I was interested enough in the old fellow to be willing to trade some information. "Thirty-five," I answered, and those bright eyes of his opened wide. "And how old are you?" I continued.

"Fifty. I'm fifty, after a fashion. But let's get back to you, if you don't mind. I know I'm being dreadfully forward, but these preliminaries are unfortunately quite necessary. Do you suppose you could tell me . . ."

"Preliminaries to what?"

"To . . . to some sort of experience, it's always different. There now, you're curious, aren't you? I beg of you, allow your curiosity to have the better of your natural diffidence, and answer my questions. Harmless questions, really. Either nothing will come of them, or they will lead you to an . . . enriching adventure. Now please, could you tell me what it is that you do for a living?"

This was not exactly my favorite question, but I was less embarrassed about answering it with this oddball than I normally was. He couldn't smirk at me any more than I was smirking at him.

"I'm a . . . writer. I'm doing . . . research for a novel. And what do you do for . . ."

"Splendid! Bravo! The most appropriate sort, I've always felt. Certainly the most congenial."

"You're English, aren't you?" I was sure the question was superfluous.

"No, of course not, dear fellow, and neither are you—you're American, as I suspected you would be. The new empire! All very fitting. But now," here he got very grim, "I must ask you your name. Such silliness. They love to play with names."

The old fellow had the candor of a true gentleman even if he wasn't English, and I had been disarmed by it.

"Alderini," I said hopefully.

"Alderini! Jolly good!"

I was getting caught up in the man's excitement. I really wanted to go all the way for him.

"Fred Alderini!" I said.

The man seemed to get very old and crumpled.

"Fred!" he moaned. "Such silliness!" Then he raised his eyes to the sky and began speaking in some strange Italian dialect. Any dialect at all would sound strange in Tuscany, because the Tuscan dialect *is* standard Italian, but the old man's dialect was really weird. Very old, full of archaisms. I couldn't get the gist of it. I stood respectfully by until he finished. Then he turned, took another long look at me, and sighed.

"You would have been fine, I'm sure. Well, I will show you how to get back to the road. You've got a car parked there, I presume?"

"Yes, a little blue Fiat. I'm staying in Florence, and today I thought I'd rent a car and see the countryside . . ."

He had begun shuffling off, with me tagging behind. I wasn't about to let this remarkable guy just walk out of my life. He could be a novel just waiting to be written. A salable novel. Comedy, tragedy, fantasy—I didn't know yet.

"Sir, may I ask you a few questions?" I said as we walked along.

"After my rather rude interrogation, I suppose the least I can do is answer your questions."

"Where are you from? I couldn't recognize your dialect."

"I'm from what was then Cisalpine Gaul—a village called Andes, near Mantua. And my dialect is the mother of all the Romance languages and dialects, my boy."

What do you do in these cases? You play along.

"Cisalpine Gaul?" I said.

"Later incorporated into Italy, of course. One of the reasons we lost our farm. Terribly messy business."

"I thought you said you were fifty years old."

"Look at this white hair, my boy! I've been fifty for a long, long time. Ever since I died."

"Oh, I'm very sorry. When did you die?"

"In the twenty-fourth year of the reign of Octavian. Today you say 19 B.C."

"And your name, sir? I mean, if I may ask?"

"Maro. Publius Vergilius Maro. In English you simply say . . ."

"Virgil. The poet Virgil."

"At your service."

Even though it was August the woods were cool and getting cooler with the advancing dusk, so I slipped my light sweater back on as we walked along. It gave me a chance to put things together. I had studied Italian back at Notre Dame, which meant I had studied Dante:

> *Nel mezzo del cammin di nostra vita*
> *mi ritrovai per una selva oscura*
> *che la dritta via era smarrita.*

Dante was thirty-five when he got lost in a forest— then there *was* a bit about a she-wolf, I could recall,

and he met Virgil, who took him through the netherworld. *The Divine Comedy*. This guy thought he was
Virgil, and waited around in the forest for some new
Dante to get lost. Thirty-five, a writer—probably not
too many come by, I thought. No wonder he was
disappointed. Only my name was wrong. God knows
what sort of "netherworld" he would have taken me
to. "Alderini" was okay, but not "Fred." Let's see,
Dante Alighieri, Fred Alderini. Alighieri and Alderini
both begin with "A" . . . I froze in my tracks.

"Sir! Mr. Maro! Virgil!" He finally turned around.

"Come along, Fred. It's getting late," he said sadly.

"Why did you choose to be called by your middle
name instead of 'Publius'?"

"In my place, which of the two would you have
preferred, my boy?"

I got out my passport.

"That's the point. I also chose to be called by my
middle name. Take a look."

There it was, indelibly, undeniably: DELBERT
FREDERICK ALDERINI.

"Delbert? Your name is really Delbert?" Virgil read
my name again: "Delbert Frederick Alderini! A marvelous name! And a marvelous time we shall have!
D.A.!" Again he looked up to the sky and started
firing away in what I now recognized to be Latin,
although I still couldn't understand anything but a few
scattered words.

"Who are you talking to?" I asked when he stopped.

"The gods, Delbert. Diana, in particular. It was she
who asked me to stay on in this world. I do so at her
pleasure. And for her amusement."

"And the D.A. business? I suppose the 'D' is in
her honor . . ."

"So is the "A," my boy. Her other name is Artemis.

At least it's a logical assumption, but with the gods, that often doesn't help: They don't like to give explanations, which they seldom have, anyway. They can be so like children, you know. Impossibly wise children. And now, step along, Delbert, my cottage isn't far."

"Must you call me Delbert?"

"I'm afraid so. And you'll have to agree to use it to sign your epic or whatever."

"How about just 'Del'? *The New Divine Comedy,* by Del Alderini. How does that sound?"

"The Del will be all right, but you'll have to do better with the title. What Dante did with my material was fine for his time—he was almost the best poet I've had, certainly—but you've got to get him out of your mind. Do your own thing, as you Americans say."

"You've had others besides Dante?"

"Oh, yes, my boy, of course I have. I'm averaging about one a century."

I did a flash review of the history of literature and didn't come up with any other D.A.s.

"The others didn't do very well, did they?" I said.

"There's no guarantee that they will, but some of them did well enough. Domitius Afer was the greatest orator of the first century . . ."

"Orator? I thought they all had to be writers!"

"Oh, many of them end up writing something, but really they can do anything they want with my . . . material. Decimus Albinus, in the second century, became a great general. I preferred that to what Decimus Ausonius did with what I . . . gave him in the fourth century. Reams of mediocre poetry, and the more he tried to imitate me, the worse it got. Inspiration is one thing, imitation is quite another. Don't try to imitate me, Del."

"I wouldn't think of it, sir." He didn't see my smile. It was getting quite dark now, and we still hadn't reached his cottage.

"I like the poetry that Daniel Arnault derived from our . . . experience in the twelfth century. As you know, his name was really Arnault Daniel, but Diana let us turn it around—it sounds so much better, don't you think?"

"Oh, definitely."

"Listen to these lines of his . . . but do you understand Provençal?

"Not when I'm sober, Virgil."

"Hah! Well, I have some good wine at home for you. Well aged."

I was curious to know just how well aged Virgil's wine might be, but I decided to wait and see. I wanted to get back to my forerunners.

"How about some recent D.A.s? I mean, I haven't recognized any of the names yet."

"Let's see . . . Denis van Alsloot, a Flemish painter in the late sixteenth, early seventeenth century."

"No, sorry. Can't place him."

"Decio Azzolino, a great patron of the arts in the seventeenth century. A cardinal archbishop."

"No, no. Excuse my ignorance. Back in Chicago these names are not household words."

"In Chicago? In the nineteenth century I had a German chap who made a name for himself in Chicago. An architect named Dankmar Adler."

"Adler! Adler and Sullivan! You talked to Adler?"

"Oh, we took a long trip together. He didn't pay much attention to what I was saying—kept staring at the buildings. When I saw that's what he was most interested in, I adjusted the itinerary for him."

"Was he your last? I mean, before me?"

"No. After him I had a Mexican over here named Doroteo Arango. A fiery fellow—too rebellious. In fact, he didn't keep his word to me. He didn't use his real name when he got back to Mexico, and brought down on his work the curse of Diana."

"What name did he go by?"

"Let's see . . . oh, yes. Pancho Villa. In 1913, when he was thirty-five, he was supposed to be hiding in the United States, but in reality he was here."

I didn't laugh. The man was deadly serious, and as mad as he was, he commanded respect. He had done his homework, I was sure of that. All those guys had existed, and Pancho Villa's real name was Doroteo Arango—I didn't doubt it. Still, I wanted to keep a certain psychological distance, to be able to jump away if it got too warm. I tried to keep things light.

"I finally thought of a D.A." I said. "Did you ever have Dean Acheson in here?"

Without turning his head the old fellow muttered, "No politicians, my boy, no politicians. I never got along well with politicians. We lost the farm because of politics. Such a messy affair. You're not interested in politics, are you?"

"Absolutely not. Strictly independent. Wishy-washy, actually."

"Hmm. We'll work on that. Anyway, here we are."

II

Where we were was in front of a very comfortable-looking log cabin, strongly built and of obviously recent construction. The inside was tastefully furnished, with Persian carpets on the floors and most of the walls lined with bookshelves containing beautifully bound books. In the middle of the living room there was a small but solid oak table with two chairs upholstered in leather. Virgil invited me to sit in one of these, and then left the room. I found myself worrying about my rented car, when I should have been absorbing every detail for the book I was going to write about this wonderful ding-a-ling. Besides, the car was hidden and locked.

Moments later he returned with a tray that held a flask of red wine, two glasses, a small salami, a large wedge of *caciotta* sheep cheese, some Tuscan bread, a cutting board and a large knife.

"I'm sorry I can't do any better," he said. "I only eat when I'm in company, so I haven't got a proper kitchen. And I never learned to cook. Had slaves for that, you know."

"Yes, I suppose," said I, accepting the glass of wine

he had poured me. It was marvelous, as rich and smooth as anything I had tasted. I told him so.

"Brunello di Montalcino, 1964—The Great Year. I have dozens of bottles of it. I know the man who made it."

"I thought you were going to say it's two thousand years old."

"Ha ha! You know, in all these centuries, the longest I've ever been able to keep a wine is about forty years. They all get decrepit, you know. I've got a bottle or two that are sixty or seventy years old, but drinking them would be like sleeping with your grandmother. Shall I get one?"

He was halfway out of his chair before I could say, "Lord, no! But even if they are decrepit they're probably worth some money."

He smiled and said softly, "My boy, I have all the money I need. I have made some sound investments over the centuries—and I collect others things besides wine in my travels. Some prove quite valuable, in time."

"Oh, so you're not always here waiting for D.A.s to come along."

"I only spend the summers here. The autumn is too dangerous because of the hunters, the winter is too wet and cold, and in the spring I have an allergy problem. I try to stay near the sea. Have some bread and salami. Help yourself."

"Thank you, it looks very good. Listen, Virgil—that is how you want me to call you, isn't it? Virgil?"

"Of course, Del! We are going to be very good friends."

"I'm sure of that. Anyway, Virgil, I've been wanting to ask you about something you said back there when we met. You said that Dante was almost the best poet you've ever had."

"That's right. He was excellent. You're a writer, you must know Dante. A sublime vision. I've learned a lot of him by heart. Especially from the *Inferno*. So much that I would be proud to call my own."

"Which makes me wonder who you could possibly have had in mind when you said he was *almost* your best poet. I mean, they don't come any better! I mean, unless you're going to tell me that Shakespeare was really a D.A. and made a sneak trip to Italy, but even he . . ."

"It isn't easy for you to take me seriously, is it? Well, you shall, in due time. And to answer your question, I was not referring to Shakespeare, whom I never had the pleasure of meeting, but to a fourteenth-century nun named Delia Alibrandi."

I sliced myself some more salami and poured some more wine. "Sure you won't have anything, Virgil? For company's sake?"

"All right, Del. For company's sake. A glass of wine and a little cheese. It's very good, you know. I know the farmer who makes it. Charming chap. I'd have put him in my *Eclogues* if I had known him then. Something of a poet, himself."

"As good as Delia Alibrandi?" I said with a smile.

The old man's eyes flashed bright and cold. "Don't . . ." he said, then he stopped and closed his eyes, and when they opened again, they were soft and serene. Now it was his turn to smile.

"You'll have to take my word for it, Del. I've known hundreds of poets over the centuries, and read hundreds more, in all the important literary languages. Delia was not "something of a poet," as you suggested. Everything she did and said was poetry."

"I'm sorry, it's just that, never having heard of her, I . . ."

"No one ever has, or ever will. Her work is lost to us. She is lost to us."

Virgil finished his glass of wine and sat back in his chair. He let his gaze find a window and the shadows outside.

"She was the youngest daughter of a baron who was rather too kindhearted to be much good at it, and in short, he had no money for the girl's dowry, so as was the practice for about a thousand years, he sent her to the convent—it was the only honorable thing. But she was a beautiful girl, full of life—a stunning woman, Del. If I could rewrite the *Aeneid*, I would use her beauty as a model for Dido.

"I think you can safely leave well enough alone."

"Oh, there are a great many rough spots in the poem, a number of scenes I was planning to revise, especially the ones in Greek waters—but I ran out of time."

"It doesn't look like it. Why couldn't you—why can't you just keep right on working on it? Not to make use of one of the mightiest creative spirits . . ."

"It is precisely that which is dead in me, Del."

"Oh. I'm sorry." There was silence. Virgil was still looking out the window. "Please go on about Delia," I said. "I'm very interested."

"Well," he sighed, "she did her best to be a good nun, and evidently she was, for almost twenty years. She read, she meditated—and she wrote. She wrote devotional pieces which pleased her superiors, who allowed her a certain amount of freedom to travel about, to use other libraries, you know, and to talk to religious men and women who appreciated her work. She made a great many friends, and used her friendships to help the poor, and to intercede on behalf of the weak. Sooner or later this sort of thing creates enemies, you know. Anyway the story got round that she was having an affair with a young silversmith she had helped. Her prioress searched through her books and papers looking for billets-doux while she was on one of her trips—and found a long manuscript. It was an epic love poem—the relationship between Saint Francis of Assisi and Saint Clare. Part legend, part invention—and all of it splendidly done. She went more deeply into the paradoxes of human love and spiritual love . . . and she did so very boldly, with great passion and imagination. She never expected to be read, at least not in her lifetime. Word got to her that she would be punished severely when she returned to the convent, so she never did. She had to flee, to hide, to travel by night—and eventually she got lost in these woods. I brought her here—not this house, of course, but one that was on this spot. We talked, much as you and I are talking now. Then I asked her to recite a few verses of her poem. Del, she went on for hours. I sat here entranced. Lines of great power, lines of great tenderness—but always crisp and pure. I remember so little:

> *"La mano sua, lo bel visin sfiorava,*
> *un cuor gia' grande in gioia s'allargava*
> *a Dio, che con si soave amor creava . . ."*

"And the rest is lost?"

"There was only one copy. After Delia had been missing for a year, the prioress declared her dead and burned all her clothes and manuscripts in a public ceremony, to purify her soul in purgatory, in the hope that was where she was."

"Where was she?"

The old man poured himself another glass of wine before answering. "My material . . . my material was too much for her. She was too sensitive—too receptive. Too empathetic. She was overcome. She needed more than a guide, and I . . . she died. Her body is buried in these woods. As for her spirit, only the gods can know."

I closed my eyes. "I'm enjoying every minute of this, Virgil, but the less you bring the gods into it, the better your story will be. Besides, I remember that in *The Divine Comedy* you repudiate the gods, you honor Jesus Christ."

"*I* did nothing of the sort. That's simply what Dante did with my material. To be honest with you, I didn't say much about the gods to him—or to anyone until the eighteenth century, for that matter. People were so touchy about religion once, you know. I hope you're not." '

"No, not particularly, but I'm not about to start believing in Diana and Jupiter and the rest of them— unless you can arrange a meeting."

"I'm afraid that's not very likely. When they appear to mortals, it's very much on their own terms. Besides, it makes no difference to me what you believe, or what you do with my material, as long as you *do* something. But just think about this from time to time, my boy. My gods are powerful but lazy, ingenious but capricious, sometimes kind, sometimes cruel, lavish in virtue and in vice; they are generally beautiful, but they enjoy taking on horrible shapes. And a great deal of the time, they don't really care what is happening on Earth. Now look at the world as you know it, life as you know it, and tell me if it seems to be in the hands of my gods, or of your Christian god.

Nothing against Christ, of course, even if he did bring down the Empire—he must have been a fine man, and a poet. Not much sense of humor, though. My gods spend half their time laughing."

"Yes. Well, as you say, I'll think about it later. Right now, if you don't mind, I'd like to know more about this 'material' you're going to give me, or show me, or whatever."

"My boy, that depends on you. I'm going to give you what you need. I'm going to show you what you need to see in order to find your focus and complete your vision. Everyone has his own hell, heaven, and purgatory, you know. But I must find out more about you. Are you tired now?"

"No, no, I'm fine—but I'm sure that you must be."

"I don't actually get tired—not physically, anyway. I close my eyes at night because there's not much to see, but I don't really sleep. I let my memory take me back over the centuries. It gives me comfort.

"*. . . relicuas tamen esse vias in mente patentis,
qua possint eadem rerum simulacra venire.*"

"That's very nice. I'm sorry I didn't understand it."

"It would translate 'yet in the mind the roads remain open, on which the images of the old things can return.' Of course, the music is lost in translation. It's from the *De Rerum Natura*."

A protest struggled out of my school memories. "Virgil, I thought Lucretius wrote the *De Rerum Natura*."

"Of course he did. The poet of my youth." He sighed, then continued. "I practically never recite my own verses—in my day it was considered bad manners. I could count on other people to recite them for me. And most of my acquaintances down through the ages have been able to do it. Even Doroteo Arango was able to recite the opening lines of the *Aeneid*."

He smiled. I must have looked appropriately sheepish.

"It's not your fault, Del. There's no time in school now for either Latin or poetry, let alone Latin poetry. But I'm not worried; I shan't be forgotten. My poetry will become more and more precious and rare, like fine pearls. And someday . . ."

" *'Arma virumque cano, Troiae qui primus ab oris,'* " I said struggling.

"Bravo, Del, bravo!" said Virgil. "But I'm sure you don't wish to sing of arms and the man—what would you like to write about?"

Right then and there, it was an easy question: I wanted to write about this fascinating loony I was sitting with. But I couldn't say that, so I reached back for the answer I had given to a girl named Tiziana three nights before.

"I want to write about Italy. I'm tired of writing about America. Everything written about America always winds up dissecting the American Dream. Which is supposed to be dead, and we all keep writing about it, telling ourselves that it's really dead. The hell it is. It's an obsession I've got to get away from for a while. Here in Italy there's no Dream, no real hope in the future. There's a Sense of History, which is a kind of hoping in the past. Maybe it's better. Certainly it's more concrete. At least the past existed, whereas the Dream never has."

I had really snowed Tiziana with this bullshit—the sort of thing that any American Lit. major can grind out on command. Maybe there was something to it. But the fact was, I had come to Italy because I had never been able to publish more than a few short stories in

America, and I was looking for something really unusual, stuff that jaded American publishers and readers might buy.

"The fact is," said Virgil, "that you have come to Italy because you've never published very much in America, and you're looking for unusual material that you might be able to sell."

I looked at the old guy, then down into my wineglass. "That's a part of it, I guess," was what I finally said.

"Don't worry, Del, because you're right—that really *is* only a part of it. There's much more to you than that. Diana doesn't let just anybody get lost in here, you know. Are you married?"

"No. I was. A sweet, sweet girl. She died . . . in an accident."

"I'm very sorry, indeed. Any children?"

"No. One that was stillborn. All deformed. Misbegotten, you could say."

"And so you don't want to beget any more children."

"I'm not looking forward to it. Could we change the topic?"

"Of course, of course. What do you think about death, Del?"

I poured a little more Brunello for inspiration. I was reminded of similar evening conversations back in Farley Hall at Notre Dame, except that the drinks were a damn sight worse.

"Well, Virgil," I finally said, "until now, I thought that the only sure thing you could say about death was that you can't avoid it. But now that I've met you, even that's not a sure thing."

"Very good, Del, very good! In fact, there are no sure things. All is whimsy."

"What's that supposed to mean? Either there's life

after death, or there isn't. Either there is balm in Gilead, or there isn't. 'Quoth the Raven: "Maybe".' " (This was probably the Brunello at work.)

"I admit that 'Nevermore' sounds better, but 'Maybe' would have been more correct. There is, and there isn't. We humans take these things so seriously. The gods certainly don't. You'll see, you'll see."

"What will I see? The Elysian Fields, or something?"

"Hah! It's possible. It might be amusing. That's what counts, you know. Being amusing, being of interest. And on rare occasions, being loved or hated by them. But it's mainly for amusement. They like having certain popes wake up after death and find themselves in Mohammed's Paradise, or Hitler find himself in Abraham's bosom—that sort of thing. I was told your General Custer is in the Happy Hunting Grounds with Manitou."

"And if a person is not of interest? not 'amusing'?"

"Oh, there are lots of those. They're just snuffed out, I'm afraid. That's why it's important to do something with your life, my boy. 'Make some waves,' I think you Americans say. Do you remember what Dante had me say about people who are afraid to make waves?"

"It's on the tip of my tongue."

"I'll help you:

"Fama di loro il mondo esser non lassa,
Misericordia e giustizia gli sdegna;
Non ragioniam di lor, ma guarda e passa."

"How would you translate that?"

I made a supreme effort:

"This world keeps no memory of them,
In the next, both mercy and justice scorn them;
Let us speak not of them: simply glance, and pass on."

"Not bad at all, my boy! A little free, perhaps, but no distortions. Oh, I think you will make waves, when we're done."

"And it evidently doesn't matter what kind of waves I make."

"Oh, but it does!"

"Listen, if Hitler managed to make it to Abraham's bosom—"

"I assure you, he wasn't very comfortable. And he didn't stay long."

"I thought the next world was for all eternity. I mean, once you get there . . ."

"That wouldn't be any fun at all, now would it?"

The old man's eyes were sparkling with his vision—a madman's vision, of course, but great entertainment. Most things are entertaining after four glasses of strong wine. Anyway, I couldn't resist. "And where did Jesus Christ wake up? In Valhalla?"

"Oh, no, my boy," Virgil said in a low, intense voice. "Even the gods had to take him seriously. He forced his reality upon them. One of the very few who have been able to do that. There is this remote possibility in every man—to kindle a divine flame and challenge the gods. They wanted it that way—to give an element of risk and uncertainty to the whole game, even for themselves. They love to gamble, you know, to make wagers, to have contests. And I think that like all gamblers, they'll play until they lose."

For a moment, I believed. The old gods were alive to me, and it felt strange and good. Then the moment passed. I looked deep into the man across the table and tried hard to think that this was the Roman poet Virgil, over two thousand years old. No luck. Not even with all that Brunello.

"What else do you need to know about me?" I asked quietly.

"That will do; that will do to get started."

"And when do we get started?"

"Tomorrow morning—if you're free."

"I'm free for as long as you can keep things— amusing. What's our first stop? The first circle of hell?"

"No, no. I didn't actually take Dante into the bowels of the earth, you know. He painted that whole marvelous canvas from—from the sort of trip that you and I are going to take. No devils, no ghosts, and unfortunately, no Beatrice. Unless of course they are all in there, waiting to get out."

With the salami knife the old man pointed at my forehead.

"Then where are we going tomorrow morning?"

"To the Aventine hill, in Rome."

It took me a long time to get to sleep that night. Not so much for the thoughts in my head. That damn dog was howling at the moon somewhere in the distance. That she-wolf.

III

I woke up the next morning to the smell of freshly brewed espresso coffee. I had slept briefly but well in a comfortable, modern bed in what was obviously a guest room; there were none of the personal touches that would indicate its regular use by anyone in particular. But the house was square and not very big; I mentally did a floor plan, and concluded there were no other bedrooms.

"Virgil, where did you sleep?" I asked when I got back into the front room. The old man was sitting in the same chair as the night before. In front of my chair there was the same tray, this time with coffee, two rolls, and butter.

"Good morning, Del! Oh, I don't sleep, I told you that. I spent the night reading, getting ready for our trip. And at dawn I walked over to old Mrs. Verano's house for those rolls. She still bakes bread every morning, bless her soul."

"So there are other houses close by," I remarked.

"About half an hour's walk from here. Beautiful, in the early morning."

The rolls were as wonderful as only freshly-baked rolls can be, but I had tasted better coffee. I didn't want to interrupt Virgil, who seemed intent on his reading, so I ate in silence. At one point I did manage to peer around to see the title of the book in his hand. It was Padovani's guide to good restaurants in Italy.

The old man smiled when he noticed me reading the title and said, "Many things don't change over the years, but restaurants certainly can. I never go to them alone, of course, so years often pass before I return to any particular establishment. I'm just checking to see which of my favorites are still open and well thought of."

"Where did you take Dante?"

"In those days there were always friends you could stay with, without its being an imposition. Everyone had guests all the time. The important houses, anyway. Well, if you've finished we can be on our way."

"Have you got a phone? I have to call Hertz—I was supposed to have that car back to them by noon today. I'll ask them if I can keep it for a couple of weeks."

"We shan't be needing your car, Del."

"It's a long walk to Rome, Virgil."

"It certainly is. I did it once, in 656. But otherwise I always had a horse or a coach of some sort. Now, of course, there are automobiles and paved roads. Not as sturdy and lovely as our Roman roads, but faster, I must say. It used to take me days to get to Rome, and now it's only about an hour."

"An hour! But it's over two hundred kilometers!"

Virgil just smiled. When he had tidied up and locked the front door, we walked around to the back of the cabin. A car was there, snug up against the wall and protected by one of those gray plastic coverings that take the place of garages for many Europeans. A two-rut road led away from the back of the house, evidently toward civilization. I helped Virgil take the

covering off, and there it was, flaming red the way it
had to be: a Ferrari Testarossa. I knew the statistics,
the way every adult male in Italy knows them: a twelve-
cylinder, 5000 cc motor, 390 hp, and, at 290 k an hour,
the fastest road car in the world. To get one, you
needed $100,000 and clout. Virgil beamed.

"The Lambourghini Countach is just as fast, you
know, but I find this auto so very—well, driver-friendly,
one might say. It cruises very nicely at about two
hundred and twenty kph."

"Two hundred and twenty?" I shouted. "I wouldn't
trust Alain Prost at that speed, let alone an old man!
I'll take the train!"

Virgil sighed hard. "There's no real danger, my
boy," he said softly. "I can't die again, as long as I
serve Diana, and you also are under Diana's protec-
tion now. But we shan't quibble about it; you may do
the driving."

My gaze fell back to the magnificent, gleaming thing
between us, and played slowly over every curve, every
feature. "Is this the Paradise part?" I asked.

First we had to take my rented car back to Florence.
I revved the little Fiat up to its top speed, about 135,
and held her there just to get in shape for the Ferrari,
which followed me no more than thirty feet behind all
the way. Then I let Virgil drive me from Hertz to my
pensione, because it was only about five blocks away. I
changed into something more suitable for a "Ferrarista"
and checked out; I put my suitcase into the trunk and
finally got behind that glorious wheel. For a few moments I stared at the famous symbol of the fighting
horse, the *cavallo rampante*. Then I started the motor
and pulled slowly away from the curb.

"You're in second gear, you know, not that it makes
too much difference," said Virgil.

And so I learned that the Ferrari Testarossa has first gear down and close, unlike most cars; but aside from that, it was wonderfully "driver-friendly," and I was as excited as a kid when we finally got back on the Autostrada del Sole heading south. There was heavy August traffic, but nothing inspires deference in an Italian like a red Ferrari. I just stayed in the passing lane, and all the cars as far as the eye could see squeezed over to the right, grateful for the chance to see me pass. I found myself doing 150, 160, 170; once a Porsche pulled up behind me, saw what I was and respectfully dropped back. I eased up to 180.

"I hope you're right about Diana," I said.

"Just keep your lights on, your left hand signal down and your eyes far ahead. There's always a Lancia or something limping along at 130 that doesn't see you in time."

"You know, Virgil, I can't understand why you have a car like this, why you want to speed around. I mean, it's not as if you didn't have the time."

"I enjoy an occasional thrill, my boy. It's almost like being alive again. It isn't easy for me to feel emotions."

"I think you felt something back in the fourteenth century. With Delia."

Virgil said nothing. I would have liked to look over at him, but I was afraid to blink, let alone take my eyes off the road. Finally he said, "I certainly think about her often enough. So young, and yet she had already understood so much. Such sweet nobility."

"Well, listen, can't you ask Diana to bring her back to life, or something? I mean, you deserve some sort of reward for long and faithful service, it seems to me."

"I deserve nothing, my boy. I am grateful to the gods

for allowing me to stay on in this world. I've grown quite fond of it. And I know you aren't serious when you speak of Diana, because you still don't believe."

"Virgil, it's hard enough for me to believe in the Prime Mover whose essence is existence and all that very metaphysical stuff I studied back at Notre Dame, without having to believe in gods and goddesses prancing around on Mount Olympus."

"Mount Olympus, indeed! All figurative, Del. But you can go right on believing in your Prime Mover, if it makes you feel better. Remember, the gods are immortal, not eternal. They were born out of Chaos, when Love issued from the egg of Night. They are only a part of the great Mystery, even as we are; but they have the power, for now. 'Essence is existence,' indeed! So scientific! So serious! I got into a terrible argument with Thomas Aquinas about this once. Nothing is that serious. Science itself is learning that reality is not based on rigid laws—everything is relative, everything is hovering between being and nothing. I predict the next great scientific theory will be called the Theory of Universal Whimsy."

I had slowed down so that I could try to follow his thinking. After a few moments I said—

"You're doing very well, Virgil, but I am strictly from Missouri, I'm afraid."

"I thought you were from Chicago."

"Even that's not quite true. Actually I'm from Winnetka, a North Shore suburb. Nice place. Anyway, to be from Missouri means you don't take anybody's word for anything; you have to be shown. Are you sure you can't put me into some sort of contact with . . ."

"Del, we've been through this." Virgil sounded depressed. I myself haven't seen a god in hundreds of years. Mercury brought me a message once. Telling me to move to another forest for a time. I still don't know why he bothered. Usually Diana whispers things like that to me in the still of the night. But they're unpredictable."

"What did Mercury look like?"

"Like a beggar. In fact, he was a beggar."

"Then how did you know it was Mercury?"

"Because he said so, and the way he said it—the feeling he gave me—left no room for doubt."

"I see. No wings on his feet, or anything."

"If Mercury has wings on his feet, then your god has a long white beard. I wish you wouldn't dawdle along like this."

I had dropped down to about 145. I started easing it up again.

"Have we got an appointment someplace?" I asked.

"Not really. Moonrise, of course, this evening. But there's a great deal to be done with you."

"Why moonrise, of course?"

"Diana is the goddess of the moon. We are going to the Aventine hill in Rome because that's where her temple stood—the spot is still sacred to her, and moonrise is the most propitious time, naturally."

"Naturally."

I want her to take particular notice of you—I think you need special help."

"Thanks a lot."

"In any case, consider it in this light: I agree with you that you need to develop your Sense of History, and for that, my boy, all roads really do lead to Rome."

We rounded a curve, and ahead there was a little old Fiat Cinquecento bravely trying to pass a truck. With respect to us, they were both practically standing still.

"Hang on, Virgil!" I said as I hit the brake. Nothing much happened.

"Pass on the shoulder!" shouted the old man. I veered to the right and whipped by the truck in the emergency stopping lane. In fact, there was a car stopped for a tire change about two hundred yards ahead, and I had to swerve right back in front of the truck to avoid him. The whole maneuver was a bit much even by Italian standards, so I got the hell honked out of me by the truck driver and a very obscene gesture from the man changing the tire. I was so shaken I wanted to stop, but I was afraid the truck might stop, too, so I kept rolling along at about 130.

"Virgil, we were almost killed back there, do you realize that?"

"The brakes are a bit slippery at high speeds. But nothing will happen. Diana . . ."

". . . is a crock of bullshit?" The old man winced.

"You see? No thunderclaps or lightning bolts! Now listen, Virgil, our tour of Rome will have to wait, because the first thing we're going to do in Rome is get these damn brakes fixed! How can you drive a car like this with bad brakes?"

"I don't use the brakes very much, Del."

"Hah! Boy, would this have been interesting on the Kennedy Expressway in Chicago! I'd love to see you explaining it to one of our patrolmen."

I tried to imitate Virgil's round British tones:

"No cause for concern, Officer. I hardly ever use the brakes. Diana is watching over me." I laughed again. "They'd use you and your car for filler on the lakefront."

"We'll get the brakes fixed; I should have told you about them," said Virgil in a cold, even voice. "I can understand your being perturbed, but I assure you there is no real cause, and I must insist that you refrain from treating me with sarcasm and disrespect. I haven't been waiting for two thousand years to be insulted by the likes of you!"

The atmosphere in the car iced over. We drove forty kilometers in silence. I didn't want to lose the old man—I was sure he represented "material" for me—so I made a move toward reconciliation.

"You know, this isn't my first pilgrimage to the Aventine hill. I went there two months ago, but not for Diana."

"Ah, yes!" exclaimed Virgil gratefully. "The Protestant cemetery is there. Keats and Shelley are buried there. Fine boys, both of them. Do you know the "Ode to the West Wind?"

I did. One of my favorites. I even remembered a few lines. I decided to rack up a few badly-needed points.

"Oh, wild West Wind," I entoned,

> *"thou breath of Autumn's being,*
> *Thou, from whose unseen presence the leaves dead*
> *Are driven, like ghosts from an enchanter fleeing."*

I stopped, and took a quick glance at the old man. His head was back on the headrest and his eyes were closed.

"Please go on," he said.

"I'm not sure I can."

The old man sighed, and took it up:

> *"Yellow, and black, and pale, and hectic red"*

—and went on to recite the whole poem, with the

sort of marvelous inflection that only comes from having meditated on every word.

"That was beautiful, Virgil."

"Thank you, my boy, but it's the poem that's beautiful. It's written in Dante's 'terza rima,' you know—on my advice. I was with Shelley the day he was inspired to write it."

"That's right, isn't it! I remember now; he was in a forest in Tuscany!" I had to laugh. "And of course, you were there."

"We became good friends. We met on many occasions. I was visiting him in Pisa when he got word from Rome of Keats' death."

"What did he think about having Virgil for a friend?"

"Oh, I didn't tell him who I was. I don't often do, except for the ones I'm responsible for—my D.A.s, as you call them. Or unless I don't mind being taken for a madman, but normally that isn't very pleasant." I was sure he was smiling.

"Well, Virgil," I said, "if you're out of your mind, then there's a lot to be said for it."

IV

In Rome it took us three hours and four hundred thousand lire to get the brakes fixed. Actually the mechanic had a four-day work backlog, but as he said, he would have left the pope's limousine stalled in the road for a chance to work on a Testarossa. I got a look at Virgil's wad when he paid, and it was clear that whatever he really did for a living, he was doing it very well. Lunchtime came and went. It was a hot day and I never got hungry, although we did stop in a bar for a glass of chilled white Frascati wine and a couple of *tramezzini*—small triangular sandwiches used for snacks.

"When does my Sense of History lesson begin?" I asked that afternoon.

"I'm afraid that there isn't much time left today," Virgil said, looking at his watch. "And I still have a little something to do in Trastevere. I promised certain coins to an old collector friend of mine. Here—I'll drive while you're taking a look at this one. We can start working on your sense of history right now. What does it mean to you?"

We got into the car and started off, laying about five yards of rubber.

"What do you think of it?"

"I'll never know unless you slow down so that I can take my eyes off the road."

"As you wish." And he did slow down; I was able to take quick glances at the coin, which was in a small plastic envelope. It was gold, and on one side it said "Louis XVIII Roi de France" around the king's head, and on the other side it said "Piece de 20 francs" around a coat of arms, and beneath it the date: 1815.

"Very nice," I said. "Probably worth a lot."

"Not really. As you can see, it's in perfect condition, so my friend will give me five hundred dollars for it. But the history, my boy, think of the history! It was minted during the famous Hundred Days, when the king was forced back into exile by Napoleon!"

"How did you get one?"

"Oh, I have lots of them. They were minted in Rome, you see, and I was very close to the Consalvi family."

I remained silent.

"Ercole Consalvi was the Cardinal Secretary of State at that time, under Pius VII."

"Oh."

And he showed me other interesting coins, and the history behind them. Nothing all that spectacular, though. Nothing all that old. I told him so, after he had sold his coins and we were driving back across the Tiber.

"Remind me to show you some of the things I have at home. I have gold pieces that were part of the ransom paid for Richard the Lionhearted. I have silver pieces that were used to buy Columbus' flagship, which wasn't called the *Santa Maria*, by the way, but the *Mariagalante*. I even have one of the Thirty Pieces of Silver used to pay Judas—at least the Jewish merchant

I bought it from in the year 96 swore to me that's what it was."

"My, my. That sure beats the Indian-head nickels I had as a kid. But you don't just collect coins, do you? You mentioned other things . . ."

"Small things. Miniatures, porcelain—and jewelry. Cleopatra once wagered Marc Antony that she could give the most expensive dinner in history. When the plates were set out, they were empty, but the goblets contained very strong wine. Cleopatra was wearing earrings made with enormous, flawless matched pearls. She took one off, crushed it, and dissolved it in the wine, which she then drank. When she offered the other pearl to Marc Antony, he declared she had won her bet."

"He didn't drink his pearl?"

"Marc Antony was no fool."

"And you've got it now?"

"Obviously."

I suppose I could have asked him how he got it, but you can only take so much cock-and-bull in one day and I knew I was in for a lot more, so I decided to take a rest. I watched the plebeians watching our car while Virgil drove us to the Aventine hill.

After illegally parking the car we began walking up Via di Santa Melania. Between two buildings there was one of the miniscule parks that dot Italian cities where there should be parking lots. Virgil led me off into this little green patch and urged me to sit down with him on a bench toward the back.

"Pleasant part of town, isn't it?" I said, thinking he only wanted to rest and chat.

"Yes, it's always been nice here, for some reason. You know, we are sitting about twenty feet above what was once one of my houses. My favorite, after the villa in Nola."

I took that one in slowly, then said, "And it's still down there?"

"Oh, yes. A good part of it. Reduced to rubble, of course, but archaeologists would have no trouble putting it back together. And there are inscriptions, mosaics, and still a few statues that would indicate it was my house. Perhaps someday I'll try to have it excavated. Not for the time being—the Italians don't take very good care of their monuments. My house is safer where it is, and I enjoy sitting here on occasion, alone with my secret, alone with my past: in the privacy of my old home."

I stared at the grass, trying to look beneath it. The power of suggestion. I seemed to sense the bond between this old man and the ancient stones below. I let him enjoy it.

But after only a minute or two he stood up and said, "Well, it's best not to tarry. Moonrise is at 7:30, and that would be the most auspicious time."

"Auspicious for what?" I asked as we headed back out onto the Via.

"Auspicious for your sacrifice to Diana."

After a few moments I said, "And just what am I going to sacrifice?"

Virgil smiled. "A lamb, of course."

I just laughed. There would be time enough to run. I had to see how far he would carry this. We reached Piazza Tempio di Diana, where there is no longer any trace of the Temple of Diana.

"First the looting, then the fires, then the popes who stripped marble wherever they could to build their tombs and churches," sighed the old man. "But that's where it stood, and that's where we shall go."

He indicated a corner building with a neon sign that was already glowing in the early evening dusk: "Ristorante Da Artemia."

"But what about the sacrifice?" I asked rather stupidly as we headed for the restaurant.

"You're going to eat Abbacchio alla Romana here— the best lamb in town, according to Padovani. Aren't you hungry?"

I certainly was, and not a little relieved. The restaurant was small but promising; 7:30 is very early for dinner by Roman standards, so the place was practically empty. We chose a corner booth and ordered Abbacchio for two.

"So you're going to eat this time, are you?" I said.

"Not because I'm hungry. For the symbolism. The sacrifice, you know. Homage to Diana."

A smiling waitress brought two aperitifs. *"Offerti dalla casa,"* she said. *"Si chiama 'Chiaro di Luna.' "* Then she sped away.

"Pear brandy and white vermouth," said Virgil after a sip. "Not bad, really. A nice gesture."

"Well, with a name like 'Moonlight' it's perfect for a toast to our friend Diana: So here's to you, Sweetheart, wherever you are," I said, raising my glass.

My companion sighed. "Del, I won't ask you to be solemn, but avoid being too flippant. A minimum of respect. She just might give you some sign of approval."

I refrained from making wisecracks, and when the lamb came I ate it with great reverence, because it was in fact a fabulous piece of lamb. But we got to the fruit course, the restaurant was filling up with people, and still no sign.

"Maybe I'm not her type," I said, unable to resist.

"That may well be, after certain of the things you've said. But no sign is necessary, you know. We've done our part—made the correct gesture. After our coffee, we'll go to the Excelsior where I always stay when I'm in Rome. We'll get an early start in the morning. I want you to see . . ."

"Your coffee, gentlemen."

So our waitress spoke some English, which didn't surprise me. What did was the fact that we hadn't ordered coffee yet. I looked up at the girl: shapely and strongly built, rich brown hair cut short, smooth Mediterranean complexion—a very pretty girl of about twenty-three, probably involved in sports or athletics of some kind. Then she looked at me. Her eyes flashed through mine with a power that made them burn.

"May I sit down with you?" she said sweetly.

"Certainly. You certainly may." I would have answered in the same way if she had asked permission to cut off my nose. I swung around to sit at the end of the table with my back to the wall. She set down the tray with three cups of coffee on it and sat down gracefully in my place. Then she put a cup in front of each one of us. I looked at Virgil, who was silent and nervous. I didn't think he was capable of being nervous. Then with his eyes fixed on the girl he leaned over the table, and in a low, slow voice asked:

"What is your name? And I shall ask you this three times."

The smile vanished from the girl's face, but the intense light of her eyes seemed to increase. She spoke with a voice that had no age, strangely soft but penetrating, a voice of aching beauty:

"That won't be necessary, old man, for I desire to speak. I am the daughter of Jupiter and Latona. I hold sway over the night even as my brother Apollo rules the day. I am Diana."

The whole thing could have been a setup, as I

realized in my subsequent frequent attempts to reason
my way back to normality. The good wine—and maybe
that Moonlight aperitif was drugged; those marvelous
eyes, the sense of expectation Virgil had worked into
me—ample explanations for the fact that when the girl
spoke, I believed her as totally as I could. Virgil
quietly bowed his head. The girl looked directly at me
and I met her glance.

"My name is . . ." I began.

"I know your name," she interrupted. "I know it
well."

"Great Diana," began Virgil, raising his head, "the
honor that you do us . . ."

"I have not come to do you honor, old man, although I am not dissatisfied with the service you have
rendered me these many years. I have come to ask . . ."
she hesitated a moment before proceeding, ". . . to ask
you and your new friend to undertake a mission. A
difficult mission. You must find my brother. You must
find the Lord of the Sun, Phoebus Apollo."

At this point I took a sip of my coffee. Both Virgil
and Diana looked at me. It was a ridiculous thing for
me to do; perhaps I was trying not to lose touch with
the real world, but it was too late. Diana smiled.

"You treat me lightly. Americans are like that, aren't
they?"

"But, Great Lady, where is your divine brother?"
said Virgil, "and why should two humble mortals be
needed to find him?"

The girl continued looking at me, but her answer
was directed at the old man:

"Virgil, old Virgil, if men cannot understand themselves, how can they hope to understand the affairs of
the gods? But I will try to satisfy you, with images
suited to your minds. My brother . . ." and here she

finally took her eyes off me and lowered them to the bowl of fruit in the center of the table. ". . . my brother has always loved the race of men more than he should. Perhaps because he sees what you do by the light of day, while I see the secrets of the night. He takes pleasure in the efforts of your minds, because by day your knowledge and power grows; so little changes at night."

Here she smiled again, and looking at me, she took a sip of her coffee. Virgil and I immediately followed suit. I noticed that no one was paying any attention to us, although the sight of a waitress sitting with clients had to be uncommon. When she put her cup down, she said to me: "No one will disturb us."

Virgil looked as if that were the most obvious thing in the world. "He is young, and unaware . . ." he began.

"You needn't apologize for him. I know of what he is capable. And incapable." She sighed, and continued. "My brother, the most brilliant of all the gods, whose power lights the heavens, wanted to allow men to partake of his power. He illumined their minds, permitting them to unbind some small portion of the force contained in all things, the force that causes the sun to burn."

"Nuclear power!" I exclaimed. Virgil shot me a look that said "goddesses are not to be interrupted."

"He is bold, Virgil, but he does not offend me," said Diana. "My brother, too, was bold, because he acted against the will of great Jupiter, our father, who wanted no such power placed in the hands of men. But the lesson of Prometheus, the mighty Titan who was so cruelly punished for giving fire to men, did not deter my brother. He believed himself too beloved, or too powerful, or too clever—but he did not escape his father's anger. He has been heavily punished, and his punishment weighs upon the world like impending doom."

"How has he been punished, Diana?" I asked, almost putting my hand on hers before jerking it back. Diana laughed! Her laughter was loud and musical. Not a head turned in the whole crowded restaurant.

"He has been punished, my bold young friend, by being made mortal. For loving men too much, he is now a man. And he has no memory of being a god."

"A man?" I exclaimed. "And who is he? Where is he?"

"Jupiter will allow me to say but little, and unlike my brother, I obey my father. He is in Italy, and he dies a tragic death. In every age, he dies a tragic death. Thus is he both mortal, and immortal."

"In every age? What do you mean?" I asked. Virgil was becoming resigned to my impertinence, and the girl continued to be amused by it.

"He is alive today, but he is alive yesterday, and in every age back to the days when you were alive, old man. He is living and dying throughout what you call time. You must begin at the beginning, and try to find him." She looked at me, evidently expecting another interruption. But I was sure that anything I might say would seem incredibly stupid.

"Virgil, you must take your friend where the stones still groan their sadness. At night, when I reign and he must sleep, I will carry your spirits back to the time of the stones. Your spirits will truly walk the earth, and you will seek out my brother. If you can cause him to recover his divine nature, the punishment will cease throughout time, and Apollo will again command the light. Thus does great Jupiter show his mercy."

"But how can we recognize your brother? And how can we give him back his real nature?" I asked.

"Ask the one who is about to die where he is from. By great Jupiter's will, if he is my brother, he will answer that he comes from a beautiful land. In this way you will know him, though he knows not himself. Then, regardless of what men may call him, ask him his name three times. As the old man knows, a god must give his true name the third time he responds. My brother's mind will open, and with his true name, his true nature will return." She turned to Virgil. "Begin now, old man. You have so little time."

The girl stood up. I made a motion to rise, but Virgil held me back. She put the empty coffee cups back on her tray and turned to leave.

"What will happen if we don't find him?" I asked.

She turned back. "I shall respond to your boldness one last time. If you fail, Phoebus Apollo cannot resume control of the power that lies deep in all things. He cannot illumine your minds. You play with this power as a child might play with the mane of a sleeping lion. And the lion will awake. On the day to me dedicated he will devour the child. Thus does great Jupiter show his wrath."

A man at another table raised and wiggled two fingers at her. *"Arrivo, Signore,"* she called in a cheerful voice, and walked over quickly to serve him. We sat watching her vacantly until she went back into the kitchen.

"Well, we'd better be on our way," said Virgil finally.

"Yes, I suppose so," I said. "Just to be sure I got it right, what she said was that if we don't find her brother the human race is going to be destroyed by nuclear power."

"That's what she said."

"On the day dedicated to her. When's that?"

"The ides of August. August thirteenth. Six days from now."

V

We strode quickly back to the car. It was 8:30 and getting dark.

"You walk as if you knew where to go," I said.

"I do and I don't. The gods expect one to follow one's best impulses in cases like this. Our search must begin in my lifetime; I must take you where there was sadness, and tragic death."

"The Colosseum?" I suggested as we drove off.

"Those deaths were almost never tragic. Just stupid. Gladiators, you know. I went very seldom to such spectacles, only when it was indispensable. And Flavian's Amphitheater, the "Colosseum" as you call it, was built a hundred years after my demise, in any case. But stones such as those do not groan sadness to me—only folly."

"You passed up the persecutions."

"Yes, I most certainly did."

Virgil was driving this time, and from the way he screeched around the first corner I realized it would be white knuckles all the way, so I cut down on my talking in order not to distract him. In the moments when I wasn't gripped by fear I tried to imagine where we were going. We whizzed by the Roman Forum.

"Not the assassination of Julius Caesar, huh? Shakespeare thought that was pretty tragic."

Virgil sighed. "Caesar's pride knew no bounds. He was the first Roman to identify his own good with the *Res Publica*, the good of the State. I was not saddened by his . . . removal. I disapproved of the way it was done. And besides," he looked over and smiled at me, almost killing two nuns trying to cross the street, "Caesar wasn't killed in the Forum. That day the Senate met in Pompey's Theater."

We went past the Pantheon and down the Via della Scrofa, and finally parked alongside the Mausoleum of Augustus.

"Caesar Augustus?" I said. "I don't recall that he died tragically."

"Anyone at the summit of power for fifty-six years cannot be said to die tragically. Octavian had time to do almost everything he wanted. Everything except ensure Rome a succession of worthy leaders."

"Octavian for his friends, huh?"

Here Virgil's sigh was especially long. "It was the Senate that started calling him Augustus." Another sigh. "A truly great man. And, yes, a dear friend."

"But he's not the reason we're here."

"No. I want you to think about this place when the mausoleum wasn't yet here—in 46 B.C., when he and I were both young men."

We got out of the car and walked onto the lawn surrounding the mausoleum.

"This whole area," he continued, "from the Tiber to the Via Flaminia and down practically to the Pantheon, was called the Campus Martius, the Field of Mars. It was an open area used for sports, military drills, and—and it was the starting point for the "triumphs," the victory parades of Rome's great generals. That's what I want you to dream about—one of the greatest triumphal parades in history. After an absence of thirteen years, Julius Caesar returned to Rome. He had conquered Gaul, crossed the Rubicon and defeated his great rival, Pompey. He had become the master of the known world, and he wanted Rome to get the point."

"That doesn't sound so tragic."

"Oh, you will see, my boy, you will see. Now come with me."

In the moonlight we walked down some steps to the base of the mausoleum, about ten feet below the level of the ground.

"This was the ground level at that time. Look at the white stones here and there—the smooth ones. They were here even then. Bend down and touch one of them, Del. They groan with a great sorrow."

I squatted down and put my hand on one of the stones. It felt like a lot of other stones I've touched. I waited a bit, but nothing happened. Then I heard a shout in the distance, and stood up—with some difficulty.

"What's happening?" I asked.

"Nothing that I know of."

"Didn't you hear that shout?"

"No, I didn't."

I thought for a moment. "Probably a close call out on the street. Somebody else that drives like you. Listen, let's head for the hotel—I feel awfully beat."

Virgil insisted on the Excelsior, even though any second-class *pensione* would have been fine with me, tired as I was. We took communicating singles; I bid Virgil good night and was barely able to get my clothes off and flop into bed before dropping off into a deep sleep.

*   *   *

And of course I dreamed. Like everybody else, I have had dreams that were vivid and real—the sort of dream that causes you to wake up with a start and sit up in bed, and it takes a minute or two to realize who you are and where you are. This time the dream went on and on. And there were other differences. The clarity, the colors and sounds! Horses, chariots, and a riotous confusion of men and women dressed in a wilder assortment of costumes than anything my brain could produce. I felt a hand on my shoulder. I spun around.

"Welcome to my world, Del!" There was Virgil, dressed in the same designer sports clothes he had had on during the day. I glanced down at myself, and I was wearing my usual dull duds—khaki slacks and a white golf shirt. I was disappointed.

"I hate it when I'm not dressed right," I said.

"So do I, but I don't think we'll need to procure different clothing. As you can see, in the center of the world one finds every manner of dress, and we are simply a part of the general confusion. And now, to the job at hand; we must find the man who is not a man."

"Where do we start? There must be thousands of people here."

"Tens of thousands. But most of them don't interest us. Let's work our way to the back, over by the river. The parade will begin soon."

We began threading our way through the babbling crowd.

"Nice of them all to speak English for my benefit," I remarked.

"I assure you they're speaking Latin and scores of other tongues. Your English at this point in history is

a Germanic dialect being grunted in the forests of the
North. But it's your dream, so you must understand,
and be understood."

"It's my dream, so if we meet somebody I don't
like, all I have to do is blink and he'll puff away,
right?"

"Hardly. As Diana said, we have come here through
your dream, but this is the real world as it was in 46
B.C. This is my world. It . . . it seems like yesterday.
Terribly exciting—but so sad."

Sad? The atmosphere was something like South Bend
an hour before Notre Dame versus Michigan State.

"The people seem happy enough," I said. "Julius
must have been well liked."

"He's promised one hundred denarii to every specta-
tor today. And five thousand to every legionnaire.
And at the end of the parade there will be a banquet.
Twenty-two thousand tables. Today, Julius is very well
liked."

We had to stop to let a litter pass in front of us,
carried by four burly slaves dressed in yellow. Inside
we got a glimpse of an old man in a bright white toga.

"Who was that?" I asked.

"Oh, a senator. Nerva, I think—I can't remember.
It's been a while, you know. The Senate and the
magistrates lead the Triumph, followed by the trumpeters, then the spoils of war—that will take a bit of
time. Then the animals to be sacrificed. Then the
hostages. Caesar has some illustrious ones today.
There's one of them."

A gilded throne was being lifted up with long, sturdy
poles onto the shoulders of two six-man rows of brown-
skinned men dressed in orange tunics. On the throne
was seated a beautiful young girl whom I instantly
understood to be Egyptian. She looked like that ex-

quisite sculptured head of Queen Nefertiti I had seen in books. She accepted the admiration of the crowd as a birthright.

"She is Arsinoe, Princess of the Nile," said Virgil. "Treated with the honors due to her station, but a hostage nonetheless. Helping to guarantee Rome's control of Egypt."

"And who is that?" A tall, strongly built black man was taking his place in the procession behind the princess. He was dressed in leopard skins that did not hide his gleaming, well-oiled muscles. On his head there was a roughly-made gold crown with an enormous emerald set in the center in front. He was on foot, but attended by four splendid black girls dressed in blue. His eyes were white and proud, but heavy with sadness. I ran up to him.

"Where are you from?" I blurted out. He looked down at me from the height of his physical superiority and natural nobility.

"You are no Roman," he said, "and your gray face comes from a land where the sun is loath to shine. You are free to return there, and yet you do not—you have no love for it. I am Juba, Prince of the Leopard People. We live where God kissed the earth, a land the Romans call Numidia. Hordes of human jackals came, and for every one we slew, ten took his place. Now I must live here, to protect my people from the jackals. But I am dead until I return."

He walked away, not caring to hear my reply. I turned to Virgil, who was again by my side.

"Well, he said lots of things, but not that he came from a beautiful land. No sense in following up, right?"

"No, no sense. It is not among the hostages that we must seek—they are in no imminent danger of death. We must go to the river bank."

When we got there, the river enabled me to do what I hadn't yet been able to do because of the crowds—take a panoramic look around. There were very few buildings in the immediate vicinity—a few small temples, or shrines of some sort. But downriver I could make out Rome on its hills. The scenery in *Quo Vadis* was more impressive, because most of the buildings I could see were made of bricks and wood; only a few were white with marble. I said something about it to Virgil.

"Octavian's reign has not yet begun. At the end of it he will say, 'I found Rome a city of brick and left it a city of marble.' But we are not here for sightseeing. Look upriver."

Coming round the bend in the river I saw what proved to be only the beginning of a long procession of barges filled to overflowing with people. As they came closer I could see that they were ragged and dirty, and wearing heavy iron collars that were chained together in groups of four or five.

"Caesar's prisoners," said Virgil. "Hundreds upon hundreds on them. They will all be killed today, to show his great power."

"In the river! In the river! In the river!" The people around us had started up a chant. When the guards in the first barge heard it, they decided to oblige. Five prisoners chained together were thrown overboard. They thrashed and struggled in all directions, strangling each other while the people roared with laughter; then they finally sank out of sight.

"In the river! In the river!" The chant started up again. But this time a centurion on shore put a stop to it. "Leave them for Caesar!" he bellowed. And so the barges began to unload their cargo on the river bank. Virgil and I watched them stumble by, some proud, some weeping, but most simply resigned.

"It will be a liberation for many of them," said Virgil. "Caesar has been saving prisoners for his triumph ever since he went to Gaul, which means that some of them have been living like that, like animals, for over ten years. This is actually the fourth day of the celebration, and Caesar has slaughtered this many every day. But he's saved the most important ones for the culmination today. Including his most famous prisoner, the great chief of all the Gauls."

I saw my chance for a point or two. I knew who that had to be, from translating *De Bello Gallico* in high school. The name was so hard and long we used to laugh about it.

"Vercingetorix!" I said.

"Precisely. And do you remember his story?"

"I remember that he laid his shield and sword at Caesar's feet after losing a big battle."

"That's correct—at Alesia, six years ago. He could have escaped, but he personally surrendered to Caesar in order to win clemency for his men. One of the worthiest opponents Caesar ever had. Certainly the bravest. There he is now."

On the last barge, just coming around the bend, there was a large cage. As it came closer I could see that the man inside was a huge hairy brute dressed in a bear skin. Dark red hair fell in a mass of tangles to his shoulders, and in profusion from his face as well.

"He used to cut such an impressive figure that now Caesar forces him to wear skins and leave his hair unkempt. He was being admired too much."

"Why can't Julius show a little mercy now and then? I mean, at least this fellow is going to be spared, isn't he?"

"He's going to be slowly strangled to death."

I shook my head and dropped my gaze to the ground.

I saw the same sort of stones that Virgil had asked me to touch at the base of Augustus' mausoleum.

"You were right about these stones groaning sorrow. Do you think Vercingetorix could be our man?"

"I'm anxious to find out."

We got as close as we could to the spot where the barge was landing. The huge man was standing in the middle of the cage now, grasping the oaken bars over his head with red, dirty hands that were chained together at the wrists. His eyes were closed. Ten legionnaires lifted the cage off the barge and onto a wagon pulled by two mangy-looking oxen and driven by a scruffy little boy. Caesar's sense of humor. The crowd appreciated it.

"The King of Gaul on his royal chariot!"

"Is that a Gaul wearing a bearskin or a bear wearing a Gaulskin?"

"It's just a farmboy taking an old boar to the slaughterhouse!"

The prisoner never opened his eyes. I swung myself up onto the wagon just as it started off.

"Be careful, Del!" I heard Virgil shout. Why should I be particularly careful? I wasn't really here. But in my strange clothes I was evidently adding something to the show, because the crowd was amused and the soldiers decided to let me stay on the wagon to see if I would do something funny, like getting myself killed. I worked my way up the wagon to the point on the side where I was nearest the prisoner.

"Where are you from . . . Noble Sir?" I thought a little respect wouldn't hurt. The shaggy head slowly turned toward me. Then the eyes opened. The pupils were green, but the whites were badly bloodshot. I wondered if he could see me. He seemed to smile. Then he worked his way over to me with his hands,

bar by bar. He seemed friendly enough. He brought
his hands down and put them on the bars in front of
my face, smiling all the while. He seemed to mumble
something. I leaned closer. Then his hands shot through
the bars and grabbed me on both sides of my head!
His chains were just long enough to permit this. He
rammed my face against the bars and held it there,
and I discovered another thing that made this dream
different: I could feel pain.

"Avernia! Avernia!" he roared at me. "The world
knows I'm from Avernia!" A belching camel has a
sweeter breath. Then he brought his face right down to
mine and said in a lower voice, "But none of you
know where I'm going. To the Land of the Ever-
young, where Lug of the Long Hand has prepared a
hero's welcome for the victor of Gergovia. And there
are no Romans!"

Then he shoved my head backward with such force
that I toppled off the wagon and onto the ground.
Two of the soldiers who had been walking alongside
the wagon ordered it to stop while they helped me to
my feet. But I had hit the ground with my right hip,
right on one of those groaning white stones, and now
it hurt so badly I couldn't stand. Virgil had finally caught
up with the wagon, and when he saw my predicament,
said:

"Brave legionnaires! We are visitors from a far-off
land, but not so far that the fame of Caesar and his
valiant legions has not reached us. Allow us to ride on
this wagon, since my companion can no longer walk,
so that we can see your great Triumph!"

As he spoke, he handed out 500-lire coins to all the
soldiers escorting the wagon. They bit into them, held
them up to the light, held a little conference, shrugged
and finally boosted us up, one on each side of the boy

driving the oxen. He paid no attention to us, and got the wagon going again. I had a lot to say to Virgil, but the first thing that came to my mind was:

"If they find any of those coins you just handed out two thousand years from now, some archaeologists are going to be pretty shaken up."

"They'll disappear when we do."

"Which can't be too soon for me. You're not supposed to get hurt in dreams, but my hip is killing me."

"I told you to be careful, Del. This is a special kind of dream. In spirit we are truly here, and all of our senses are with us."

"My sense of smell certainly is. Don't let our bear friend here breathe on you."

We both looked around. Vercingetorix had resumed his position in the middle of the cage with his eyes closed and his hands on the bars overhead. I noted with satisfaction that we were out of his reach.

"So he isn't Apollo," said Virgil.

"He's from Avernia, he said. No prize for that answer. Now whom do we ask? Ouch!" I was doing my best to keep all my weight on my left hip, but sometimes the wagon hit a stone or something and threw me over on my right, and I would see stars.

The boy looked over at me and said, "I'm looking for the smoothest ground, but it isn't easy." He was small and thin, but his grimy face was more than a child's; I took him to be an undernourished fifteen-year-old.

"You're doing fine, son," I said. "It's not your fault." Then I looked over his head at Virgil, who was shielding his eyes from the sun and peering ahead.

"There he is," he said calmly.

"Who? Apollo?" I said as I turned to follow his eyes. Virgil didn't answer because it wasn't necessary.

There, in armor of burnished gold only partly covered by a purple tunic, standing in a white chariot drawn by four white horses, was Julius Caesar. Behind him the soldiers were getting into their ranks, and directly in front of him the prisoners were being herded into some sort of order. That was obviously where we were heading. As we drew nearer, I could make out the shouts that were coming from the troops behind Caesar:

"Viva Julius!"

"Not a man he cannot slay, nor a maid he cannot lay!"

"Let's hear it for Old Skinhead!"

I was a bit taken aback. Virgil looked at me and smiled. "These are his veterans, they've been with him for years and years; he owes everything to them. They can say whatever they like. If you shouted something like that, those same men would run a spear through you lengthwise. I've seen it done."

Now we were passing close to Caesar's chariot. An old man in a simple tunic was standing next to him, holding a golden crown suspended over his bald head. Now and then he would whisper something into Caesar's ear.

"Who would that be?" I asked Virgil.

"I don't know—some trusted slave. It's his duty to remind the victor that he is only a man. That's what he keeps whispering to him. I don't think Julius is paying much attention."

I opened my mouth to say something, but the trumpeters started up, and even though they were over a hundred yards away there were so many of them that they drowned out all other sounds. When they finished their fanfare, Virgil said, "That means the parade is starting."

Our wagon was being positioned directly in front of

Caesar's chariot, behind the great mass of prisoners
that were now slowly beginning their long, final
procession.

"No lack of tragedy and sorrow here, Virgil, but
where do we begin? And how much time do we have
before these poor devils are killed?"

"Oh, there's time. Hundreds of thousands of people
have to see them first. The parade will take hours
before we stop at the Capitoline. Through the triumphal arch you see ahead, then a few laps inside the
Circus Flaminius and the Circus Maximus, then all
around the Palatine, then down the Via Sacra . . ."

"My hip feels a little better. I suppose we should get
down there with the prisoners and start asking them
where they're all from."

"No, I don't think the gods mean for us to do that.
There's a certain style in everything they're involved
in."

"Maybe we're in the wrong place at the wrong time."

Virgil didn't answer. I had cast aspersions on his
ability as a guide. Well, it certainly looked as though
he had choked. We rolled along in silence for a while.
I kept scanning the prisoners ahead, not really knowing what to look for. They were heading to the slaughter, yet some of them either didn't realize it, or were
caught up in the festive spirit, because they were smiling and waving back to the happy crowds lining our
path on both sides. Virgil was paying no attention to
them; he seemed to be sightseeing, looking up and
around at the buildings and monuments.

"Nice to be home, huh, Virgil?" I said.

"No, not at all," he answered coldly. "Not in these
circumstances. But I was thinking, perhaps when we
pass in front of the Temple of Apollo . . ." he paused.
Then the boy between us spoke.

"Have the Romans no god of Fortune? For it was only Fortune that gave them the victory over us."

"Of course, my boy!" answered Virgil, amused. Here in Rome there are gods for everything. The temple of the Goddess of Fortune is just up ahead on your right."

"I would like to put Caesar's luck to the test," said the boy.

"So you're a prisoner, too," I said.

"Of course. And Caesar thinks he will kill me for sport. But I'll choose my own way to die, and he won't enjoy it." He looked at me closely. "Are you friends of Rome? Where are you from?"

I smiled. He was stealing my lines. "We are no friends of Rome—not today, at any rate. And I'm from Winnetka. That's way west of here. Are you from Avernia, like your friend in the cage?"

"That barbarian is no friend of mine, and I am no Gaul! If Caesar wants to conquer, let him conquer all the forests and savages that he likes, to the north— and to the west," the boy sneered. "But when he invades the East, then he is the barbarian. A soldier forced me into these rags, but my people already wore silk when the Romans were still naked in the trees. I come from a beautiful land in Anatolia, and I am the son of the chief scribe in the court of King Pharnaces."

Virgil and I stared at each other over the boy's head. Then I put my hand on the boy's shoulder and said forcefully, "What is your name?"

"You needn't shout. I am Sarthos, son of Athradates."

Again I said, "What is your name?"

The boy shook his head, turned to Virgil and said, "Tell your deaf friend that I am Sarthos, son of Athradates, and tell him also to jump down now, together with you!" At which the boy stood up and started whipping the oxen and pulling them to the right into the round, open courtyard in front of the Temple of Fortune. No one knew what to make of it, least of all the poor oxen, who responded to the screaming of the crowd and the panicky efforts of the guards to head them off by barreling all the way around the courtyard as fast as they could. Now the boy pointed them straight at Caesar's chariot, stalled by the confused crowds, and shouted, "Your good fortune is running out, Tyrant!"

I was holding on for dear life, but somehow I found the presence of mind—or the madness—to shout, "What is your name?" the third time. But my words reached the boy's ears a second after a spear and two arrows reached his chest. He whipped his head around and gaped at me as if I had said the most astonishing thing he had ever heard. Then his eyes glazed over and he fell backward against the cage. An instant later the terrified oxen crashed into the side of the great white chariot. I heard the loud crack as one of its wheels buckled, and I felt myself launched forward, straight toward Julius Caesar. I landed on the floor next to my bed in the Hotel Excelsior.

VI

The next morning at breakfast Virgil and I did a lot of staring at each other, but very little speaking; each of us was too immersed in his thoughts. Virgil was obviously thinking about where to go next; I was still trying to understand more about where we had been, or hadn't been, depending on how you looked at it. And Virgil had definitely been with me, in some way; his first (and practically only) comment that morning had been, "The boy sitting between us! Sarthos, indeed! Jupiter must have enjoyed it immensely."

The search for Apollo would have to continue. How crazy could you get? I again attempted a few "rational" explanations, adding hypnosis and micro-transmitters implanted in my brain to the list. For some reason it all seemed more farfetched than Virgil's gods. And when I remembered the eyes of that girl in the restaurant, I knew there had to be something behind them that was not a waitress. I seemed to have no choice but to go along. Like Alice in Wonderland, hoping that some white rabbit would lead me back to my old world. Or was I really hoping that?

"If you've finished your cappuccino, we can be on our way, Del."

"In space or in time?"

"Both, unfortunately. In space today, in time tonight."

"I have a question or two."

"We can have a nice talk in the car. It's a long way to Pavia."

"Not the way you drive."

"You can drive if you like, if you promise not to drop under one hundred forty. I think it's bad for the motor."

"Why Pavia?"

"It's a long story."

We checked out of the hotel, but before we started for Pavia I bought the *Herald Tribune* and a thick paperback called *Storia di Roma Antica*. When we picked up the car I said, "Go ahead and drive the first leg, Virgil. It's better to take turns anyway. I'll take over at Prato for the drive through the Apennines, if you don't mind."

"That'll be fine with me. Why did you buy the book?"

"To have something to bury my head in while you're driving."

"I shall be a model of caution."

He did slow down to a point where I wasn't expecting to die any moment, and could look at my reading material. According to Diana (or whoever she was) we were all going to be nuked in six days—five days—unless we found her brother. You wouldn't have guessed it from the newspaper. The Arms Reduction talks were evidently making some progress. The pope was on his way to Russia for a historic visit. All was quiet in the Middle East. The Cubs and Sox had both won. The world seemed to be in pretty good shape, all things considered. I said so to Virgil.

"You know as well as I do that things can happen in minutes in this push-button world."

"I find it hard to believe that there would be no warning, no buildup, no background crisis."

"Oh, it's probably brewing somewhere already, but there's no guarantee it will ever get into the *Herald Tribune*. Still, you might find something. For all the good it will do."

"It would do me good. It would be a connection between the real world and . . . and what we're doing."

"Is that what the book is for, as well?"

I put down the paper and picked up the book. "I want to check on what we saw last night."

"Oh, it all happened. But that doesn't mean it will all be in the history books. They are worse than the *Herald Tribune*."

It took me a while, but I found the story of Vercingetorix, and of Caesar's Triumph. The substance of it was all there. Even Caesar's "accident" in front of the Temple of Fortune, but without details.

"I'm sure Caesar did his best to hush it all up—a bad omen, you know. As it indeed proved to be. I'm surprised that even that much made it into the records."

"Then there was something else I wanted to bring up: just how much danger is involved in these crazy dreams? I mean, my hip still hurts!"

"I heard you fall out of bed."

"Wrong hip. I hit the floor with my left side, and it didn't hurt much. It's my right hip that hurts—the one I fell off the wagon onto."

Virgil thought a moment before answering. "I'm afraid it's quite simple," he finally said. You are dreaming with your whole spirit, with all your senses. Anything that happens to you during the dream is vicariously undergone by your body as if it were physically there. A psychosomatic phenomenon, if you will."

"And so if one of those arrows had hit me . . ."

"You may well have died. Of shock. Of the conviction that you had been killed. We'll simply have to trust the Queen of the Night to keep you from dying in your bed during these dreams. If for no other reason than that she seems to have taken a liking to you with all your impudence."

"I hope you're right. It would be kind of silly to die in a hotel bed because of an arrow some Roman shot two thousand years ago. We'll have to be more careful, Virgil. If your gods are anything like the one I'm used to, they only help those who help themselves."

"Quite right. Indubitably."

"You know, Virgil, I recall that in mythology the gods were not above having occasional love affairs with humans."

"Quite right again."

"Do you suppose Diana will want to reward me if we do a good job? I mean, if it's true she likes me . . ."

Virgil winced hard and almost drove off the road. Then he untensed and sighed. "You're dealing with the wrong goddess, my boy. Diana is the Moon Virgin, and she gets extremely . . . upset, when men show . . . special interest in her. Turns them into stags and that sort of thing. You are stretching her benevolence to the limit."

"Okay, okay. I didn't know. But hasn't she ever been in love?"

"It is said that she loved Endymion."

I had heard the name, but that's about it. I figured he couldn't really expect much more, so I plowed ahead.

"Can't remember much about him."

Virgil sighed, of course. "The sleeping shepherd! Don't you remember Keats' poem, my boy? What literature courses do you people take in America these days?"

"Updike, Mailer, Vonnegut . . ."

"I rather like Vonnegut. He seems to understand that all is whimsy."

"Listen, what we're doing is pretty serious. I mean, what's whimsical about trying to save the world from nuclear destruction?"

"Everything, my boy! Everything about it is whimsical! The fate of the world hangs on an old man's memory and a young man's dreams. And we saw last night that finding Apollo isn't going to be a straightforward affair—the gods are determined to have their fun."

"Well, if it's just fun, then they have a happy ending planned. They'll just watch us run around a while, then . . ."

"Oh, no, no, no my boy; that wouldn't be true whimsy, you see. They must leave all possibilities open, including the last: Jupiter is quite prepared to let the world blow up if we don't find Apollo, regardless of the consequences—even for himself. Divine whimsy is never under control. At its core you find Divine indifference."

"That's comforting."

"It certainly wasn't meant to be."

We made it to Prato by 11:30, and I took the wheel. I zipped over, around, and through the Apennines as fast as I thought was humanly possible—Virgil complained only once about the slow pace. By 12:30 we were in Bologna ordering *tortellini alla panna* in one of Padovani's restaurants.

"Actually I would prefer the *lasagne con porcini*," said Virgil, "but to come to Bologna and not eat tortellini would be like going to Naples and not eating pizza."

"The pizza I had in Naples wasn't bad, but it can't compare with Chicago pizza. You know—deep-dish."

Virgil gave me a baleful glance and then muttered something about *"de gustibus non est disputandum."*

"What do you care anyway?" I said. "You never eat."

"I eat for the company—because the table is the best place for a good conversation."

I had to laugh. "You know, Italians haven't changed much since your day in that respect. I was just thinking; if we were in America trying to save the world, we'd grab a hamburger someplace without getting out of the car. And here we are taking the time to eat *tortellini alla panna.*

"A world where you 'grab hamburgers' isn't worth saving, my boy."

"Climb down, climb down. Sometimes you can't beat a Big Mac."

"Here comes our waiter. Why don't you order one?"

He set our tortellini in front of us and asked us what we would have for our second course. Virgil was ready for him: *"Per me, il 'filetto di tacchino con tartufi,' e per il mio amico un 'Big Mac,' per favore."*

"No, no," I smiled, *"il tacchino va bene anche per me."* The waiter went away relieved. "Turkey with truffles?" I said to Virgil.

"They do great things with turkey in Bologna, I'm told—and I've always had a weakness for truffles."

"Expensive weakness—five hundred dollars a pound."

"Let me tell you about the time when Horace and I bought a basket of truffles . . ."

"Listen, Virgil, right now I would rather you told me about Pavia and the sort of nightmare I'm going to have tonight. I mean, we should give at least some of our time to the business of saving the human race."

"If you insist. Tonight we are going to pay a visit to the last of the true Romans. And one of the greatest, in my opinion. Not in terms of power, but in terms of Roman wisdom and virtue. Even if he was a Christian, of course. But his philosophy was Greco-Roman: Plato, Aristotle, Cato, a little Marcus Aurelius. Care to guess?"

I raised my glass of Sangiovese and critically examined its ruby-red reflections while I tried to think of something cultured to say. "Let's see, now," I began, the last of the emperors in the West was Romulus Augustulus . . ."

"The poor lad. He knew less about being a Roman emperor than you do. No, our man died in Ticinum— today called Pavia—about fifty years after the fall of the Empire in the West. In 524. His name was Anicius Manlius Torquatus Severinus Boetius. Severinus for his friends."

"And Boethius for the world. The author of *The Consolation of Philosophy*."

"Bravo, Del! So you read something besides Vonnegut at Notre Dame!"

"Oh, I never read Boethius, but I remember his name from a History of Philosophy course I took. I know that that book of his was very important in the Middle Ages."

"For eight hundred years it was the most widely-read book in Europe. After the Bible, of course."

"And you think he's a likely prospect."

"He was a senator and a consul, of the noble Roman family of the Anicii. The Ostrogothic king Theodoric made him 'magister officiorum,' the head of the entire civil administration of the court in

Ravenna. What happened to him was complicated, but I'll try to simplify it as much as I can."

The waiter brought our turkey. Virgil pronounced it reasonably good, and continued his story. "Theodoric was an Arian Christian, a heretic, you would say, whereas Justin, the Emperor of the East, was in communion with the Roman pope, John I. So were Boethius and many other senators, who therefore felt closer to the Emperor of the East than to the barbarian who was king of Italy. Still Boethius was a loyal servant, who administered the state bureaucracy with wisdom and honesty. One day certain letters were brought to his attention that had been written by a friend of his, the Roman Catholic senator Albinus, to the Emperor Justin. The content of the letters made little difference; the simple fact of being in correspondence with Justin was treasonous under Theodoric. Boethius tried to cover up the whole thing in order to protect his friend, but Theodoric somehow got wind of it."

"And that's when the shit hit the fan."

Virgil paused only for a moment. "No, not really. Not for Boethius, at any rate. But Albinus was put on trial, and Boethius let his courage get the better of his prudence, and publicly came out in his friend's defense, passionately arguing for the right of any Roman senator to write to whomever he pleased. At one point in his speech he said, 'If Albinus is guilty, then so am I,'' and that's when the sh . . . patience of Theodoric ran out. Boethius was charged with treason, Theodoric twisted arms in the Senate to make the charge stick, and after a rather farcical trial before the tribunal of Ticinum, Boothius was sentenced to death. But he had about ten months before the sentence was carried out, and in that time he wrote his famous book."

"Maybe we should buy a copy. I could bone up a bit."

"I don't think that's necessary. But if you like, I think I remember a few of the nicer passages."

He remembered a great many of the nicer passages, and that's how we passed our time in the car from Bologna to Pavia.

"Boethius understood Fortune for what it was—the whimsy of the universe," he said, as we whipped by Piacenza. "And in the *Consolation* he abandons Lady Luck for Lady Philosophy. At one point Philosophy says to him: 'So you want Luck to help you out? Then you have to play by her rules. You can't stop her from turning her wheel, O greatest of nitwits, because she would cease to be herself.' "

"What was the Latin for 'greatest of nitwits'?" I asked.

"Omnium mortalium stolidissime."

"I'll have to remember that. And what does he decide to do about Lady Luck?"

Lady Philosophy tells him: "Fight against Lady Luck, so that she doesn't get you down when she's bad or corrupt you when she's good. Play it cool."

"Where did you learn that last expression?"

"One must try to keep up with colloquialisms, my boy. They are the lymph of language."

"And how does it sound in Latin?"

"Firmis medium viribus occupate."

"I'll amaze my friends and confound my enemies with what you're teaching me, Virgil. If I can remember some of it."

"And if we're not all blown up in five days."

"We'll just have to play it cool."

"Quite right."

Pavia is an elegant little city of about 100,000 people, which in the Middle Ages battled nearby Milan to a standoff time and again until the great Visconti family finally forced her to her knees in the fourteenth century. We drove by the beautiful Certosa, the Carthusian Monastery on the outskirts of the city, then by the park where, as Virgil took pains to explain, Francis I of France was defeated and captured by Charles V of Spain in 1525 in a great battle that proved the superiority of firearms over cold steel, putting an end (militarily) to the Middle Ages. Virgil himself was in Milan at that time, picking horses for the Duke, Francesco Maria Sforza.

"Picking horses?" I asked.

"Oh, I was famous for that in the old days, you know. Octavian wouldn't have a horse unless I looked at it first. A real eye for horses has always been a rare thing—perhaps rarer than the gift of poetry. I have often used this gift down through the centuries—to make the acquaintance of powerful men, and more importantly, because it still gives me great pleasure."

Now we were going by the colleges of the University of Pavia, founded in 1361, but with a law school dating back to 825. The slogan of the moment was white-washed onto the walls: "Stop al Nucleare!" Fallout from Chernobyl: the students wanted to close Italy's one nuclear power plant and stop work on the two under construction. Stop al nucleare. That's what we're here for, boys, I thought. But cheer up, we might be crazy.

Virgil pointed out to me that the street plan still followed the outline of the old Roman *castrum*, showing that for almost seven hundred years Ticinum was a bastion of Rome's defense network. Finally he stopped the car in the center of the city, in front of the cathedral with its huge cupola.

"Are the stones that groan with sorrow here?" I asked.

"Perhaps, but I wouldn't know which ones they were. The tower in which Boethius was imprisoned was somewhere here, but no trace of it is left. The cathedral is comparatively quite recent—begun in the fifteenth century and finished in the nineteenth."

"Took their time with it, didn't they?"

"Chi va piano, va sano e va lontano."

"Haste makes waste."

"Quite right."

"So where do we find the stones that groan?"

"I think we can do better than stones. The bones, my boy. Boethius' bones."

"And where are they?"

"In a church called San Pietro in Ciel d'Oro."

As it turned out, the church wasn't hard to find. Virgil confessed he might have had trouble finding it on his own after so many years—three hundred and nineteen, he calculated—but Democrazia Proletaria, a small political party on the way-out left, had put discreet little signs on the city's corners to help tourists find all the important sights. The signs also said: "The city government doesn't seem to understand that tourism can provide jobs."

"They've got my vote," I said.

"For the Ministry of Tourism, most certainly," said Virgil.

The church was out of the way, on a corner next to a military school. When we got there, it was after five o'clock, but the summer sun was still high and hot.

"What have we here?" exclaimed Virgil, looking at a stone plaque at the entrance to the church. "What a fine idea! Dante's verses, in *Paradiso*, you see, where he writes about Boethius and this church:

*"Lo corpo ond'ella fu cacciata giace
giuso in Cieldauro ed essa da martiro
e da esilio venne a questa pace."*

"What do *'ella'* and *'essa'* refer to?" I asked.

"To Boethius' soul: 'The body whence it was chased lies down under the Golden Ceiling, and from martyrdom and exile came unto this peace.' "

"So you came here with Dante."

"Well, no. We confined our movements to Tuscany. Travel was fraught with inconveniences, you know. But we did discuss Boethius at length, and I told him about this church."

As we went in I looked up, expecting to find a *ciel d'oro,* a golden ceiling, but it was only brick, except over the altar. Virgil saw me staring.

"Oh, the whole vault used to be covered with gold, my boy. Most of it was stripped away, to pay for someone's wars."

"And is that where Boethius' bones are?" Now I was looking above the main altar at what was clearly the tomb of someone very illustrious, judging from the fine marble statuary with which it was surrounded so as to form a three-arched Gothic chapel that protected the sarcophagus.

"Beautiful, isn't it? Fourteenth century. No, that isn't Boethius, but someone considerably more famous: Aurelius Augustinus—your Saint Augustine. A fine Roman, in his own way. Heard him speak once, in Ostia. Quite moving."

"That's where Saint Augustine is buried?"

"Well, the Pavians paid the Arabs a fortune for the skeleton that's in there. The suspicion has always remained, however, that it belonged to a Saracen pirate and not to the great bishop of Hippo. The gods, of course, enjoy that sort of thing. My own bones were supposed to be in a sepulcher near Naples. I was there when they opened it. I was hoping that some sort of skeleton would be in there, but it was simply empty. A great disappointment for everyone."

"Then I suppose that's Boethius in that tomb on the right."

"Hardly. That's Liutprand, a Lombard king. Kept trying to take Rome, in the eighth century. A very messy century. Come along now. Our man is over here."

Virgil led me down into the crypt where, on a little altar in the center, there was a small container with glass sides; inside there was a rather random assortment of dry, gray bones. The name was faintly inscribed underneath: SEVERINUS BOETIUS.

"How was he executed?"

"Barbarously, of course. They tried strangling him, but botched the job; a friend of the family told me that one of his eyes popped out. So they clubbed him to death. Tonight I want you to dream about the day it happened: October 23, 524."

I put both my hands on the inscribed name and closed my eyes.

"Legend has it that . . ."

"Shhh!" I was listening to something—listening with my hands. A low moan that was slowly working its way up my arms. I jerked back from the tomb.

"What's wrong, Del?"

"Let's find a good hotel with king-size beds. It's going to be a tough night."

VII

After falling asleep I found myself in a large market-place, and my nose was filled with interesting smells, the least interesting of which was the unwashed odor of the people hurrying all around me. The next thing I noticed was that it was cold; the clothes I had been wearing on a day in August many hundreds of years in the future were inadequate here. I rubbed my bare arms.

"It's October 23 today, remember?" Good old Virgil was by my side. "A chilly autumn day," he went on. "Since we're in a market place, I suggest we purchase some sort of appropriate clothing."

And so we walked around the marketplace of old Ticinum, which differed only in secondary ways from open markets in the Mediterranean countries of our century. The same hawking, the same haggling, the same basic merchandise—pots and pans and cheese and vegetables.

"Trout! A beautiful trout from the Ticino River! This morning at five he was still alive!"

"He smells like he died of the plague!"

"Olive oil from Liguria! Pour it on your food, rub it on your body!"

"Not at those prices, bandit!"

We came to a stand where an old man and two small girls were selling cloth and yarn; behind them we noticed a small selection of cloaks.

"I know someone who might need two cheap cloaks," said Virgil to the old man.

"Then don't send him here. We have only fine cloaks."

"I was referring to those rags hanging behind you."

The merchant took down two brown cloaks and threw them on the table in front of us. Virgil fingered them as if they were used handkerchiefs.

"I don't think my friend is this desperate," he finally said, "unless the price were very low."

"For two fine cloaks like these, ten pieces of silver is nothing."

"My friend might be persuaded to give you two. Two lire-pieces."

"Two what?"

"He comes from a rich land, far to the east. Look at these." And here Virgil took two 100-lire coins out of his pocket. The old man looked one of them over, bit it, and shook his head.

"You could buy a horse with these!" protested Virgil.

"Your coins contain no gold or silver. Your country far to the east must be poor indeed."

I was really getting cold, so I decided to intervene. "Don't sell your cloaks to this man, old merchant. He doesn't appreciate their quality. I can see that they are truly fine cloaks." Both Virgil and the merchant stared at me, speechless. "Such cloaks are worth many pieces of silver," I continued, "or even more." And here I took off my digital watch. "Even a powerful talisman such as this."

The old man called upon all of his professional

reserve to hide his amazement at the strange glowing symbols that magically changed.

"It's a language that only the spirits understand," I said. I was beginning to enjoy myself, and Virgil had started to smile. "It commands them to protect you. And if you press this button," I pressed the date button, "it tells them to give you good fortune." I kept staring at the date: October 23, 524. A damn good watch.

"Well," said the old man, fumbling to get the watch on, "it's a worthless trinket, but my grandchildren might like it. What are the other buttons for?"

"Oh, you must never press those!" I couldn't resist. "Or at least, please wait until I am far away before you do!" I snatched up the cloaks and walked away, with Virgil tagging behind. They were a bit rough and smelly but not too heavy; enough to keep us warm, however.

"Nicely done back there, Del."

"He won't be able to find anyone who can read those numbers, will he?"

"Not for another five hundred years."

"I suppose my watch will disappear when we do."

"Of course."

"So the poor devil will be out two cloaks."

"I rather expect they will reappear on his rack when we've done with them."

"In other words, Diana will tidy up after us."

"Quite. Now let's hurry to the tower."

There was much to look at as we walked along: the old Roman temples could still be seen, but large slabs of marble had been stripped away, and many of the walls had been scorched. On the side of one large building, however, a team of workers on a rickety scaffolding were scrubbing the wall with big bristly brushes.

"Ticinum fell on bad times, you know," said Virgil. "First Attila seventy-five years ago, then Odoacer fifty years ago." Virgil shook his head. "*Homo homini lupus.* The town lost half its population. Then Theodoric came with his Ostrogoths, thirty years ago. He considers himself the defender of Roman civilization, you know. He has done a great deal to stop the pillaging of the temples, and has even restored a good number of buildings around Italy, especially in Rome. But it is all for naught. The long night is coming. These are the twilight years. Theodoric knows Latin and Greek, but doesn't know how to write!"

Bearded soldiers dressed in hard leather could be seen standing around in small groups, talking and laughing.

"The Ostrogoths have made Ticinum one of the three capitals of their kingdom, along with Verona and Ravenna; but the court is in Ravenna. Still, this city is growing in importance. Look down the street to the left: those are Theodoric's new baths. And there is his amphitheater—not bad for a barbarian. And that huge new building ahead is one of his palaces."

I was impressed. "It looks like a town making a comeback. There's a lot of vitality here."

Virgil gave out one of his longer sighs. "In ten years the Eastern Emperor Justinian will invade the West, trying to restore the old order, but causing more havoc and destruction than the barbarians ever did. The Ostrogoths will be forced to abandon Ravenna, and move the court here to Ticinum. Then even Ticinum will fall. But the Byzantine peace will be short-lived. In 572 the city will fall to the Lombards, after a three-year siege, and become their capital. And they will have no desire at all to preserve Roman ways. They will change Ticinum's name to 'Papia,' and as such she will sadly preside over the progressive benightening of the Western world."

"That must be our tower," I said. It wasn't very tall, as towers go: rather squat and stocky, and made of sandy-looking bricks.

"Indeed it is," replied Virgil. And what is to be our strategy?"

"Let's wing it."

"I beg your pardon?"

"Play it by ear."

"Ah, yes. Quite. Well, *audaces fortuna iuvat*, you know."

"HALT!" It was just about the biggest, burliest, ugliest Ostrogoth I had ever seen, and he was barring the entrance to the tower with an ax.

"My good man," began Virgil, "we are friends of the prisoner Boethius, and have come to see him."

"No visits this morning. Orders." The ax didn't move. I tried a different tack.

"You obviously don't know who we are. Don't let these simple cloaks fool you. We are special envoys traveling incognito."

"Keep traveling." He turned the blade of the ax toward us.

"We are prepared to reward your kindness, if you allow us to comfort our unhappy friend," said Virgil— and he took off *his* watch. It was a gold Patek-Phillippe, studded with small diamonds. It was undigital. The barbarian took the watch with one thick grimy finger and stared at it disdainfully.

"It's a device for determining the hours of the day and night," said Virgil. Those little needles move with such regularity that you can always tell exactly what time it is."

"Who in hell needs to know that?"

"Maybe your wife would like it," I suggested.

"My wife. Hah! My wife's been dead for fifteen years. In the other country."

A thought hit me. I wasn't going to get fooled twice. "And where are you from?" I asked.

"I was born in Thrace. But my father was born far to the north. I don't know where I'm from. A Goth makes his home where he pleases. And does what he pleases." He dropped Virgil's watch into a leather pouch attached to his thick belt. "And now it pleases me to let you speak to the Roman. For a few minutes. And I, not your bauble, will decide when the minutes are finished." With that he lowered his ax, and we were able to enter the tower.

"It would have been shocking indeed if that great oaf had turned out to be Apollo," said Virgil as we began winding our way up a tight and gloomy stone staircase. "Nonetheless, I suppose you were right to try."

Every ten steps there was a small landing and a cell door with a little barred window. The first cell was empty. The second held a man too young to be the forty-four-year-old Boethius. "Where are you from?" I called in through the window.

"Mediolanum," the young man replied in a thin voice. "And I believe that the Son is of one substance with the Father."

I looked at Virgil. "That means he's Roman Catholic, not Arian," he said. "But that can't be why he's in there, unless he really made himself obnoxious. Keep going."

The third cell contained a mean-looking old woman.

We moved on. "I don't suppose Apollo could be a woman, could he?" I asked.

"Unlikely, but not impossible. Vertumnus, the god of the seasons, changed into an old woman in order to get close to Pomona, the man-hating object of his affections. But I refuse to entertain such conjectures as of yet."

"There's another thing I wanted to ask you." I stopped on the stairs for a moment. "Is there any chance that this guy will recognize you? I mean, did you know him personally?"

"No. The real me right now is a monk helping Benedict found his monastery on Monte Cassino. I was his first librarian."

"A monk!"

"Anything to help preserve Latin literature. Move along now."

In the fourth cell a middle-aged man was looking through a small barred window in the back of the cell. He was short and stocky, brown-haired but balding, and he was wearing a dirty white toga. It had to be Boethius. I got right down to business.

"Where are you from, sir?"

"And who is it that wishes to know?" he answered without turning around. His voice was soft but firm—a voice used to speaking with authority.

"Friends, noble sir," said Virgil. "Friends from far away who have come to offer the warmth of companionship in exchange for the light of your wisdom."

Now he slowly turned toward us. His eyes were deep-set, but clear and bright. "Come in, then, for it is an exchange I would gladly make, and make, and make again for many a day. But I have no days, only hours. And perhaps not hours, but minutes."

The door was bolted but there was no lock, so we

were able to let ourselves into his cell. "It shouldn't be too hard to organize an escape if they don't even bother to lock your cell," I said.

"I gave them my word I would attempt no escape in exchange for certain privileges." He indicated a corner of the cell, where there was a small desk covered with writing materials. On the floor next to the chair there was a pile of scrolls. "And the word of a Roman senator is still worth something—although I don't see why it should be."

"You don't see why it should be!" said Virgil. Why, Rome taught the world the meaning of the word 'honor'!"

"Yes, indeed, in the Golden Age, when Cicero, and Cato, and Seneca, and Horace, and Livy, and Virgil, and great Ovid walked in splendor and strength. But since then Rome has taught many other lessons to the world. Duplicity, cruelty, and now—now even cowardice. It is right that Rome should die, for her spirit died long ago. Far better these barbarians in their vigor and ignorance. They are children who will grow. Rome is an empty old harlot."

"It was a barbarian king who unjustly imprisoned you."

"Acting out of pride. And out of love for his Arian god. And from the Roman Senate in Ravenna, the Senate I was trying to defend, not one voice was lifted in my behalf. Out of cowardice."

"Were you born in Ravenna, sir?" I had to try to get us back on the track.

He smiled. "No, sir. The Anicii are born in Rome. But I was raised in a fine villa in the Alban hills. Oh, I come from a beautiful land, good sir, but not half so beautiful as the one I hope to see before today's sun is set." Virgil smiled from ear to ear, which struck

Boethius as an odd reaction. "Good sirs, do you not share with me the Christian hope for resurrection in Jesus Christ? Today I shall cast off this body like an old garment!"

"We believe this most firmly, great sir," said Virgil warmly. "And now, please tell us: what is your name?"

The man looked surprised. It was his turn to smile. "Strange friends you are, that don't know my name! And you come from far away indeed, if you don't know that this evil tower holds the ex-consul Severinus Boetius."

It was my turn. "Please excuse me; what is your name again?"

Boethius looked at me long and hard. "No excuses are needed, for now I understand. You have come to help me prepare for death, to teach me the humility I will need in the presence of God. For what does a noble name and a fine title mean before the Judgment Seat? There we all have but one name: Sinner, miserable Sinner. You said that you have come for the light of my wisdom, but my wisdom is the old wisdom of an unredeemed world, a wisdom based on what a man can do with his reason to find consolation here below. I have written of these things because I believe this wisdom must not be lost, for it is not opposed to the new wisdom of the children of God, the wisdom that surpasses understanding. Good sirs, if you are, as I now believe, priests of the Lord's true church, pray with me now, for the old philosophy can lead a man safely to the very doors of death, but only faith in Jesus Christ can open those doors." And with that, he got down on his knees and bowed his head.

"That's no good, is it?" I whispered to Virgil. "I mean, he didn't give me his name."

"I'm afraid not." And Virgil went down on his

knees in front of Boethius, put his hands on his shoulders and said, "You must trust us for a moment, good sir. Please tell us a second time: What is your name?"

Heavy steps on the tower stairs. We were going to get screwed again.

"What is your name?" I fairly shouted. But the cell door swung open and a procession of five people came in. There was the oaf with Virgil's watch in his pouch, plus two other bad-looking Ostrogoths who were evidently his fellow guards, and two other men, one of whom ran to embrace Boethius, who was getting to his feet.

"Severinus!"

"Memmius!"

Virgil pulled me aside. He looked resigned. "This is Memmius Symmachus, Boethius' father-in-law. He is here because he tried to defend his son-in-law, and he will die today with him. Now, it would seem." Virgil was looking at the two new guards, who had leather cords and knotty clubs.

The fifth man now took out and held up a small piece of bread and said "I have brought Holy Viaticum for your journey to the Lord."

Boethius looked at us and said, "Are we then blessed with three priests in this our final hour?"

"But we are not priests, sir," I said. "We . . ."

"These men falsely claimed to be your friends!!" It was the oaf. He moved toward us with his ax. Boethius headed him off.

"They are more than friends, they are my brothers in Christ, and have brought me comfort. Let them go in peace, I pray you—or remain, if they so choose."

"They cannot stay! No witnesses except the priest. These *brothers* must leave. Now!"

Virgil held Boethius' hands for a moment. His face was a mask of sadness.

"Courage, good sir," said Boethius. "I wish there were more time for conversation."

"So do I, noble sir. So do I." And Virgil turned to go.

I shook the philosopher's hand, rather too hard under the circumstances. To come out with another "What is your name?" at this point would have been not only futile but dangerous. I simply said, "Good-bye."

"We shall meet again in Heaven," he said, "and continue our talk." I smiled weakly and walked out of the cell.

As we went down the stairs I asked Virgil, "Is there any point in our sticking around?"

"None whatever. I suggest you try to wake up."

I knew pinching wouldn't work, because even getting badly hurt hadn't done the trick in Rome. I concentrated hard. "Wake up, wake up, you dummy!" I thought. No soap. "This isn't going to be easy, Virgil," I said.

"Then we'll just have to wait."

"Wait for what?"

"For Boethius to die. Evidently you can't wake up until Apollo dies. It won't be long. Come with me."

We walked back to one of the old temples and went inside. It was clean, but completely empty. "The statue of Apollo would have been right about here," said Virgil when he reached the back. Then the temple started to tremble. It wasn't like an earthquake. The building was shuddering in silence, alone. Then I woke up.

VIII

Breakfast was another sad affair. We peered at each other with bleary eyes over the tops of our cappuccini.

"There are better ways to spend a night," said Virgil.

"And better company to spend a night in—no offense intended."

"I never liked sleeping—not even when I needed it. Now that I do it only to be your guide, I like it even less." He was holding up his cup with both hands, and I could see his wrists.

"Watch in good shape?" I asked.

"It seems to be. No thanks to that oaf. And yours?"

"Date button doesn't work."

"If we survive this, I'll take you to Switzerland and get you a decent watch. With hands instead of neon lights."

"Where are we going today?"

"To Naples."

"Oh, Lord. All the way back down. Couldn't you come up with someone a little closer?"

"Yes, I could. In fact, I did. But the days are passing. We have to go where we have the best chance of success." I was sullen. Virgil continued. "This morning, after we returned from old Ticinum, my first thought was of Arnold of Brescia."

"Who the hell . . ."

"Oh, he was a fascinating person, a man who fought against every power figure he encountered. He collected more reprisals than Martin Luther. He was declared a schismatic by one pope, a heretic by another, and by means of a third, Adrian IV, he earned a historic distinction indeed."

"And what was that?" I muttered.

"The only man to succeed in getting the city of Rome placed under a papal interdict."

"Sounds pretty bad."

"If you believe as firmly as they believed in the Middle Ages, nothing can be more terrible. In fact, it worked. The Romans, who loved Arnold, had to turn him over, and he was hanged."

"Must have had some weird ideas."

"Only one, really. He believed that the pope and the church should avoid material wealth and power."

"Lots of people have said that. Saint Francis, Saint Bernard . . ."

"Arnold made a point of saying it in the wrong way, in the wrong place, at the wrong time. He was an impossible man, really. Absolutely no tact, and no patience. A tragic case."

"Sounds like our man."

"Oh, I'm sure he is. I'm certain he was Apollo. But can you imagine trying to talk to such a one, trying to get him to repeat his name? They say he even refused confession; he would entrust his sins to Christ alone. But if you insist, we can see if it can be done."

I shook my head slowly. "Could you think up somebody who isn't so awfully religious? I mean, that was our problem with Boethius."

"I think I've found just the man. Or boy, rather. A boy of sixteen. It should be easy to talk to him, to impress him, to get him to answer our questions. He died in Naples about a hundred years after Arnold—in 1268. On October 29. How very unfortunate. All Italy talked about it for years. Shocking. Quite shocking."

"Let's get going, Virgil. Naples is quite a hike."

I bought a newspaper before we left, and found I was able to read it calmly enough—I was getting used to Virgil's driving. Well, the choice was between that and ulcers. And there was nothing much in the paper; nothing to suggest that in five days all those red buttons were going to be pushed. The pope was doing his thing in Kiev. East Germany had agreed to talks with the West that would include a discussion of the possibility of tearing down the Berlin Wall. Both the Cubs and the Sox had won again, and were leading their divisions. I remembered that one of the prophecies of Nostradamus had been interpreted to mean that the world would end on the opening day of a World Series between the Cubs and the Sox; but that would have to wait until October in any case. Then I noticed that an American track and field team would be going to the Soviet Union for a big meet in a few days.

"Hey, Virgil, what do you think would happen if the Russians wiped out an American track and field team?"

"They do that often enough, don't they? It seems to me that except for the dash events . . ."

"No, no, I mean really wipe them out. Kill them all, or hold them as hostages or something."

"Whatever would bring them to do a thing like that?"

That was a tough question. Virgil answered it.

"I imagine they might be induced to hold them as hostages by some enormous provocation on the part of the Americans."

"Such as?"

"Direct intervention in Afghanistan, perhaps. But this is all bootless bar room speculation, my boy. We'll just have to wait and see."

I sat back and closed my eyes. It would have been nice to get some normal sleep for a change. I thought about Concetta. Concetta was a girl I knew in Naples.

I woke up about an hour later with a fine idea in my head. I didn't expect Virgil to like it, but I was determined to be firm.

"I'm glad you were able to take a nap, Del. The last few nights have not been particularly restful."

He had given me a perfect opening. "No, they haven't. And they've been dangerous, too. And I didn't particularly like the fact that I wasn't able to wake up when I wanted to. I mean, things could go wrong. I'd hate to get stuck back in some godforsaken century."

"You're forgetting Diana."

"And you're forgetting the whimsy of the gods you like to talk about."

"Del, my boy, faint heart never . . ."

"Never filled a flush. I know."

"Never filled what? I've never heard that."

"Then you've never played poker."

"No, indeed. But I should like to learn."

"Let's not get off the subject."

"What is the subject?"

"My nights."

"What else is there to say?"

"Tonight I'm going to have some company. Real company." Virgil said nothing. "I know a girl in Naples. A nice girl, very attractive. And very understanding. And affectionate. I'm going to ask her to spend the night with me."

"Del, only the two of us can travel through time together."

"I know that. But I want her there in bed with me. For two good reasons. The first one is obvious. I'm getting very uptight, and a little Tender Loving Care is just what I need. And the second one is more important. If I have a heart attack or convulsions or just trouble waking up, someone will be right there to help me." There was a third reason, perhaps the most important. But I wasn't going to tell Virgil about it.

After a minute of silence, Virgil said, "There's a third reason, isn't there, Del?"

"Do I need one?"

"The first two are a bit weak."

"The flesh is weak, my dear Virgil."

"But what you are seeking from this girl is more than fleshly comfort."

"Perhaps." The old devil was uncanny.

"You want to renew contact with other people—with normal people. You're afraid of losing all touch with reality."

"Something like that." It was exactly like that.

"You're not out of your mind, you know."

"Coming from you that isn't much comfort. But coming from a normal person it might help . . . No, I don't mean that. I know I can't talk about all this to anybody. That's not what I want to do. I want to spend some time with somebody who knows absolutely nothing about all this. I just want her to touch me and tell me I'm real."

"You can't deny that what's happening to us is real."

"At this point, that would mean denying myself. I have no choice but to go along. But I'm being carried beyond all contact with . . . look at those people,

Virgil." We were flying past a family sedan full of kids; a luggage rack on the roof was loaded with camping equipment. "They're going on vacation. They're going to hike and swim and fight mosquitoes for a couple of weeks. There are lots of people like them, Virgil. A whole world full of them."

"If you quit now, there'll soon be very few of them, indeed."

"Oh, I know I have to see the thing through. Helluva game, though, with all these new rules."

"Think for a moment of that chap driving that automobile full of family back there . . ."

"*Way* back there. You're doing two hundred."

"Yes. Well, quite likely he feels much the same way. He has to see it through. I doubt that he's terribly keen about what he's doing."

"At least he knows the rules of the game."

"Does he really?"

"He thinks he does."

"Really?"

"How about turning on the radio?"

I took a while for us to decide on a channel. I wanted Vivaldi's *Four Seasons* on FM stereo, but Virgil had found a station that was doing nonstop Bob Dylan.

"You've got to be kidding," I said.

"I rather like him. He's something of a poet."

"He certainly isn't a singer."

"Listen to the words, my boy."

"The words are completely outmoded. Like my high school letter sweater."

"Would you please listen for a moment?"

Old Bob sang it right on cue, and grudgingly, I had to give it to Virgil, it *was* a hard rain, and it *was* a-gonna fall.

We had a quick lunch in Florence. "Quick" means an hour and ten minutes. I had a "Fiorentina," which is a pretty good steak. I said *"al sangue"* about three times, but it still wasn't rare enough to suit me. It was pink, not red.

"Italians have never learned how to cook good meat," I complained to Virgil. They're great with tripe, pig's feet, cow's cheeks, rooster combs and all that crap, but if you give them a decent piece of meat they just cook the hell out of it."

"There is an element of truth in what you say." Virgil was nursing along an *antipasto misto,* a plate of cold cuts, which was all he wanted. "But this is the greatness of Italian cuisine. The poor people created it from what the rich did not deign to eat. The ingredients of real Italian food are always the commonest, most inexpensive things: polenta, pasta, pizza . . ."

"You should see what a plate of pasta costs in an Italian restaurant in Chicago."

"How regrettable. But with regard to what you were saying, it isn't altogether true that Italians don't know what to do with the better cuts of meat. A good *brasato* . . ."

"I know, I know. I told you I'm up tight. How about telling me about tonight? Who's the kid we're going to look up in medieval Naples?"

"The Italians call him 'Corradino.' In English it's 'Conradin,' I believe. In reality he was Conrad V, Duke of Swabia, and the last of the Hohenstaufens."

"The who?"

"Oh, come now, Del, you must have studied the great European dynasties. You know, the Hapsburgs, the Savoys, the Bourbons . . ."

". . . and the Hohenstaufens. Yes, I remember the

name now. Not much else. They produced some emperors, didn't they?"

Virgil thought for a moment. "Three. The most famous was Frederick I—Barbarossa. Remember?"

"Vaguely. I was never a big star in history."

"Evidently not."

"Let's get back to our boy Conradin."

"Yes. Well, I'll try to make it simple. In those days you either had to be a guelph or a ghibelline. The guelphs were, roughly speaking, supporters of the political power of the pope, whereas the ghibellines, roughly speaking, sided with the Holy Roman Emperor."

"And of course Conradin was a ghibelline."

"Not really, but the ghibellines wanted to use him against the pope, Clement IV, who was getting too powerful. Clement had just put his friend and fellow Frenchman Charles of Anjou on the throne of Sicily. The ghibellines asked Conradin to come down from Germany and take Sicily, which was rightfully his anyway. Rightfully, if you're a ghibelline."

"I'm not sure."

"Anyway, the lad came sweeping down with a fair-sized army, passing triumphantly from one ghibelline city to another; Verona, Pavia, Pisa, Siena—he fell in love with Italy, and thought that all Italy loved him."

"He didn't know about the guelphs?"

"He didn't take them seriously. How much did you take seriously when you were fifteen?"

"Oh, I took some things very seriously."

"But not the guelphs."

"No, not the guelphs." I slowly chewed on my last piece of steak.

"Finally he reached Rome, where he got the warmest welcome of all."

"What? Even Rome was ghibelline?"

"Predominantly. The guelphs had fled, and so had the pope. But Charles of Anjou hadn't fled; he was an old fox, the veteran of many battles. He waited with his army in Abruzzo, east of Rome, and when the boy went out after him, he was routed."

"Who? Which one got routed?" My mind had done some wandering.

"Conradin, of course. He fled to Nettuno, to the castle of one of the noble Romans who had applauded him only weeks before—a man named Giovanni Frangipane."

"And Giovanni sold Conradin to Charles of Anjou."

"You do remember some of the story."

"None of it, but back in Chicago it happens all the time."

"And Charles had the boy beheaded in a public square in Naples. Does that happen all the time?"

"Not in public squares. I think we should get the show on the road, Virgil."

"Wouldn't you care for dessert?"

"No, thank you."

"Fruit?"

"No, thanks."

"Not even coffee?"

"Not even coffee. I'm already nervous enough."

"And you're looking forward to seeing your lady friend."

"If you like, I'll ask her if she has a friend for you." He didn't like it, but it got him out of his chair.

In the car I pursued the subject. "I already know that you don't normally eat, drink, or sleep. Am I to understand that you don't have sex either?"

"I have never been a man of passion—not even

when I was alive. My experiments with Eros were limited—and uninspiring, I'm afraid.''

"And since you died—nothing?"

"Death takes a lot out of you, Del."

There had to be some truth to that, but I still wasn't completely convinced. A few minutes later I played my last card. "You know, I was just thinking about Delia Alibrandi's father not having enough money for her dowry, and having to send her to a convent—could that be because he guelphed when he should have ghibellined?"

"Extraordinary. Yes, that was a part of it. You Americans take such liberties with language."

"I thought you liked it."

"Up to a point. The point where liberty becomes anarchy."

"Getting back to Delia . . ."

"We weren't talking about Delia. We were talking about her father. *You* were."

"You'd better slow down if you're going to get touchy."

"I'm not touchy, but I know what you're driving at, and I'm not sure I don't resent it."

"What's wrong with my wondering whether or not your relationship with this very special person went as far as making love? I'd be anything but displeased, you know."

Virgil was silent for sometime. Then he said:

" *'Twere profanation of our joys
To tell the laity our love.''*

I slumped down into my bucket seat. "All right. But you did love her. Not just her poetry. You loved a woman, body and soul. And you still do."

Virgil slowed down. Then he said:

*"But we, by a love so much refined
That our selves know not what it is,
Inter-assured of the mind,
Care less, eyes, lips and hands to miss."*

"Virgil, notice that Donne says 'care *less*,' he doesn't say 'care *not*.' There's a difference."

"I know. I know. Would you mind driving for a while, Del?"

I didn't mind at all, and in fact I drove the rest of the way to Naples. Virgil wasn't very good company—he kept staring out the window on his side. He didn't even complain when I found some Monteverdi on the stereo.

IX

Virgil had me head straight for the waterfront, and there we started south with the city on our left and the bay of Naples on the right.

"Didn't you live in Naples for a time, Virgil?"

"I had a very nice villa at Marechiaro on the Promontory of Posillipo, which was not a part of Naples at the time. We've already passed it."

"Didn't you want to see it?"

"Oh, there's nothing left of my villa. And besides, nostalgia is only to be taken in small doses. Pull over and stop here for a moment." We were in front of "Castel dell'Ovo," the old castle built on a strip of land that juts out into the bay.

"This is where Conradin awaited his execution. It was quite different then, of course. Considerably smaller. It's been redone several times. That little round fort facing the sea is only about three hundred years old. And I remember when the Spanish seriously damaged the whole castle at the beginning of the sixteenth century."

"How did it get its name—'Castle of the Egg'?"

"Hah! That's a good story, and I'm supposed to be at the bottom of it. You know, Del, I had quite a reputation in the Middle Ages, and especially here in Naples, for being a sorceror."

"A sorceror! Virgil the poet!"

"I was supposed to have freed a devil imprisoned in a bottle in exchange for immortality, and for the secrets of magic. All sorts of strange things were attributed to me. I was rather amused, and I must confess I took no steps to put an end to it all."

"I'll bet you didn't. In fact, I'll bet you actually did some of those strange things."

"Don't be silly! I have no special powers at all."

"Superior knowledge is the greatest power, and you've always had that. What did you do here?"

"*They say* that I put an egg in a pitcher and put the pitcher in an iron cage and hung it from the ceiling in one of the rooms, and that I tied the fate of the castle to the fate of the egg."

"Okay, so what happened to the egg?"

Virgil smiled. "It broke. During the reign of Joan I."

"And the castle?"

Virgil's smile got wider. "It sort of caved in. Joan had it rebuilt, and put a fresh egg in the pitcher."

"And of course, you had nothing to do with all this."

"I don't even like eggs."

"Shall I go over and touch the castle? The stones that groan, you know. That way I can dream this place up tonight."

"No, I don't think we should try to meet with Conradin here. He and his companions will be under a heavy guard. The people felt sorry for him, and few were enthusiastic about having Charles as king. In other words, he still represented a dangerous political threat. I doubt that anyone was let in to see him here.

Out best chance to talk to him is at the site of the execution. A condemned man always has the right to speak."

"You're the guide. But I have a suggestion. Why don't we buy a few more watches or trinkets of some sort, to have in case we have to do some purchasing or some corrupting tonight?"

"It certainly can't hurt. Come, let's proceed to the place of execution—Piazza del Mercato." We started up and continued along the waterfront, past the enormous Castel Nuovo which Charles of Anjou built after the execution, past the 'Molo Angioino,' the pier built by his son, Charles II . . ."

"So the Angevin dynasty did a lot for Naples, I gather."

"Charles I made Naples the capital of a kingdom, something she never again ceased to be until 1860."

"But this was a foreign dynasty."

"Nothing odd about that. Naples was in the hands of foreign dynasties starting from the Normans in 1140 right down to Garibaldi."

"Who was also considered a foreigner, I suppose."

"Of course. Piedmontese. Turn left here." I turned into Piazza Masaniello where we parked, illegally, but there didn't seem to be much choice. Virgil went to buy some trinkets. I went to make a phone call.

"*Ciao*, Concetta!"

"*Ciao*! Who are you?" This was all in Italian, of course—mine with an American accent and hers with that Neapolitan tone pattern that makes everything sound so dramatic, at least to me.

"I'm Fred! Fred l'americano!"

"Freddino mio! Where are you?"

"Here in Naples, Concettina mia! But I'm afraid it's just a one-night stand. How about meeting at "Giovanni's'? We can start the night with some boiled octopus!"

"Freddino, I'm busy tonight."

"Concetta, I was really looking forward to seeing you."

"But this is my—what's that expression you taught me—my 'sugar daddy,' Fred. He doesn't like it if I come up with excuses. Can't we make it tomorrow?"

"God knows where I'll be tomorrow. Concetta, I need help. I need you."

"I like you a lot, Fred, but I need my sugar daddy."

"Concetta, I can give you all the sugar you need tonight. I can pick you up in a Ferrari. We can spend the night at the Santa Lucia Hotel."

"Fred! You've published a book!"

"Well, almost. Someone else is involved. You'll see when we meet."

"We're not going to meet tonight, Fred."

"What if I told you the fate of the world might depend on your helping me tonight?"

"In bed."

"Well, yes."

"You need help, Fred, but not the kind I can give."

"Concetta, this means a lot . . ."

"Don't be a bore, Fred. Call me again sometime, *Ciao*."

"Concetta!"

Click. I hung up slowly and turned to leave the phone booth. Virgil was standing there waiting for me.

"Perhaps it's for the best, Del."

"If my cracking up is for the best, we're sailing right along. You were quick. What did you buy?"

"These." He held up a box of plastic ballpoint pens and some pocket-sized notebooks.

"Think they'll do the trick?"

"They would have with me, in the thirteenth century. Writing was very laborious, you know. You had to . . ."

"Okay, Virgil, I'm sure you're right. Let's get on with it. Where's the place of execution?"

"Very close. Come along." We walked over to an adjacent piazza where there was a very old church, Santa Maria del Carmine.

"The bones of Conradin are in there," said Virgil, "but few places groan with sorrow as much as the piazza here before us. Piazza del Mercato, the Market Place, but for over five hundred years it was the place where Naples rid herself of her worst citizens— and of some of her best. There in the center, where the fountain is now, there used to be a block for the beheading of nobles and a gallows for the hanging of commoners. Go and touch the old stones around the base of the fountain. Countless times they have been washed with blood."

I walked over and first touched the new stones, the fountain stones which were cool and dry; the fountain wasn't running. Then I let my hands slide down its smooth white side to the old gray stones at the bottom. They felt warm, and wet. I even thought I could smell the blood—so much that I could almost taste it. I straightened back up and returned to Virgil.

"You know," I said, "this stone-touching business can all be explained by the power of suggestion. You say blood and I feel blood. How much of this whole experience can be explained the same way? I mean, what's happening to us objectively? Because subjectively, I might be . . ."

"Subjective, objective! Just how much difference do you think there is? Your subjective is my objective in the first place, and in . . ."

"Let's go get something to eat."

"I propose we check in to our hotel, have a shower, and change our clothes first. No one eats before nine in Naples anyway."

After doing these very sensible things we went to Giovanni's, my favorite restaurant in Naples because I love octopus. Usually I'm a meat-and-pasta kind of guy, but I have this thing about octopus. The meat is so clean and white. The taste is so uncomplicated. Anyway there I was, slicing up a tentacle and listening to Virgil who was trying to cheer me up with some droll stories about the various times Vesuvius has erupted, when in came Concetta.

"*Ciao*, Fred!"

Virgil and I stood up. "*Ciao*, Concetta! It was great of you . . . Concetta, this is my friend, uhhh, Virgil. Virgil, this is Concetta."

Virgil took the girl's hand and kissed it the way George Sanders used to do in the movies.

"Virgil!" she gushed. "What a marvelous name! And I'm sure you're a poet, too!"

"Of sorts, Signorina. But a splendid young lady like you would inspire anyone to poetry."

"Shall we all sit down?" I suggested. Virgil held Concetta's chair for her. I wondered if he knew that she was partial to older men.

"Well, can I order some octopus for you? It's very good."

"No, thanks, I'm not very hungry at all—I had a big lunch. I'll have some dessert with you—but perhaps you won't be having dessert. Your friend doesn't seem very hungry."

In fact Virgil had only ordered a small shrimp cocktail, which he hadn't even finished. "Oh," he said, "but I've already noticed that they have my favorite dessert here—profiteroles—and I'm sure they'll be doubly sweet in such lovely company."

Virgil seemed to be genuinely impressed by the girl. Well, she was very pretty. Long, shiny black hair down over her shoulders, large eyes, delicate nose and mouth, and the sort of figure that managed to be slim without being at all flat.

"Your Italian is so elegant, Virgil—may I call you Virgil?"

"It would give me great pleasure, my dear."

"May I ask where you're from? I don't think you're an American."

"Good Heavens, no!! I am really quite Italian, from Mantua. But I have traveled and lived in many different places, and my speech has become terribly bland—none of the regional flavor I find so delightful."

I had to break this up. "You know, I can't thank you enough for coming, Concetta. Breaking an important date like that . . ."

"I didn't break the date, Fred. My . . . my *commendatore* phoned to say he had an absolutely splitting headache, and would have to postpone our date till tomorrow night. Very strange."

"Why so strange?" I asked.

"He once told me he'd never had a headache in his life."

I looked at Virgil. His eyes said "Don't look at *me!*" Then he quickly turned to the girl:

"Perhaps he drank some altered wine, my dear. That can give a headache to anyone. You'll see that a new day will restore him to you in fine form."

I put my hand on hers. "And you were lucky to find me. Us."

"*We* were lucky," Virgil corrected.

"I remembered you mentioned this restaurant on

the phone, and hoped you would come anyway. I counted on your passion for octopus."

Her and Virgil's attention focused on the tentacle still on my plate. I finished it quickly, and we ordered dessert. Concetta and I both had lemon sherbet, while Virgil worked with obvious pleasure on his profiteroles—soft, airy pastry balls covered with chocolate sauce. We talked about Naples. Virgil tried to stem the tide of his knowledge, but only with limited success.

"Miseria!" said Concetta finally. "Virgil, you must be a professor. A history professor. At the university. Am I right?"

I jumped in. I had an answer all prepared. "Virgil is a doctor, a neurologist. Sort of. He's trying to help me."

Concetta squeezed my hand. A look of great tenderness came into her eyes. She looked at Virgil who was wisely nodding his head, and then at me. "I think you've found the best possible doctor. And if there's anything I can do to help . . ."

"There definitely is," I said. "My problem is basically nightmares."

"Nightmares?"

"Terrible nightmares that sometimes I can't wake up from. Nightmares that are so real to me that they can be dangerous, because I could have a heart attack or something."

Concetta looked at Virgil again. He simply closed his eyes.

"And what can I do to help you?" Her hand was still on mine.

"You can help me relax. Get rid of my tension." Virgil's eyes were still closed. "You can stay the night with me. Just your presence next to me might give me the confidence I need. Right, Virgil?"

He opened his eyes and said serenely, "The affection of such a sweet young lady would be a powerful remedy, indeed. If she agrees to the experiment."

Concetta caressed my cheek. "Of course I do. I'll do my best. But what should I do if it doesn't work? If you start having a nightmare?"

"Nothing, my dear," said Virgil. "There's nothing you can do."

"If you see that I'm having a heart attack or something you can call a doctor."

"I can call Virgil—where will you be, Virgil?"

"Oh, he'll be in the next room—but sometimes he's a very heavy sleeper. If he doesn't come to his door immediately when you knock, don't waste a lot of time—call down to the desk for help."

"None of this will be necessary, my dear," said Virgil. Don't be bothered if he tosses and turns. Del—I mean Fred—we'll have to ask for different accommodations anyway, so I suggest that we have a single bed put into your new room—along with your double—so that Concetta can have a place to sleep if you become too agitated."

"I won't sleep if he becomes agitated. I'll be too worried."

"Virgil's idea is a good one, Concetta. I mean, at least you'll have a safe place to lie if I get restless. I wouldn't want to elbow you in the mouth or anything."

"Who's going to explain these arrangements to the room clerk?" she asked.

I smiled. "My friend Virgil here could smooth-talk Death himself into an indefinite postponement."

We finished dessert and had coffee—decaffeinated on Concetta's suggestion, immediately seconded by Virgil. Then we walked to the hotel—a half-hour stroll on a warm, starry night. Concetta and Virgil both saw shooting stars.

Virgil got the rooms and beds that we wanted and bid us good night, kissing Concetta's hand again like maybe not even George Sanders used to.

Concetta really did do her best. The force of her desire to give herself to me was tangible, and irresistible. I was not in top form . . . too anxious. But she had a great lover's ability to make everything seem right. I finally dozed off in her arms, happy enough, under the circumstances.

X

Virgil and I were standing on the steps of that same church, Santa Maria del Carmine, where Virgil had said that Conradin would be buried. But now it was October 29, 1268. We were no longer in the city. Wooden shacks and workshops could be seen everywhere as if they grew from the grass and dust, and here and there a few other churches. But at a distance of about a mile I could see a long, gray stone wall that reached all the way down to the bay.

"That's old Naples, still within her Roman walls," said Virgil. But she will begin to grow now. Look off to the right." Up to the right, about a mile inland, a large castle could be seen. "That's Castel Capuano. Charles has already decided to start the new wall of the city from there. He wants to give importance to this area."

"He already has." I pointed to the wooden platform in the center of the large space that opened out in front of the church, a bit to the right. On it were the block and the scaffold that Virgil had told me about.

"Yes. In fact, this open area would normally be a marketplace, full of tables and merchandise. But important executions are something special."

"A crowd seems to be gathering."

"Yes, it shouldn't be too long now. The prisoners will pass right by us, on this dirt road that comes from the city."

"You know, Virgil, I've been meaning to ask you something. Supposing we finally get through to one of these guys—I mean if Conradin is Apollo and we get him to give his name twice, and we ask him a third time and that wakes him up, he declares he's Apollo and gets back his true nature . . ."

"Yes. That will be a great moment."

"Okay, but then what happens? I mean, he has to die anyway, doesn't he? Whatever happens here has already happened, and everybody knows Conradin lost his head."

"Everything has already happened, everything must still happen. Cronos, the god of time, allows his fellows to dance freely throughout his reign."

"That clears it up. Thanks a lot."

"Del, in discussing these things we are like two deaf people discussing music. But we can try. Apollo has already been punished in every age up to our own. When—and if—he recovers his true nature, it will change nothing in time, but he will resume his divine existence, free to roam Cronos' kingdom but never to leave it, for the gods are immortal, but not eternal. And he will save the world in our time."

I thought about that for a minute, but it didn't help much. "So Conradin is going to get the ax in any case," I thought I'd say.

"Of course. Because even if he is Apollo and becomes aware of it, he has obviously already decided to let the execution take place anyway. Which would seem logical enough. If I were Apollo, I should have no desire to continue being Conradin . . . at least I don't think so."

"Well, I suppose Apollo will be able to figure it all out."

"Very good, Del. After all, it isn't our problem."

"Look at the shawl that woman is wearing! You don't suppose there's a way I could bring something like that back as a souvenir for Concetta?"

"No, I don't suppose there is. How did it go, by the way?"

"Just what the doctor ordered. She's a great girl."

"She seemed so. Quite attractive. Charming, really. You have good taste. I still have my doubts as to the wisdom of it, however."

"Virgil, knowing that in reality I'm in the arms of a beautiful girl is doing wonders for my morale. Besides, Diana must have thought it was a good idea."

"Do you really think so?"

"Who do you think hit Concetta's *commendatore* with that headache?"

"Leave the gods out of your life as much as possible, Del."

"Look who's talking."

"*Pax vobiscum,*" said someone behind us.

"*Et cum spiritu tuo,*" I fired back. Five years as an altarboy. We turned around. There were two Franciscans, looking just like they look in our century, except that their brown robes were made of very coarse cloth. Each had a sack thrown over his shoulder, and one of them had a long staff with a short piece of wood strapped on toward the top that turned it into a cross.

"Can you gentlemen tell us when the execution is to take place?" said the one with the cross.

"We aren't certain," answered Virgil, "although I should imagine it to be imminent. But how is it that such a hateful spectacle can be of interest to men who preach the Gospel of Love?"

"God's justice is not a hateful spectacle, but a lesson which all would do well to heed. This ghibelline did gravely offend Clement, Christ's Vicar on earth, for which he has been solemnly excommunicated. His body will be thrown in an unhallowed grave, and his soul will fall into deepest hell. For terrible is God's holy wrath."

"But because no one can ever be said to be beyond the reach of God's holy mercy," began the other one, "we have come to see if he can be brought to repentance in his final hour. For although one who is excommunicated can normally be pardoned only by His Holiness, even the humblest priest can receive his confession *in periculo mortis*."

The first friar sighed. "It's a futile gesture, Fra Tommaso. *Fiat voluntas Dei*."

"But Fra Gioacchino, God never wills the damnation of a sinner. We must hold out His saving grace to this miserable creature and to his companions one last time."

"Good friars, my friend and I are greatly interested in the outcome of your pious endeavors," said Virgil, glancing at me. "Before you approached we were debating whether a mere lad of sixteen can have hardened his heart beyond all entreaty. It is a subject—the sinfulness of the young—which I have even discussed with your most worthy minister general, Fra Bonaventure."

The eyes of both friars opened wide. "You—you have spoken with Fra Bonaventure?" asked Fra Gioacchino.

"Oh, yes, many times," answered Virgil. "We were both teachers in Paris."

"Our general is not in Paris now. He is touring the provinces of our order here in Italy. Some say he will be here in Naples before next Easter," said Fra Tommaso.

"Unfortunately we will have already left. But when you see him," here Virgil reached into his pocket, "please give him these." He took out a ballpoint pen and a small pad. "I bought them in—in Constantinople, from a Venetian merchant named Polo. Niccolo Polo. He got them in Cathay, along with other things even stranger than these. Bonaventure and I often talked about the wonders of the East."

"Good master, I pray you, what are they?" asked Fra Tommaso.

"A pen and paper, for writing. Look, I will write my name." And he carefully printed PUBLIUS on the first page.

"This is indeed a marvel," said Fra Tommaso.

"Magic, it is!" said Fra Gioacchino. "The Devil has had a hand in every strange thing I have seen. Fra Tommaso, you are as simple as a dove, but you must also learn to be as prudent as a serpent."

"Observe carefully, Fra Gioacchino," said Virgil, and he printed the words LAUDETUR JESUS CHRISTUS on the second page of the notebook. Then he said, "Could the Devil's tools be used against him?" and handed the pen and pad to Fra Tommaso, who said:

"Master Publius, forgive the diffidence of my companion. Rest assured that your gift will be delivered to Fra Bonaventure." He carefully fingered the pages of the notebook, and tried to focus his eyes on the point of the pen. "How fine a thing, to be able to write so freely!" he added.

"And yet, the merchant told me that they are common things in Cathay; in fact he had a good number of them, for his son Marco and the rest of his family and friends, to whom he was returning. I was able to buy several, and it would be my pleasure to give the same to you—and to Fra Gioacchino—in exchange for a little favor, which I'm sure Bonaventure himself would hasten to grant us if we were with you. Allow us to accompany you when you make your effort to save the boy from the jaws of hell. We will surely be edified by the eloquence which the Holy Spirit grants to His servants on such occasions."

I nodded my head and smiled as seraphically as I could. The two friars looked at each other in silence. Virgil got two more pads and pens out of his pocket and gave them to the two Franciscans.

"Good sirs," said Fra Tommaso, "it is doubtful whether anyone not dressed in religious garb will be allowed to approach the prisoners."

"Especially anyone dressed as strangely as the two of you, with all due respect;" said Fra Gioacchino; "did you also buy your clothes in Constantinople?"

"No, we—we are fulfilling a vow. But isn't it true that you have an extra robe in your sack? Which you wear on the Lord's day?"

Gioacchino put down his sack and began taking out his Sunday robe. Tommaso was still hesitating.

"But your hair—and the cincture . . ."

"In fact, we have no right to either the tonsure or the cincture. We are simple postulants," said Virgil, smiling.

Fra Tommaso smiled back. "Simple postulants. Well, I suppose there's no harm. For a friend of Fra Bonaventure."

The Sunday robes were cleaner and not so coarse, but they didn't fit. Actually the one Tommaso gave

Virgil wasn't so bad, but Gioacchino's stopped at about mid-calf on me. Luckily I had on brown slacks and shoes, so the overall effect could have been worse. I asked Gioacchino for his opinion, but he was engrossed in his pen and notebook. "Fine, fine," he said, without looking up.

"Here he comes," said Virgil. A procession was coming into view from the left. Two men in armor on horseback led the way, and they were very efficient at clearing a wide path through the crowd; in fact they and their horses looked as though they would like nothing better than to trample a few peasants. Behind them came a contingent of foot soldiers, about forty, marching along in pairs with their spears pointed at the sky.

"You know, Virgil," I whispered, "there's a grim sameness about all this. Every night we see big uglies with spears. We might as well be back on the Fields of Mars. No difference."

"Hush. There certainly is. These are good Christians."

"Cheap shot, Virgil."

"Look! There's Conradin."

The boy was on a horse, dressed in a simple brown tunic, with his hands tied behind his back. A soldier walking alongside held the reins. He was a long-boned lad and he held his blond head high, gazing straight ahead with clear blue eyes set in a strong, handsome Teutonic face.

"Well, this is the first one that looks like he might be a god," I said.

"And yet, he may be just a boy, trying to die like a man—like a king."

"Who are the other ones?" Behind Conradin came eight other prisoners being led along in line on horseback. Most of them seemed young, but none as young and fair as their leader.

"The one behind Conradin is Frederick of Baden, the Duke of Austria. I don't recognize the others."

"Will they all get the ax?"

"Of course. They lost."

"Helluva way to make war. Thank God for the Geneva Convention."

"On the contrary. Warlords should always be put to death. They'd think twice before doing it again."

"What if they're sixteen years old?"

"Perhaps a sound thrashing would suffice."

The two Franciscans had been standing a bit off to one side, talking intently about the pens and about Fra Bonaventure. Now, however, they came closer.

"Master Publius, I think we should begin moving up to the place of execution," said Fra Tommaso.

"I quite agree," said Virgil. "Lead on boldly, good friars, for our mission is divine!"

Fra Gioacchino held his long staff up like a cross and led our little procession by shouting: *"Parate viam Domini! Rectas facite semitas Dei nostri!"* It did the trick pretty well, but, when necessary, Gioacchino also knew how to use the pointed foot of his staff to "make straight the paths of our God."

We reached the place of execution shortly after the prisoners who, still on horseback, had been brought up behind the platform and surrounded by a barrier of soldiers. The last of them to arrive was now pulled from his horse directly up and onto the platform. Conradin's young voice rang out:

"I led these men into battle, and into defeat, and now I shall lead them into death, and beyond. Take me first!"

The officer on the platform smiled cruelly, walked

over to the youth and said loudly, "This isn't a game, my proud little brat! When you've seen a few heads roll, you'll realize that!" Then he ordered Conradin's comrade-in-arms to be forced to his knees and his neck to be stretched on the block. A short, stocky executioner stepped up. He had the same black hood and ugly ax that we've all seen in a hundred movies. A hush fell over the crowd.

"In God's name, give him some time!" cried Fra Tommaso. All heads were turned in his direction. "This is no animal, to be dispatched in such haste, but a man about to face his God! Let him compose his thoughts, let him express his hope in God's mercy, with the help of divine grace! *Laudate Jesus Christus!*"

"*Sit semper laudatum!*" I shouted, and my cry was taken up by the crowd, and even by the head on the block. Virgil looked at me approvingly. The officer walked over to our side of the platform. "They've had time enough, and priests enough, to prepare their souls," he said gruffly. "And I have my orders!"

"Which you must zealously obey, my good sir!" said Virgil. "But if you could obey them, and also keep the crowd and the Church content, would this not redound to your credit? All we ask is to speak with them in their last moments, for their spiritual comfort."

The officer considered this for a moment, then said, "Go and talk with them while they're waiting their turn, if you will. But I can allow no one up on the platform."

Fra Tommaso took the long cross from Fra Gioacchino and handed it up to the officer. "Take this, then," he said, "to show the people that you, too, wish Jesus Christ to be praised. And may you know His mercy!"

The officer took the cross, found a knothole in the planks of the platform and drove the pointed foot down into it so that it stood alone. The crowd cheered. The head on the block kept repeating *"Sit semper laudatum!"* more and more wildly until the officer gave the signal to strike. The executioner was evidently a little nervous, because his ax missed the neck and hit the ear, but with enough force to cut right through anyway. I decided then and there I wasn't going to watch the other executions.

The four of us worked our way around to the back of the platform, and at a word from the officer we were allowed through the barrier of soldiers that surrounded the horses with their hapless riders. We all headed straight for Conradin.

"A moment, a moment, good friars!" said Virgil. "The young prince will be the last to meet his Maker. Look! Even as we speak, the next lamb is being led to the slaughter. Let the two of you, who have long walked in the Lord's path, speak the last words of solace to these souls as they are taken. We two novices will do what we can to prepare their minds and hearts to receive the saving grace you will offer them."

It was obvious that the two friars where not particularly pleased with this arrangement, but then and there they could think of nothing to say against it. "Let it be as you say, Master Publius," said Fra Tommaso, "and may the Holy Spirit move us all to wisdom."

"Amen, Brother, amen," I said, with enough feeling to startle myself. Our two companions hurried over to the man who was being pulled off his horse and onto the platform; we started working our way over to Conradin. Virgil had words of comfort for each one of the doomed men we passed. I was too ashamed of the hypocrisy involved to say anything more than an occasional "Courage" or "Peace be with you." By the time we made it to Conradin, the ax was

coming down on its fourth head of the day. One look
at the boy told us that it was getting to him, just as the
officer had predicted. He was pale and sweating.

"My young lord," began Virgil, "we bring you a
message of hope."

"It is not hope I need, good sir, but strength. I must
show these people how a Hohenstaufen dies. But I
. . ." he lowered his head and his voice, ". . . I'm only
a boy. I want to run away. Thank God my hands are
tied."

"Think sweet thoughts of your homeland, and it will
give you peace. Where are you from?"

"Wolfstein," the boy said, "how wonderful in winter! all of Swabia . . . I come from a beautiful land,
good friars, and I wish I had never left it."

"It was your duty," said Virgil eagerly. It was your
royal blood that led you forth. You have lived more in
sixteen years than other men do in seventy."

I had to give Virgil credit: he could shovel the old
bullshit like a Chicago politician. I wished I had the
stomach.

"Think of who you are," he went on. "What is your
name? Let your royal blood speak for you!"

His head came up, and he answered determinedly: I
am Conrad the Fifth, Duke of Swabia and rightful
King of Sicily." A cry of terror came from the platform. Number five was being forced to his knees behind the block. Conradin winced and looked away.

"All my fault," he sobbed. "So much death and
misery, and all my fault." He looked at us. "Talk to
me, men of god. You see that if left to myself, I shall
break down like a baby. Tell me of the world to come.
Although to be honest, I wish I had had more time in
this world."

At this point I don't know if Conradin was in real danger of breaking down, but I certainly was. *Skishunk!* Down came the ax again. I looked at the boy's neck, and felt terribly sick.

"The world to come?" said Virgil. "It can take care of itself, my boy. We live one moment at a time. This is a great moment for you, if you live it well."

"Strange words for a man of your cloth."

"Say it again, Conrad! Say it to the Universe, and the sound will reverberate forever! What is your name?"

"Conrad!" But it was not the boy who called out, it was number six on his way to the block. "God save Conrad the Fifth! God save Swabia!"

"God save Swabia!" echoed the young prince, "And God be with you now, my noble Otto!"

"Your name," I said hoarsely. "What is your name?"

"Good sirs, I thank you for your concern, but I have found a better use for my voice. It must accompany those who are dying for me. Courage, Otto!" he shouted, "We shall all soon laugh together with our fathers!" And Otto started to laugh, and didn't stop until the ax forced him to.

This time I almost retched. The boy immediately called out to number seven; he had found the way to maintain his own courage. Virgil took me aside. "This won't be easy," he said.

"And it hardly seems right to interfere," I added. "This is all so terrible, and serious, and beautiful in a way, and here we are playing this damned party game your god friends invented."

"Whimsy, Del. Gruesome, but we have no choice that I can see. You stay with Conradin—I'm going to try something with Frederick of Baden."

Virgil went back to talk to Frederick, who would be

number eight, the last before Conradin. Meanwhile number seven was being hauled up onto the platform, followed by his young leader's cries of encouragement. But number seven had decided to put up a fight. He lurched from side to side, and was a big enough brute to require four soldiers to bring him to the block.

"Bastards! You can't do this! Let me go, for God's sake! Filthy dogs! No, no! Why . . .?" Then the ax hit. I wasn't looking, but at the now-familiar *Skishunk!* the octopus I had eaten seven hundred years later came climbing up into my throat, and I had to choke it back.

When I could, I looked at Conradin. His eyes were closed, and his body was shaking in his struggle not to weep. I could think of nothing to say. The boy opened his eyes. He had won his battle. I loved him with all my heart.

"Frederick!" he shouted, "Have they got good Austrian beer in Paradise?"

"Whatever they have, it can't be worse than your Swabian swill! Hah hah! You're a good lad, Conrad, and I want to hear your voice as the ax falls. Shout your name loud and clear for me!"

I shot a glance at Virgil, who was moving back our way, smiling like a smuggler crossing the border. I was almost angry.

"How did you talk him into that? Oh, never mind. Get ready."

Frederick proudly strode over to the block and knelt down. "What is your name, my prince?" said Virgil in a voice rich with urgency. "Call out your name to your noble friend!"

Frederick laid his head on the block and the executioner raised his axe.

"I am Conrad, Duke of Swabia and your friend to the death!" the boy shouted.

Skishunk! Up came my octopus again, and this time there was no holding him back. I barfed all over. In my misery I heard Virgil solemnly start the third question: "What is you . . ." and *whack!* I got slapped in the face, in my real face—hard! Hard enough to wake me up.

XI

—

Well, I had actually thrown up in bed, and Concetta, understandably alarmed, had slapped me back into the twentieth century.

"You could have choked, Fred! I mean, it was frightening! I didn't think anybody could . . . could do that in his sleep!"

"I'm sorry, Concetta. I'm really sorry," I said as I staggered toward the bathroom. When I came back out ten minutes later she was already dressed, and Virgil in a silk lounge robe was sitting with her on a small sofa. I was in my underwear, so I quickly dressed. As I pulled on my pants I said in English, "I'm sorry, Virgil. A huge choke, in more ways than one."

"History has often been a question of good or bad digestion. And from what Concetta has told me, it may well be that she saved your life."

"Non capisco," said the girl.

"Please excuse our rudeness, my dear," said Virgil in Italian with his hand on her knee. "I was just saying that you probably saved Fred's life. And that until he gets over this nervous condition of his he would do well to watch what he eats." He looked at his watch.

"It's 6:30. Why don't we go down for some breakfast? A cup of tea might do you good, Fred."

That's what we did, and I drank my tea in silence while Virgil tried to put to rest Concetta's various fears for my health. After breakfast we drove her home. I rather lamely tried to give her some money, for saving my life, I said. For all the trouble, and the mess.

"Buy yourself a present from me," I said.

"You buy it for me someday. When you're better." And she kissed me. Then she kissed Virgil just as warmly. "Where will you take him now?" she asked.

Virgil was off balance. "I . . . I'm not sure, my dear."

"But you can't stay here in Naples."

"No, I'm afraid we can't."

"On the phone Fred said something about the fate of the world."

Virgil smiled. "I can understand why he would say anything for the pleasure of your company."

She looked at me for a moment and then said, "Okay, I won't ask any more questions. Good luck with whatever it is. Good luck to you both."

"Concetta, my dear," said Virgil, "you are a rare young lady, indeed. You will certainly see your Fred again, but perhaps you won't see me, and so I beg you to accept this little token of my esteem." It was a pendant. It was a huge gold pendant, with an onyx cameo showing the head of a man, exquisitely engraved.

"Take care of it, my dear—it's two thousand years old."

"Two thousand years old! But the man looks just like you!"

"That's the poet Virgil. I'm sure he would want a

splendid girl like you to have it." She accepted it, and Virgil got an even nicer kiss this time.

Back in the car, I said "I want to thank you for doing something for Concetta. I'm glad you're not mad at her."

"Mad? Of course not!"

"Well, you know, by waking me up she probably destroyed the world. Ha ha! Whimsical, isn't it?"

"We have to be on our way, Del." He gunned the motor and off we went, heading for the autostrada.

"Back north, I suppose?"

"Yes. Florence. I think we should try Savonarola."

"Savonarola! That fanatic priest who got burned at the stake?"

" 'Fanatic' is a bit strong. It's more charitable to say 'zealous.' "

I slumped back in my seat. Ten minutes later I said, "After Boethius, you asked for my opinion. Aren't you going to do that anymore?"

Virgil hesitated. "It's just that I feel quite certain that Savonarola was Apollo, and that it would be fairly easy to get a wild fellow like him to shout his name as often as we like. There's a chance, anyway."

"Virgil, I'm making a supreme effort just to sit here and continue this madness. I'm losing my grip, and it's a feeling I don't like. You've got to help me along." He said nothing, so I went on. "I don't feel up to another execution scene. Can't you come up with somebody that doesn't know he's going to die?"

"Del, with the fate of the world at stake . . ."

"Virgil, the smart thing to do would be to rest up and wait until the last possible night to make one big attempt. I mean, don't you have the feeling we're running all over for nothing? The gods aren't going to let us win until we come down to the wire—assuming they do let us win. They'rę having too much fun with us."

"And they're taking their chances. Remember, the gods can be outsmarted. It's been done. And we have a powerful goddess on our side. Besides, you know what the Italians say, don't you? *'Siamo in ballo . . .' "*

". . . balliamo," I finished.

"Can you give me a good translation?" Virgil asked.

"How about 'We're out on the floor, we might as well dance'?"

"Hmm. A bit long, but accurate enough."

"Listen, I read about a pope once that got crushed when a church ceiling collapsed someplace. A very good pope, very learned. Might be Apollo, don't you think? I mean, that'd be plenty whimsical, having a pope be Apollo."

"It would be, but he wasn't. You mean Pope John XXI. It happened in Viterbo. And it wasn't a church, it was the ceiling of the papal palace. A worthy man, but not Apollo."

"You're sure of that?"

"Quite sure. He died in 1277, nine years after Conradin. They were contemporaries, and couldn't have both been Apollo."

"All right, all right. Pull over to the curb at this corner, please."

"As you wish, Del. But why?" He braked smoothly but firmly and was able to bring the car to a halt where I wanted.

"Two reasons. First, I want to get a newspaper at that newsstand. Second, there's no point in going on until we know where we're going, because I don't want anything to do with Savonarola. I'm positive he's not my type." I got out and went to get a paper. When I came back, Virgil was smiling.

"Savonarola is not my type either. I was in Florence in 1497 for his 'Burning of the Vanities.' Copies of my poetry were thrown into the fire! No, no; if it's going to be painful for both of us, there's no sense to it. Not yet at any rate, when we have a number of choices. And I no longer think Savonarola was Apollo. Or rather, I believe that since this mission was entrusted to both of us, a clear rejection on your part must be given as much weight as any feelings I might have. I'm not infallible, as we've already seen with Vercingetorix, so I'm willing to consider my judgment overruled in this case. By means of your refusal, Diana is telling me that Savonarola wasn't Apollo after all, and it would probably be another night wasted. Besides, I have another candidate to propose to you. A very interesting fellow. A painter, a Renaissance painter who died in Ferrara in mysterious circumstances."

"What was his name?"

"His name was Giovanni Antonio de'Sacchis, but he was known as 'Il Pordenone,' after the town in Friuli he came from. An extremely good painter—I especially like the crucifixion scene he did for the cathedral in Cremona. So chaotic! So sharp and colorful! You'd swear it was alive and moving . . ."

"Okay, start the car. Let's go to Ferrara. Anything's better than another execution."

As we rolled smoothly along toward the autostrada in the cool of the morning, I started glancing through the paper. The Cubs and Sox had both lost, which was a relief. There was a picture of the pope and a Russian Orthodox Metropolitan embracing. Then I noticed it.

"Hey, Virgil, here it is. Evidently an attempt was made to assassinate Colonel Qaddafi."

"It wouldn't be the first time."

"He's accusing the C.I.A."

"He does that every day."

"He's really mad this time. He says he's got nuclear bombs hidden in America and in other countries that will be detonated if he's ever killed."

"Detonated how?"

"Let's see . . . 'by loyal martyrs of the Libyan Revolution.' No shortage of those, is there?"

"I suppose not, but do you think the Libyans have the technology . . ."

". . . to build the bomb? What they don't have, they can buy. And assemble the bombs, simple ones, right there in the U.S., with all the enriched uranium that's disappeared in the past few years. College kids can build A-bombs, Virgil. The real high-tech is needed for the delivery systems, but if the bombs are sitting in basements with a lot of hyped-up dingbats ready and willing to touch two wires together . . ."

Virgil thought for a moment. "Still, I think he's bluffing."

"So does the State Department," I said. "But if you're both wrong?"

"Then you might have something. But I doubt anyone will try to kill him in the next few days, so soon after a failed attempt."

"Maybe that's what everybody thinks. Maybe that's why this would be the best time. Maybe . . ."

"Maybe, maybe," said Virgil. "We aren't involved in that particular part of the pageant. Let's concern ourselves with what concerns us."

I folded up the paper and stuck it down beside my seat. "I suppose that means my history lesson for the day, all about this painter of yours. What's his name?"

"Pordenone."

"Never heard of him."

"Then you're no student of Renaissance painting."

"Can't say that I am."

"The story involves another painter you must have heard of, Tiziano Vecellio."

"In English that would be . . ."

"Titian. Do you know anything about him?"

"Only that he painted in Venice."

Virgil sighed. "That's something, anyway. Well, the fact is that both Titian and Pordenone . . ."

"Virgil, I'm not in the mood."

He was silent for a moment. Then: "You're absolutely right. Lets's get our minds off this strange business whenever we can. You know, that's probably why you . . ."

". . . are going bonkers."

". . . are feeling depressed. This thing is too obsessive. Just for conversation's sake, where would you most like to be right now?"

"In my mother's womb."

"Hah! Jolly good. I mean, besides that."

"At Ravinia, stretched out on the grass listening to the C.S.O."

"I beg your pardon?"

"The Chicago Symphony Orchestra. Best in the world. They give summer concerts in Ravinia Park."

"Yes, I've heard that they're very good, but . . . the best in the world?"

"We say that. In Chicago we like to say things like that. We've got the tallest building, the busiest airport, the noisiest subway . . ."

". . . and the best pizza."

"Absolutely."

"Look at that Japanese girl. At least I believe she's Japanese. It's hard to tell with the sunglasses."

We were in line now, waiting to get our toll card.

As usual, there were young hitchhikers standing around hoping for rides, some with signs saying "Roma" or "Francia" or simply "Nord." The girl that had attracted Virgil's attention had a sign saying "Orvieto"—a beautiful medieval hill town between Rome and Florence.

"That long, black hair is really something," I said.

"Notice how Oriental her movements are. Delightful."

"Yes, very graceful. So petite. Beautiful."

"Del, I think she's small enough to sit between us. These seats are wide, and what's more, this arm rest is low enough and big enough for her to sit on, it seems to me."

"Let's ask her."

Virgil motioned to the girl, who skipped happily over. "Orvieto?" she said sweetly.

"Con piacere, Signorina, se non si formalizza . . ."

"Not speak Italy. Speak small English." I got out as she hurried around to my side. She slid lightly in and sat right down on the armrest as if she did it every day. She had only a light duffle bag which fit nicely behind my headrest.

It was enjoyable having her aboard, even though her English was very small indeed. Her name was Shoda, she was nineteen, she was born in Yokohama but lived in Osaka, she was hiking around Italy on vacation and in October she would start work in a toy factory. We were already close to Rome by the time I had worked that much out. Then Virgil took over—in Japanese. It turned out he had learned a few words from a Jesuit friend of his who had spent twenty-five years there in the seventeenth century. Shoda was delighted, and laughed like a string of silver bells.

"Ask her why she's going to Orvieto," I said and

Virgil put together some strange sounds with the word "Orvieto" in the middle; the girl laughed again, and fired back a much longer string of sounds.

"Well?" I said.

"She wants to see the famous facade of the cathedral, and then she said something else I couldn't make out."

I turned back to the girl and asked, "Does he speak good Japanese?"

She repeated my question to herself until it made sense, then said "Hah hah hah! Speak old Japanese, old old! Hah hah! I rike! I rike very much!"

A car passed us. For a moment it meant nothing, then I recalled that I hadn't seen a car pass since I met Virgil, so I shot a glance at the speedometer: 120 and sinking. I also saw why. The temperature gauge was moving into the red.

"We'd better take a look," said Virgil. "I'll stop under that overpass, so that we'll be in the shade."

Well, the fan belt was broken; it must have been defective. I was just setting out to trot up to the nearest emergency call box, which I could see about a half-mile ahead, when a gray Lancia stopped in front of us. Three husky guys got out.

"Got a problem?" said the oldest one, with a big smile showing through his brown beard and mustache.

"I'm afraid so," said Virgil. "A broken fan belt, as you can see."

All three men examined the broken belt, with the oohs and ahhs suitable to anyone admitted into the presence of those twelve red-headed cylinders. "Too bad, too bad," said the bearded one. And it won't be easy to get a replacement. This isn't a standard size. And I'm afraid I've got more bad news for you two."

One of the younger men had moved over next to

me, and the other was next to Virgil. I turned to look in the car for Shoda, but she wasn't there!

"I want you to take out your wallets and hand them to my friends," the bearded man continued. "And don't do anything stupid, because plaster casts are uncomfortable in the summer."

Cars kept whizzing by, but any temptation I might have had to signal or put up a fight was easily overcome by the thought that I didn't want the girl to be frightened and discovered by these thugs. I figured she must be hiding on the floor of the car. Virgil and I took out our wallets. The men beside us snatched them, took out the money and gave them back. "Thanks," I said. "Have a nice day."

"We will, we will," said their leader. "Now would you gentlemen please get back into your marvelous car?"

The two flunkies followed us to the doors. "Now they'll see her," I thought; but she wasn't in the car. We sat down.

"Fasten your seat belts," said my guardian gruffly. The bearded man had walked back to their car, and was getting something out of the trunk. A white plastic bag.

He calmly ambled back so as not to attract undue attention and said, "Now lean forward slowly and put your hands behind your backs." Slowly, because otherwise the shoulder strap wouldn't have permitted the movement. Then he discreetly took two pairs of handcuffs out of the bag, and passed one pair to the flunky on my side of the car; my cuffs and Virgil's snapped shut behind us almost simultaneously. Then our seat belts were pulled so tight I could hear poor Virgil wheeze. He said nothing; obviously he, too, was thinking of the girl, wherever she was, and hoping as I was that they would go as soon as possible. Then the bearded man turned on the car's battery and ran the windows up, leaving a crack on my side, which was a nice gesture.

"It'll get a bit hot in here, because I can't turn your air conditioning on; the battery would run down too soon, and we need that to run the radio, to cover any shouting you might do. Eventually someone will stop. *Arrivederci*." But as he leaned across Virgil to turn on the radio, he looked out the windshield and saw what we saw: Shoda, standing calmly next to their car.

"What have we here now?" said the leader. "I don't know where you came from, sweetheart, but I know where you're going. Take her, boys."

The two thugs jumped forward, but there was no hurry; the girl didn't move. Not until the men reached her. I didn't see what happened next very clearly, because the two men partially blocked my view. The girl somehow whirled and kicked both men, one, two, right in the family jewels, so hard that Virgil and I both audibly winced. The men doubled up, and she chopped them on the backs of their necks. They fell hard and didn't move. Then she started walking toward the bearded man.

"That crap won't work with me, sister," he hissed, and flipped out a switchblade. The girl kept coming.

"Look out, Shoda!" I shouted. The man lunged at her. She stepped aside, and as the man's outstretched arm plunged by her she came down hard on it with her forearm, just the way you see the karate champions do when they break through boards and bricks. The same thing happened; his arm cracked audibly and bent like a new elbow. The man shrieked in pain, dropped his knife and hugged his shattered arm.

"Le chiavi delle manette, subito!" Shoda said per-

fectly, and moaning with pain, the man gave her the handcuff keys. *"Ora sali nella macchina,"* she said and the man went to his car.

Some of the cars that passed slowed down, but then speeded up again. The girl went to the two men lying on the ground, took our money out of their pockets and then kicked them both sharply till they got to their feet, still bending over, holding on to their jewels.

"Filate via di qui, porci!" she said. The two obeyed as best they could, and soon the gray car was moving away. Then she came around and opened my door.

"That was incredible," I said. I was sure she understood; she had pretended not to know Italian, and I didn't doubt that she had also been pretending with her "small" English. "You were great, Shoda," I continued. But she said nothing. She put our money on the dashboard and reached behind my seat for her duffle bag. She put it on my lap, opened it, and took out a fan belt. A Ferrari fan belt! Then she walked to the back of the car, lifted the hood, and changed belts as fast as if she did nothing else all day long. We could follow her movements with our ears and rearview mirrors, but we were still belted and handcuffed. After closing down the hood she came back to me; I said nothing this time. She reached behind me and unlocked my cuffs. Her hands were cool, and when she was close I caught the scent of a Michigan forest after a rain. Then she picked up her duffle bag, went around to the other side of the car and did the same for Virgil. Now at last she took off her sunglasses. Almond eyes, but Diana's eyes all the same. Their power and purity held me once again.

"What is written, is written," she said, "but it is you who write. Continue on your way, but search your heart for a different peace." Then she put her hand on

Virgil's head. "You serve me well, old man," she said with a smile, "although your Japanese is painful indeed." Then she closed the door, put her sunglasses back on and started walking backward down the road with her thumb out. The first car that passed stopped to pick her up.

XII

The car was back in top form, but we took our time, not wanting to overtake any gray Lancias, even though I'm sure they got off the autostrada at the first opportunity. It turned out that by noon we were no farther than Orvieto, so we stopped to have lunch there, close to the famous cathedral. I decided to go easy on my stomach for a while, so I had *risotto colla radicchiella*—rice cooked with dandelion greens—and breast of chicken in a light wine sauce. Virgil had a small portion of *coniglio in umido*—stewed rabbit.

"Americans don't eat much rabbit, do they?" he asked.

"Some do," I answered. "For most it would be like eating squirrel."

"How silly. It's so good."

"What is? Squirrel?"

"Well, that too, probably."

"Think we'll see her again?"

"Not unless we need help again."

"You know, I don't think that sort of highway robbery would be possible back in the States. Not on a toll road in broad daylight. Too many bears."

"I beg your pardon?"

"Too many State Highway Patrolmen. And too many guys with CB radios. They'd be taking a helluva chance. It isn't easy to get off a tollroad."

"Here in Italy they do very little patroling."

"Lucky for you."

"Quite."

"I'll bet we see her again when this thing is finished."

"That may depend on how it finishes."

"I must be doing something right. She wasn't mad at me,"

"Avoid familiarity with the gods, my boy."

"Do you remember what Mussolini said?"

"So little of what he said was memorable."

"He said 'Better one day as a lion than a hundred years as a sheep.' "

"If you try playing the lion with the gods, they may well turn you into a sheep."

"Some people say that Orvieto has the best white table wine in Italy."

"One of the best, surely."

"But not the best?"

"A simple matter of taste. My choice would fall on the white wines of Friuli—Tocai dei Colli Orientali, for example."

"Perhaps our wanderings will take us through there."

"I hope not."

"Why not?"

"Because I fervently hope we shall find Apollo tonight, putting our search to an end. Friuli-Venezia Giulia is our last resort. I pray the gods it won't be necessary. The blackest, most sorrowful page in the whole history of Italy was written there. It would be terrible for us both. Conradin's execution was a child's birthday party in comparison."

"Count me out. Find something else."

"Oh, I shall, I shall. As long as I can. You know, if we finish eating in a hurry, we'll have a few minutes to look at the cathedral. Food for the soul, you know."

"And perhaps she'll be there."

"I hardly think so."

In fact, she wasn't. "Let's go," I said, after we had been standing there for a few minutes.

"My boy, you're standing in front of the most beautiful Gothic cathedral in the world!"

I felt like a fight. "It's stupendous," I said. "sumptuous, yet extremely elegant. But it isn't Gothic. There's no real Gothic in Italy, not even in Milan. You Italians have never understood Gothic."

Virgil was ill-prepared for an attack of these dimensions, and a long half-minute passed while he rallied his defenses.

"And I suppose you Americans understand it?"

"Have you ever heard of 'Chicago Gothic'?"

"By all the gods . . .!"

"Well, it exists, and it isn't Gothic either, of course. Gothic architecture is uniquely spiritual. This beautiful building," I gestured grandly towards the cathedral, "follows certain tenets of Gothic architecture, but looking at it is only a rich aesthetic experience, not a spiritual experience. Go to Chartres, my dear Virgil." And with that I made for the car.

Virgil hammered away at me for the next hour, all the way to Florence, but I remained serene and immovable. I had written a great term paper all about this for my sophomore Art Appreciation course at Notre Dame, and no poet was going to talk me out of it.

"Gothic is ascetic, almost mystical," I said patiently. "You Italians have always been lush and worldly in religion, and it all comes out in your church architecture and in your religious art. Look at all those fat, sensual Madonnas."

The Testarossa did a short wobble. "Tonight," said Virgil slowly, "when we're talking to Pordenone, please refrain from any discussion of art and related subjects."

"Why, did he do lots of fat Madonnas?"

"Of course. Rotundity was beautiful in those days. But let me tell you about him. We shall see him on January 12, 1539. He was fifty-six years old and at the height of his powers. In Venice he was chipping away at the artistic domination of the mighty Titian. In 1537 the sisters of St. Mary of the Angels preferred Pordenone's painting of the Annunciation to one done for them by Titian . . ."

"So Titian threw his into the Grand Canal."

"No, he was not a temperamental man. He gave it to the Empress Isabella. But then, still in 1537, the government of Venice took the 'Sensaria del Fondaco dei Tedeschi' away from Titian and gave it to Pordenone."

"That sounds pretty tough."

"The word 'sensaria' is obsolete—it meant a living, a sort of salary paid to artists in return for a certain amount of work each year. Actually Titian didn't need the money, but it was a blow to his prestige; before him the 'sensaria' had been held by his great teacher, Giovanni Bellini, and Titian had worked there at the Fondaco dei Tedeschi—the German Exchange—with his friend Giorgione. He attached great sentimental value to the position."

"Why did they take it away from him?"

"Titian was very casual about meeting deadlines. And that is also the reason behind the 'unkindest cut of all,' which came the following year. The Doge took an important commission away from Titian—a paint-

ing for the Hall of the Great Council—and gave it to
Pordenone. Titian had taken twenty-four years to do
an earlier painting for the same Hall.''

"And this was in 1538?"

"Yes. In November.''

"And two months later Pordenone dies in mysterious circumstances.''

"Yes. And five months after Pordenone's death,
Titian gets the 'sensaria' back.''

"Hmm. And what was Pordenone doing in Ferrara?"

"The Duke of Ferrara, a fellow named Hercules II,
had been begging him to come and do the drawings
for some tapestries that would portray the life of Ulys-
ses, or some such. He traveled there by night, on a
boat from Padua. And perhaps he caught pneumonia.
In any case, we do know that he worked hard for the
few days he was there before dying. And there has
always been a popular tradition that he was poisoned.''

"By Titian.''

"By someone sent by him. But I personally have
never believed it. I met Titian in Venice in 1559. Such
a wise old man, so pleasant in his ways!"

"What were you doing there?"

"I made a great many ducats during the Renaissance giving Latin lectures on Classical Literature.
Actually I didn't do it for the money—it was a fine
way to meet all the best people.''

"What did you call yourself?"

"Various things. In Venice I was 'Ser Teofilo
Pagani.' Anyway, I've never been able to believe that
such an agreeable man would have been capable of
anything so vile. He even let me make suggestions
about his painting.''

"Oh, no.''

"Oh, yes. he was painting 'Diana and Callisto' at the time. You know, the one with . . ."

"No, I don't."

"I suppose not. Well, because of me there's a golden canopy on the right above Diana; I suggested it would be a suitable indication of her divinity."

"It sounds to me like you should stick to poetry."

Virgil fell silent. I had been overdoing it. "Sorry, old friend. It's just jealousy, you know. I have to take a few shots at you now and then. Listen, if you don't think Titian put the contract out on Pordenone, who did?"

"Pordenone's brother, Baldassare. He may well have hired his brother's killer, assuming that's what you meant by that 'contract' business."

"Ah-hah! And the motive?"

"Their father's inheritance. They got into a terrible fight over it. In 1534 Baldassare had his brother charged with trying to steal certain things of their dead father's which belonged to both of them. A week later Baldassare was ambushed by a band of killers, but he managed to kill one of them and escape. Naturally he accused his brother Antonio, our painter, of sending the killers. There was a trial, and Antonio was acquitted. But it is said that from then on, he painted with a club and a sword by his side."

"Sounds like a case for Lieutenant Colombo."

"Yes. Quite. I rather like him, you know?"

"Virgil, what if he really died of pneumonia after all? Apollo always dies a *tragic* death, supposedly. The 'stones of sadness,' or whatever it was."

" 'Tragic' doesn't necessarily mean 'violent,' as I can tell you from personal experience, for what is sadder than the premature death of an artist, be he poet or painter, who still has so much to give?

Pordenone was just beginning to explore Mannerism, you know. He was quite ahead of his time in this respect. Who knows what he might have done?"

"Hmm. Maybe."

"Furthermore, I've got a strong feeling about him now—that is, of course, unless you're opposed . . ."

"Anything's better than Savonarola."

By the time we got to Ferrara late that afternoon I knew more about the town than I really cared to. The big tragedy for Ferrara came in 1598 when it was abandoned by the princely House of Este, which had governed the city for over three hundred fifty years. The town fell to the pope, and gradually lost all its splendor and importance. Virgil said that when he went there in 1845, it was a sleepy little farm town. In this century it was one of the towns where Fascism really got underway: Italo Balbo's town. I knew about Balbo because Chicago's the only city in the world that has a street named after him. He flew there from Italy in 1933, at the head of a squadron of hydroplanes, which was quite a stunt for those days. Now Ferrara has swung way over to the other side, politically, and is one of the reddest towns in Italy, Virgil said. As we drove in, we could see that it was a prosperous, fast-growing little city. About like South Bend.

"South what?!" exclaimed Virgil. "My boy, this city was one of the jewels of the Renaissance! Pisanello, Mantegna, Pier della Francesca all painted here! Tasso and Ariosto wrote here! This city was called the first modern city of Europe because of its public parks! Five hundred years ago! What has South Fork given to the world?"

"South *Bend,* Virgil. Have you ever heard of Knute Rockne?"

My companion fell silent. We headed through the city's modern outskirts into the old city center with its glorious old palazzi that Virgil couldn't resist pointing out to me: the Diamond Palace, built with eight thousand five hundred diamond-shaped marble stones, the Schifanoia Palace with its splendid coin collection (which Virgil would have liked to show me, coin by coin), and the beautiful palace built for the great Ludovico il Moro, Lord of Milan. Then, at one point Virgil started off with:

"That's my last Duchess painted on the wall,
Looking as if she were alive. I call
That piece a wonder now."

"Browning!" I interrupted. "And you're reciting 'My Last Duchess' because the duke in question was a Duke of Ferrara." I sat back, satisfied.

"And also because we just went through Piazza Alfonso II, named after the duke in question. A man of great munificence, and even greater licentiousness."

"Ever meet him?"

"The Duke? No. Browning, yes, many times. I was a friend of the family, you might say. He and Elizabeth had a flat in Casa Guidi in Florence. I helped their little son Robbie with his Latin. We're getting close."

"Close to the place where Pordenone died?"

"No, to Ariosto's house. I have to get my bearings. Pordenone died in an inn, a place called Osteria dell'Angello; which I'm sure has long since been destroyed. But I stayed there once for a few weeks when I was visiting my friend Ariosto, and starting from his house I should be able to locate the spot where the inn stood."

"Was this before or after Pordenone?"

"Before, before. Ten years before his death. Dear old Ariosto! I used to read back pages of *Orlando Furioso* to him."

"If you were such good friends, why did you have to stay in an inn? Why didn't you stay with him?"

"Here we are. See for yourself." The house was small. We got out and stood in front of it.

"You see, Del? Only two bedrooms, and the other was for his son, Virginio. Here, read that inscription. I helped Ariosto with it." It said:

Parva sed apta mihi,
Sed nulli obnoxia, sed non sordida,
Parta meo sed tamen aere domus.

"That's not so hard, you know; I think I can translate it," I said courageously.

"Give it a try, Del!"

"An unimposing house, but it suits me; it's subject to no one, sordid it's not, and anyway I used my own money."

"Ha ha! Ragged but robust. You've got the idea."

"Do you want to go in?"

"No, we'd best be about our business. Let's see now. To come here I used to walk down this road . . ."

And off we went, retracing a path three hundred fifty years old. Virgil was able to do it because, as is usually the case, the basic street plan had never been seriously altered. After about a half-hour walk he said, "This is it. This was it. Oh, dear."

We were standing in front of a sleazy old movie theater. The movie playing was entitled *Super-sexitation nella Porno-pizzeria.* The poster showed a girl curled up in a huge pizza dish, dressed only in olives and anchovies.

"Are you sure it was here?"

"Quite sure. I remember the curve in the street. And that church we just passed. No question about it."

"No point in going in, is there? I mean, there's nothing left of the old inn."

"I'm afraid we're expected to go in. A symbolic gesture, you know. The old stones under the building will sing their sadness to us, if we concentrate."

"That won't be easy."

Inside the theater there were about ten men sitting here and there, and a group of three adolescent boys giggling in a corner. We sat toward the front, where Virgil imagined the center of the inn had been. On the screen the girl we had seen in the pizza dish was bouncing around serving pizzas to very hungry-looking men. Now she had on a tiny apron, and nothing else. I closed my eyes, put my hands on my ears and tried to concentrate on old Pordenone. Nothing came through. "My word!" That came through. It was Virgil. He was thoroughly enjoying the movie. The girl was stretched out on a table, and the men were decorating her, using tubes of tomato paste.

"You know," whispered Virgil, "this reminds me of an orgy I attended at Gaeta once. But we started with olive oil, and . . ."

"I'm sure they'll get around to it, Virgil. Now what about Pordenone, remember? I'm not getting any signals. That's why we're in here, you know."

"Of course. I suggest you try repeating his name over and over to yourself in your mind," he said without taking his eyes off the screen.

"Aren't you a little old for this crap?"

"Oh, but it's quite interesting. Amusing, after a fashion."

I closed my eyes and put my hands on my ears again, and started thinking "Pordenone, Pordenone" until it made me sleepy. I stopped. I mean, *I* stopped, but the word kept repeating itself in my head. It sounded much different . . . older, sadder, and with a strange accent. I let the voice go on for some time, then I opened my eyes. It stopped immediately. Back in the porno-pizzeria, the pizza girl was fighting back with handfuls of shredded mozzarella.

"We can go now, Virgil. I got the message." We stayed until the end of the film.

"Extraordinary," said Virgil as we walked out.

"You're a dirty old man, Virgil. Maybe not the dirtiest, but certainly the oldest."

"Nonsense. Simple curiosity. I don't go to the cinema very often. I had never seen a picture of that sort. Fascinating."

"Listen, the stores are still open. I think we'd better buy some warm clothes if we're going to be here in the month of January tonight."

"Good thinking, Del! Let's hurry back to the car and drive into the center of town."

Which we did. Virgil insisted on going to Armucci's, the most expensive clothing store in town. Virgil walked straight through the men's department into the ladies' where, fortunately, the fall styles had already started to arrive. We bought two long capes, one beige trimmed in yellow and the other yellow trimmed in beige. As I was trying mine on (the yellow one) I said to the puzzled saleslady, "Men wore this sort of thing in the sixteenth century, you know." She nodded readily.

Then we went to the men's department and bought

beige wool pants and cashmere sweaters—mine was beige and Virgil's was yellow. As we paid, or rather as Virgil paid, the confident salesman smiled at us in his friendliest manner and assured us we would make a charming couple. I smiled back and said, *"Vaffanculo."*

"You shouldn't have been rude," said Virgil when we were back out on the street. "He had made a perfectly logical deduction, you know. Nothing to get excited about. In my day in Rome it was quite normal to . . ."

"I know, I know. Great switch-hitters. Let's find a hotel."

Before going to bed that evening we briefly put on our new clothes, to be sure we would find ourselves in them back in 1539. We certainly did make a darling couple.

"These things are hot and I'm tired," I said. "Let's go to bed."

"Each in his own, I presume." I wheeled around. Virgil was grinning mightily.

"Ho ho! We are touchy, aren't we? Up tight, or hung tight, or hanging up, or whatever it is you say."

"Ho ho. Very funny. Go to bed and dream about your pizza girl, old man."

XIII

Well, we looked pretty fruity, but it *was* cold back in Renaissance Ferrara, so we were glad to have the outfits. Besides, I had to admit that we fit right in. There were capes of all kinds and colors hurrying past as we walked along the wide cobblestone street that Virgil assured me would lead us back to the Osteria dell'Angello. But first we had to walk through the large piazza in front of the enormous, moat-circled castle of the House of Este, handsome yet cruel-looking, around whose turrets and towers many guards could be seen walking slowly back and forth. We made our way over to the moat, not without having to dodge horses and carts and dozens of workmen with wooden wheelbarrows.

"What are they building?" I asked.

"Oh, many things. Most of them seem to be heading toward the cathedral over there. And what do you think of the castle?"

"Some shack. One would say that this Este family means business. I like those battlements up there."

"A fire will ruin them thirty years from now, and they'll be demolished."

"Too bad. Who's in charge here now? I know you told me, but . . ."

"Hercules II, and his French wife Reneé, or Renata as they call her here. Over there on the right is her private chapel. Inside there's nothing pictorial, no statues, just colored marble. She's a Protestant, a Calvinist. Calvin was here three years ago, you know. But her husband will eventually estrange her, take away her children, and even imprison her for a short time, because of her faith. A poor political move."

"Why so?"

"Because her father is Louis XII, King of France."

"I see why he needs the moat."

"Let's move along now. What a pity. Pordenone would be here in the castle now, working on those tapestries if he weren't dying. That way. It's not too far. You'll recognize the church, and the curve in the road."

"You mean he's already dying?"

"Oh, yes. He's fallen quite ill. But still hanging on."

"Sounds like slow poison, if it was poison."

"Among other arts, the Italian Renaissance brought the art of poisoning to new heights."

"I thought poisoning was mainly a Roman custom. You know, Lucrezia Borgia . . ."

"Then you don't know who was the Duchess of Ferrara before Renata."

"Here comes a wild guess—Lucrezia Borgia?"

"Quite so. Hercules' mother. She was born in Rome, but lived her adult life here, for the most part. She died about twenty years ago, much lamented. A great patron—I suppose one should say matron—of the arts."

"Not 'matron.' 'Patroness.' "

"How illogical."

"Whimsical, if you please."

"I'm afraid it's about to rain. Let's hurry."

It did rain, but we made it to the inn before getting too wet. It was built with thick, dark beams of oak and abundant mortar. The was a fire blazing in the large fireplace in the center of the back wall. There was a sort of bar to the left, and about seven tables to the right; the two tables closest to the fire had three men sitting at each of them, drinking something—wine, I suppose. A fat, bald man with a beard came through a door at the far end of the bar.

"At your service, gentlemen," he said. The voice struck me as being the one which had repeated "Pordenone" in my head in this same spot, four hundred fifty years from now. "A cup of hot spiced wine is what a body needs in this weather."

"Perhaps later, good host," said Virgil: "our business here may be urgent. Is it true that Giovanni Antonio de'Sacchis, the painter from Pordenone, is lodged with you?"

"He is, curse my bad luck, but the doctor says his soul will soon be lodging elsewhere. If your business is with him, you'll have to wait for the doctor to come back. The doctor left instructions that no one should be allowed to see him. The painter's an irascible sort, you know. Not at all pleased to be dying. Visits make it worse, and hasten his end."

Virgil smiled broadly. "And his doctor is quite right, but our visit will do him no harm, and may well do him good, for we are physicians also."

"That changes things a bit—but not enough. The doctor was very explicit. You're asking me to take a chance. Why should I take a chance for nothing?"

"Sir," said Virgil sternly, "if you refuse us access to this man you may well be held responsible for his death by him who has sent us here from Venice—a powerful man, sir, far more used to sending emissaries of vengeance than of comfort, such as I assure you we are. Let us pass, sir, for this painter's work is much admired by one who will be terribly displeased if there can be no more of it."

"And is it given to know the name of this great man, and of the worthy professors he has sent to my humble establishment?"

"I am Dr. Publio Maro, and this is Dr. Deliberto Alderini. As for the painter's benefactor, a name pronounced with reverence in the Great Council of the Most Serene Republic is not to be bandied about in an inn. And now, by your leave, good sir, precious minutes are passing."

The innkeeper gave us one last hard look, then bowed and gestured toward a door to the right of the fireplace.

"He's in the first room at the top of the stairs—my best room. He's being attended to by the doctor's assistant. There is a bell to ring if you have need of me."

We bowed and made for the door the man had indicated. The eyes of all six drinkers followed us in silence. On the way up the dark stairs I said "Why 'Deliberto'? I'd have preferred "Federico.' "

" 'Deliberto' has an air of importance."

"I feel fruity enough without a name like . . ."

"Hush! Here we are."

We had reached the first door after the stairs. Virgil knocked softly. Moments later the door opened slightly and the face of a blond fellow, probably about twenty years old, peered out at us."

"Young man," said Virgil, "I am Dr. Maro and this is Dr. Alderini. We have been asked to give our professional opinion on the condition of your patient, Messer Antonio de'Sacchis."

"Gentlemen, I have strict orders not to . . ."

"Who is it? Open the door, *deficiente!*" The voice was weak, but the tone was imperious. The boy's head turned.

"But Messer Antonio, the doctor . . ."

"The doctor is a bigger *deficiente* than you are! Now will you open the door or must I do it?"

The door was reluctantly opened, and we entered a hot, spacious room, well-lit with gardenia-scented oil lamps and well-furnished—the red rug on the floor was thick and clean, and all the furniture was beautifully carved. The large window on the left was streaked with rain, making the fireplace glowing in the corner near it seem even cozier. On the right was a large square bed, actually more of a wooden dais than a bed, upon which there was a thick, lumpy mattress covered with silk sheets and one heavy orange blanket. On each side of the bed there were two braziers full of hot coals. And in the middle, head and shoulders propped up on pillows, lay Pordenone.

He was naked to the waist, and his breathing was short and fast. His skin was bluish and sweaty. He had a fat black leech attached to each temple. Apart from that, he was a handsome, strong-looking man with fiery eyes. His hair and beard made you think of one of the Apostles. But not his words.

"Who the Devil are you?"

"We are doctors of physick," said Virgil, "come from Venice to see if we can be of service to you, Messer de'Sacchis. The world must not lose an artist of your great talent."

"From Venice? Hell and damnation! I didn't want Venice to know I'm ill!" At this he clutched his chest and began coughing violently—a wheezing, liquid cough.

"Bronchitis," I whispered to my colleague.

"Yes, but that's not the half of it, I'm afraid."

When the coughing fit stopped, the artist began again. "I'm not going to die anyway. They'll not have that satisfaction. If I can keep all you doctors away from me long enough to get well."

The young assistant came between us and the patient, and spoke to us softly: "As you gentlemen can see, he suffers from a serious imbalance of humors, probably provoked by a poison of some sort. The only cure is rest and sweating, and occasional blood-letting."

"Yes, of course," said Virgil. "We have no intention of interfering, and our visit will be brief. Messer de'Sacchis," he continued, raising his voice, "you need not fear us, for we shall not lay hands on you— our medicine does not require it. Only one favor we ask of you—that we might see your ankles."

"His ankles?" asked the assistant. With effort I refrained from asking the same question. Pordenone looked surprised, but not angered.

"My ankles? Yes, I'll show them to you. I've wondered about them . . . don't stand there like a fool, Domenico, help me with these sheets. Come close, Professors, and look for yourselves."

The heat up around the bed—and the smell, regardless of the scented lamps—was almost unbearable. The ankles were blue and puffy. "Too much blood," said the assistant.

"Nonsense," I ventured. "Poor circulation."

"Poor what?"

"Circulation. Blood circulation. The blood isn't circulating through the body properly."

"Good Doctor, you can't be serious. The blood doesn't circulate in the body. Any student who has read Galen knows that."

Virgil stepped in. "Messer Domenico, my colleague has never read Galen."

"Never read Galen? Then how . . . ?"

"He learned a different kind of medicine in the New World."

"In the New World?" said both Domenico and Pordenone.

"Yes. Dr. Alderini was with Alvar Nuñez Cabeza de Vaca on his mission to the New World—to the land called Florida." I began nodding sagely. "And while there he learned the secrets of healing from the natives—from the tribe called the Seminoles." Pordenone's bright eyes were riveted on me. I kept nodding.

"Fascinating! Wonderful!" said the artist. "One hears so much about the strange lands that Genoan discovered —it's so hard to believe—on the other side of the world! What a shame! What a terrible shame!"

"Why is it a shame, Messer Pordenone?" I said. "Excuse me, I meant Messer de . . . de . . ."

"No, no, you may call me Pordenone. I come from a beautiful land, and I'm proud to bear the name of its first city."

I shot a glance at Virgil, whose eyes had brightened. We were doing great. "Thank you, Messer Pordenone," I continued. "I wanted to know what it is that you consider a terrible shame."

"The fact that this New World has been visited only by sailors, soldiers, adventurers, priests—even by doctors—and never by an artist capable of bringing back true images of the marvels you must have seen. How I would like to go! Tell me—is it true that there is a city of gold—El Dorado?"

"No, sir—at least, not in Florida. The only city I've seen in Florida is called Fort Lauderdale."

"And now," said Virgil hastily, "if you'll excuse us,

I must consult with my colleague." We turned and walked toward the fireplace. I began.

"Virgil, a little whimsy can't hurt. You know that."

"All right, all right. But we have a good chance here, Del. Ask him his name three times as part of your healing ritual—do you understand?"

"Got it. Good idea. Hey, he's in bad shape, isn't he?"

"Heart failure. Whether brought on by poison or not, I don't know. We've got to keep him calm, and not waste any time. Come on."

We turned and went back to our patient. I stood at the foot of the bed, and took off my yellow cape, mainly because I was overheating, but also to add some flair. I spread the cape carefully on the bed, pointedly covering the man's ankles. I even shoved my beige sweater sleeves up past my elbows. Pordenone looked impressed. I began making mysterious motions in the air.

"And now, good sir," I began solemnly, "I must ask you to answer my questions, simply and truthfully. You are unknown to the spirits we are calling upon, so I must first ask: What is your name?"

The doctor's assistant crossed himself. My patient looked up at the ceiling and said, "I am Giovanni Antonio de'Sacchis, from Pordenone."

The door swung open. In strode an angry old man, obviously the real doctor.

"What's the meaning of this?"

"Good Doctor," said Virgil hastening to him, "we have almost finished, and I assure you we are doing your patient no harm."

"No harm?" said Pordenone loudly. "Why, I feel better already. Stand to one side, Doctor, and let this gentleman proceed."

"Proceed with what? This is highly . . ."

"This man is from the New World!" Pordenone's blue tinge was turning to purple. The doctor wisely stood aside. I began my hand motions again.

"The spell has been broken, the spirits are confused, so I must ask you again: "What is your name?"

"I am Antonio de'Sacchis, from Pordenone."

Made in the shade. I hastily leaned forward over the foot of the bed. "For one last time, for your salvation, I ask you . . ."

"For your damnation, he means!" shouted the doctor. Spirits, spells! Sir, we are Christians in a Christian land! *Vade retro, Satana!*" In the meantime he had grabbed a crucifix that was on a small bedside table, and jammed it into my face. "He's calling the devils to come for your soul! I'll not let them do it! *Vade retro, Satana! Vade retro, Satana!*"

Virgil had been moving toward the bewildered painter to try to ask him his name, but the young assistant had jumped in front of him and taken up the cry: *"Vade retro, Satana!"*

Well, if they could shout, so could I. I bellowed "WHAT IS" and got to "YOUR" before I got the crucifix rammed into my mouth.

The door burst open, and in charged the innkeeper. "What in the name of God and Saint George . . .!" he roared.

"In the Devil's name, you mean!" roared back the doctor. "You let these demons in, now help me throw them out!"

The young assistant had already wrestled Virgil all the way over to the window. My mouth was a bloody mess. I grabbed the crucifix, fell on my knees, and started kissing it. It worked. At least, all the shouting gradually stopped. Everyone was staring at me. I swallowed blood, smiled seraphically, then shouted painfully but clearly, "Pordenone, what is your name?" Then I cringed, awaiting a blow; awaiting also the manifestation of the Sun God. Zip on both counts.

"He's dead," I heard the doctor say. "Messer de' Sacchis is dead. Your hellish incantation was too late, *Stregone!*" The innkeeper standing over me swung his booted foot way back, but then I woke up.

XIV

—

"Well, we've solved one of history's mysteries," I said that morning at breakfast. "We know who killed Pordenone. We did."

"How's your mouth?"

"A little sore, but all my teeth are back in place."

"We're running out of time, you know."

"We've still got about four hundred fifty years to screw around in. Plenty of time."

"I meant that we only have two more nights."

"I know that's what you meant, but the only way I'll ever get through this madness is to slip in a few chuckles. Like the pilots in World War I. So where does our next mission take us, Commander? As if it made any difference."

"It does make a difference, Del. Don't overdo it."

"Let me guess. We're going to storm down to Sicily in order to be with Garibaldi when he lands with his Thousand Men."

"Heavens, no! Del, I'm not up to this right now."

"But you've decided where we're going, haven't you? I mean, you've always been ready with an idea."

"Yes, I suppose so. Venice, if you must know. I

think we should go to Venice. But don't ask me why. Not now."

"Depressed, Virgil?"

"We came quite close this time, you know."

"Close only counts in horseshoes, old friend."

"It also counts in *boccie*."

"That's the spirit! Listen, Venice isn't very far, and I've never been there, so why don't we . . ."

"Never been to Venice?"

"No. Never got around to it. So we could . . ."

"You've never been to Venice."

"It can happen, Virgil. I'll bet there are dozens of people in the world who've never been to Venice. So why don't you show me around? I mean, you're history's most famous guide, and we'll have most of the day, so . . ."

Virgil's eyes had gone dim. His head slowly drooped to one side.

"You okay, Virgil?"

"No."

"Let's just hit the high spots. You know, Saint Mark's Square . . ."

"This is August, Del. You can't see Saint Mark's for the tourists. It takes forty-five minutes to cross the Rialto. The *vaporetti* are like cattle barges. And in the best of times, having a scant day for Venice is like having three minutes alone with Sophia Loren."

"Sophia Loren? Oh, yes, my grandaddy told me about her."

"And I hope you paid attention."

"Listen, if you could show Dante around Hell, you can show me around Venice in August."

The old man sighed. "Well, let's get underway. Even finding a table for lunch will be a problem, you know. We'll have to go somewhere extremely exclusive."

"When the going gets tough, the tough get going."

"Come along, then."

Before getting into the car, I bought the morning papers. And there it was, the real thing this time: ATTENTATO AL PAPA, big and black. The pope had been shot—again, poor devil. In Vilnius, by some Lithuanian loony.

"History is full of these sick little men," was Virgil's comment.

"I guess this is it: the first spark, the first domino. This sick little man has probably ended history."

"Not necessarily. How is His Holiness faring?"

"Hard to say. He's in a hospital, but nobody gets in or out. No medical bulletins. He could be dead. The Western journalists who were present say that the pope took the bullet full in the chest, a bit to the right."

"Oh, my. And the sick little man?"

"The Russian police practically blew him to pieces a second after he shot. They wounded four other people, one seriously. Bystanders.

"And the reactions around the world?"

"What you would expect. And everybody's offering to send their top surgeons, but the Russians are stonewalling."

"A reflex. A knee-jerk. Provoked by embarrassment."

"Their biggest problem is with the Lithuanians. Rioting in the streets, evidently."

"Well, this is all very terrible, Del, but it doesn't sound like the beginning of World War III."

"The day after they killed that archduke at Sarajevo it didn't sound like the beginning of World War I, either."

"It did to me."

"Listen, the day after tomorrow the world ends, right?"

"Not with a whimper, but a bang."

"Very good. You believe that, don't you?"

"Unless we find Apollo . . ."

"Okay, okay, so it's logical that something like this pope business . . ."

"Has logic been very useful to you in the last few days, Del?"

I turned on the radio. The Russians were saying that the pope wasn't dead, but in very serious condition. Certain foreign surgeons would be allowed in for consultation. Several hundred people had been arrested. Colonel Qaddafi was blaming the C.I.A., and had reiterated his threat to have his hidden bombs set off if they ever got to him. The Italian coalition government was crumbling. Another Russian submarine had run aground in Sweden. The big track meet in Moscow had been canceled, and the American team was on its way home. All the American nuclear carriers had left their ports for unspecified destinations. The decision had been taken to launch the newest European telecommunications satellite a week earlier than planned, in order to provide the best possible live coverage.

"Of what?" Virgil asked the radio announcer, "of the end of the world?"

"No," I volunteered. "I think CBS has already bought exclusive rights to that. They're thinking of the pope, basically. Today you can slow down a bit—we've got plenty of time."

We were already on the A 13, the autostrada that would take us to Padua where we would pick up the A 4, the *Serenissima*, for the short run into Mestre and Venice. All told, about 110 kilometers. It looked like it was going to be a beautiful day, and not too hot.

"Come on, Virgil, let's try to loosen up." I finally found some music on the radio—it sounded like Boots

Randolph and his yakkety sax, but it wasn't—it turned
out to be an Italian named Fausto Papetti. Pretty
sweet sax, I thought. Virgil seemed unimpressed, but
at least he had slowed down to 145. We crossed the
Po, wide and lazy as it approached its delta.

"Is Venice your favorite town, Virgil?"

"Del, my boy, Venice isn't a 'town.' Venice is a
little old lady dressed in silken damask and yellowed
lace. She lies on a bed of tarnished gold, receiving her
friends for the last time, waiting serenely for death.
But she was Mistress of the Adriatic for a thousand
years. No one can take that away from her, and she
knows it."

"You're really in a melancholy mood, aren't you?"

"So it would seem."

I left him alone for a while, and read my *Tribune*
sports page. The Sox had lost a heartbreaker, 15–3.
Guys on the roster I'd never heard of. I didn't think I'd
been away that long. They say it's one of the first
things you notice, getting old—the teams change. The
real Sox for me will always be the first ones I knew:
Nellie Fox, Luis Aparicio, Sherm Lollar, Minnie
Minoso, Billy Pierce—and no one can take that away
from me, either. God, how maudlin can you get? The
sax music had stopped. I decided to give something a
try. I turned off the radio and in my best glee-club
baritone started booming out:

"Gaudeamus igitur,
Juvenes dum sumus!"

I was hoping Virgil would chime in. Instead he
stared intently at the road and even speeded up a bit.

"Come on, Virgil, my voice isn't that bad."

"No, but the song is."

"Okay, what's your idea of a good song?"

The old man gave me a baleful glance, then put his eyes back on the road in silence. A full minute passed. Then in a reedy but well-modulated tenor he started in on "Stardust."

I slipped into the song with some close harmony, and Virgil smiled. We sang all the way into Venice. His Classical American repertoire was pretty copious—more than mine, anyway. I needed some help with the words to "Stardust," for example. But thanks to my mother, who had sung them all while washing dishes, I was able to hang in there with him pretty well. Virgil kept slowing down. On the long causeway out over the lagoon from Mestre to Venice we were even passed by a Fiat Panda. Virgil didn't even notice—he was too busy with "Begin the Beguine."

We parked in the parking silo in Piazzale Roma and then immediately looked for a gondola; when I saw the *vaporetti* with people bulging out wherever possible, I understood why.

"How about hiring a speedboat-taxi?" I suggested.

"I thought you wanted to see Venice."

The gondolas ranged from plain to luxurious, but they were all the same shape and color: black. We hired a plain one, got in carefully (they have no keels) and started off.

"Why are all the gondolas black?"

"Because of a law passed in 1562. An attempt to bring a little sobriety back into Venetian life. Everything and everybody was so sumptiously decorated—a visual orgy. Especially the boats. So the Magistrato alle Pompe toned things down a bit."

"What's that thing with the prongs on the prow?"

Virgil smiled. "It's called the *ferro*. It's a symbol. Ask the gondolier what it means."

"Scusi, cosa significa quel 'ferro' a prua?"

"Significa la vita, Sor."

"Life? In what way?"

"The big blade on top means that life is a battle. The six prongs facing forward mean that for six days a week we must move ahead and fight this battle. The single prong facing backward is the day on which everyone rests—except gondoliers."

"Hah hah! Bravo, molto buona, questa!" said Virgil. Then he leaned close to me and said, "Every gondolier has a different explanation. The truth is that no one really knows the meaning of the *ferro*. It's one of the secrets of Venice. Now coming up on the left is the railway station, of course, while on the right we have the Church of San Simeon Piccolo."

"What about San Simeon Grande?"

"A little farther down on the right. It may interest you to know that . . ." And off he went, for the whole length of the Grand Canal, all the way to San Marco. Virgil told me many things about the great families that had inhabited and given their names to the palaces we glided past—the best morsels from hundreds of years of gossip from Casanova to Peggy Guggenheim. At one point I made the mistake of asking him how the dogi were elected.

"It's a bit complicated."

"Okay, forget it."

"The Great Council was convened—all the members over thirty years of age. They then put little balls into an urn—as many as there were councillors—but thirty of the balls were painted gold. Then each councillor was given a ball drawn out by a blindfolded boy. The thirty councillors with golden balls were the first electors."

"And they elected the Doge. Not bad."

"But not correct. They were only the *first* electors. Thirty balls were then put back into the urn, of which only nine were gold. The nine who got the golden balls then nominated . . ."

". . . the Doge, finally."

"No, they nominated forty electors."

"They did what?"

"They chose forty men who . . ."

"We were down to nine, now we're back up to forty guys to choose the Doge?"

"They did nothing of the sort. Twelve of them were chosen by lot to name twenty-five men from whom nine were chosen by lot to name forty-five men from whom eleven were chosen by lot to name the forty-one men who, if accepted by the Great Council, were allowed to elect the Doge."

I sat stunned, until the beauty of it all became clear to me. Here was an electoral system that not even the Chicago Democratic Party could rig. "Great Balls of Fire," I finally said softly.

"I participated once," said Virgil. "I was one of the forty-five in the 1355 election, after Marino Faliero was beheaded. You see . . ."

"Are you sure our gondolier doesn't understand English?" I whispered. "If he does, he'll steer us straight to the funny farm."

Virgil smiled. "That brings to mind *Julian and Maddalo*. Shelley and Byron in a gondola, remember?

> 'What we behold
> Shall be the madhouse and its belfry tower'
> Said Maddalo, 'and ever at this hour
> Those who may cross the water, hear that bell
> Which calls the maniacs, each one from his cell,
> To vespers.'

*   *   *

Look up on the left, Del. That's Palazzo Mocenigo, where Byron was staying at the time. I met him at a party once. Charming man. Here in Venice he made himself a remarkable reputation for sexual prowess."

"Another switch-hitter."

"The ladies of Venice didn't mind. Dozens and dozens of them. I'm beginning to think you're a puritan, Del."

"And I'm beginning to think you're a Romantic. You keep quoting Romantic poets."

"I invented Dido. I invented Romanticism."

"I'm getting hungry."

"I've got a nice place in mind."

XV

Virgil gave our gondolier a bunch of lire and we left him smiling in front of the Doge's Palace. We threaded our way through the brightly colored, sunglassed crowds into Piazza San Marco.

"Well, what do you think, Del? It's considered the most elegant square in the world, you know."

"These twenty thousand other people detract from the elegance."

"So do we, then. One must be democratic in these situations." Shall we go into the basilica? Glorious mosaics, you know; and I would like to show you the Zen chapel, because . . ."

"The Zen chapel! I know Venice was influenced a lot by the Orient, but Zen Buddhism . . ."

"Don't be silly. You've got your tongue in your cheek, haven't you? Of course I'm referring to Cardinal Zen, and his marvelous tomb.

"Of course," I deadpanned.

"It was terribly important to him, you know. I had a chance to ask him about it once, and he . . . *Merda!*"

Virgil's exclamation was both descriptive and expletive, in that one of the thousands of pigeons that were surging around in waves above us had been inspired by my friend's venerable head to relieve himself. I did what I could with my handkerchief, but further tourism was out of the question. We headed directly for the restaurant, a place called Do Veci, which was also a hotel, Virgil explained, and would do quite nicely for the night. It wasn't at all far, but because of the crowds in the narrow walkways that riddle Venice it took us fifteen minutes to get there; I could see that it was very close to the Rialto bridge.

Virgil reserved our rooms for the night and went upstairs to wash his head. I told him I would wait in the restaurant, with an aperitivo. It was a smallish place, with old wooden beams over your head covered with Venetian proverbs such as:

Chi ga pan, no ga denti; chi ga denti no ga pan.
O Franza o Spagna, basta che se magna.

On the walls instead of windows there were photographs of the great and famous who had eaten there—a touch I never like. Lack of class. Strange, because otherwise the place reeked with class, from the ancient bottles of wine hanging in brass holders from the ceiling to the black-suited waiters crisply striding around, looking proud of what they were a part of. I was led to a square table; I ordered a Negroni and began to peruse the menu. If the prices were any indication, this was going to be quite a meal. Then a voice behind me disturbed my savory reverie:

"Well, I'll be a son of a bitch!"

He was right about that—it was Ed Dohler. Big Ed.

"Fred! Fartin' Fred Alderini!"

"Hello, Ed. It's certainly a small . . ."

"Millie Kay! C'mon over here, Sweetie!" Millie Kay was an abundant blonde. She was dressed the way a harem girl would dress for tennis. She was chewing gum.

"Fred, this is my little lady, Millie Kay!"

I stood and shook her flaccid hand. "Pleased to meet you, Millie Kay."

"This is Fred Alderini, Sweetie! We were at Notre Dame together!"

"That's very nice. Eddie, I can't find the toilet!"

"Ask somebody where is it."

"You know I always get ones that don't know English."

Big Ed accosted the first waiter that came by and said, "Where's the toilets, amigo? Por la Senorita."

With a moment's glance the waiter gave new meaning to the word "contempt"; then he said smoothly, "Right this way, Madam," and led her away. Big Ed sat down at my table, and so did I. He was dressed like a Highland beachcomber.

"Hey, you gonna eat here?"

"Well, I . . ."

"That's great! You can help us with the menu! You speak Eye-talian, don't you? Hell, you're right at home over here!"

"Yes, but I'm not alone, I . . ."

"You're married, aren't you! I remember hearing you got married! To a St. Mary's girl I set you up with, wasn't it?"

"Her name was Daphne Milo."

"And now her name is Daphne Alderini."

"It was for a while. She died."

"Oh, God. That's a damn shame, Fred. How'd it happen?"

It was not something I liked to talk about, but it was true that I had met her through the good offices of Big Ed Dohler. She was a friend of one of his many women, and they set us up as a blind date once. So maybe I owed him an explanation.

"She fell out of a chestnut tree and broke her neck. On a picnic."

"Well, I'll be damned."

You won't, but I will, I thought. I was throwing chestnuts at her. "That's the way it goes," I said, and finished my drink.

"I'm really sorry, Fred." For a moment I felt his compassion; it was sincere. I hadn't thought he had it in him.

"What'll you have, Ed?"

"A Manhattan for me and a Daiquiri for Millie Kay, if they can swing it in here."

"No sweat, Big Ed." I ordered their drinks, and two glasses of chilled Riesling.

"Okay, so who are you with?" asked Big Ed.

"Here he comes now. Virgil!" I motioned to my old friend who hadn't yet located me. When he came over, I said, "Virgil, I want you to meet a college friend of mine, Ed Dohler. Ed this is Virgil—Dr. Virgil Maro."

"Doc, any friend of Fred's, and you know the rest." He pumped away at Virgil's hand.

"How do you do, Mr. Dohler. Quite a stroke of fortune, I should say, that two old acquaintances should meet so far from home."

"Hey, you're English, aren't you?"

"By no means. I'm quite Italian, but I have made a careful study of your lovely language, and I'm afraid my first teachers were British. Now, however, my enjoyment of English is being enhanced by exposure to Americanisms in all their color."

"Doc, you're beautiful!" cried Big Ed, and we all sat down. The voice in me that still wanted to be a writer

started whispering that this was a confrontation de
voutly to be wished. Big Ed Dohler and the poe
Virgil. Crass meets Class, Apeneck Sweeney versu
Western Culture. In short, I resolved to make the bes
of an otherwise embarrassing situation.

"Here's my little lady now, Doc!" Ed was saying a
Millie Kay found her way back to her husband. Virgi
and I stood up. Ed looked at us and followed suit.

"I can't wait to get back home where they have rea
toilets!" said Millie Kay. "In most places there's jus
a hole in the floor. Here it's all right, but you're
supposed to reach in with a little brush afterwar
and . . ."

"Shut up a minute, Sweetie. I want you to meet a
friend of Fred's. He's a doctor."

Virgil took it from there. "Dr. Maro, dear lady.
am delighted to make your acquaintance." And he
kissed her hand. The girl took it back slowly, staring a
it.

"Ain't that somethin', Sweetie? Ain't he beautiful
Come on, let's all sit down!"

Our drinks had come. As I handed them around
Virgil said, "And so you were students together! A
Notre Dame, I gather."

"Damn right!" said Big Ed. "Golden Domers, both o
us."

"And did you both take your degrees in Literature?
That was for Ed to handle. The truth was I had
never understood how a cheesebrain like Big Ed had
ever been admitted to Notre Dame. He was no jock
and even the jocks were smarter than Big Ed. The
only exams he passed were the ones he managed to
cheat on. But to N.D.'s credit, he was thrown out in
the middle of his sophomore year. It was Millie Kay
who answered Virgil's question.

"Eddie took his degree in Economics. That's what lots of football players do. Eddie was a football player at Notre Dame. They graduate in Econ so they can manage their money."

Eddie shot a pleading look at me, but it was unnecessary. He could tell her he won the Heisman Trophy and a Rhodes Scholarship for all I cared. Maybe he *had* told her that.

"And I'll bet Eddie has lots of money to manage," I said to Millie Kay.

"Truckin', Fred!" said Big Ed, brightening up. "Got myself a fleet of trucks. Make more damn money than I know what to do with. Truckloads of it! Hah hah! That's why I married Millie Kay. She goes around all day buying all kinds of crap. That's why we're over here, to buy more crap. But it's hard to do with this toy money they use. You pick somethin' up for hunnerds of thousands of lire, you think maybe you've actually spent somethin', turns out to be about sixty bucks."

"Think there's something on this menu we can eat, Eddie? I don't even see spaghetti."

"No sweat today, Millie Kay; our friends both speak Eyetalian. Take a look, Fred. Anything on here looks like a rack of ribs?"

"A rack of ribs?" said Virgil slowly. He seemed to be in a daze.

"Yeah, that's what I always eat in restaurants. I'm an expert on ribs. But sometimes I learn somethin' new. Don't suppose the Eyetalians know much about ribs, though. Any luck, Fred?"

"No luck, Big Ed. No ribs."

"Anything like a chicken-fried steak?" asked Millie Kay.

"A chicken-fried steak?" said Virgil even more slowly.

"You'll have to excuse Millie Kay, Doc. She's from the Texas Panhandle, where they don't know nothin' about fancy food."

"Sorry, Millie Kay, there's nothing like it. Listen, there's lots of seafood: shrimp, lobster, salmon . . ."

"I can't stand fish," said Big Ed. "There must be a steak on there somewhere."

"How about a nice big Chateaubriand—it's a thick steak with potatoes and béarnaise sauce."

"Fry the potatoes, gimme ketchup instead of the sauce, and that'll be fine."

"It's for two, Ed. Millie Kay, does this sound good to you, too?"

"Nope, I think I'll have the salmon. With tartar sauce."

Virgil was sitting back in his chair now, smiling with his arms folded. The tartar sauce didn't even faze him.

"And I'll have the steak for two," said Big Ed.

"That's a lot of steak, Big Ed, fifty-six thousand lire worth."

"What's that in real money?"

"About thirty bucks."

"Bring it on, but it better be good for thirty bucks. I don't pay that at the Stockyards Inn in Chicago."

"Aren't you going to have a first course?" I asked. "Or an *hors d'oeuvre*?"

"What they got?"

"Salted Hungarian goose, octopus salad . . ."

"Skip the shit and find the food, Fred."

Virgil frowned at me. "I think our friends might like some *prosciutto crudo*. It's Italian ham, cured and salted in a special way, to be eaten in very thin slices. It makes an excellent *hors d'oeuvre*."

"Okay, Doc, we'll give it a try. With a little mus-

ard. Okay, Sweetie?" Millie Kay shrugged her freck-
ed shoulders.

"And for a first course," I said, "one of the big
specialities here is rice cooked in squid ink."

Millie Kay put her hand to her mouth. Big Ed
laughed out loud, really loud. Virgil leaned over and
took the menu out of my hands. He studied it for a
few seconds, closed it with a sigh, and asked, "How
do you like your spaghetti, Madam?"

Millie Kay said, "Like the canned kind. Nice and
soft, in lots of tomato sauce."

Without flinching he turned to Big Ed. "And you,
Mr. Dohler? Will you have some spaghetti?"

"Is there the flat kind?"

"Let's see . . . yes indeed: Fettuccine alla Bolognese."

"Well-cooked. I like it soft."

"I understand. And what about you, Fred?"

"Gamberetti, Vermicelli, and Capitone alla brace."

"Fine. I suppose the house wines will suffice."

"No wine for me, Doc, I'll have beer."

"And I'd like a Pepsi, please," said Millie Kay.

At this point the waiter came over. *"I signori sono
pronti a ordinare?"* he asked. Virgil and I looked for a
moment at each other; I deferred to his *savoir faire,*
which he would need every bit of to place our order
without getting us tossed out.

"Vede," he began in a confidential tone, *"i nostri
amici sono americani con gusti un po' particolari . . ."*

"That's great, bein' able to talk like that," said Big
Ed to me in an equally confidential tone, which was,
however, loud enough to disturb Virgil and the waiter,
who turned away somewhat to continue their arduous
task.

"You know, you meet a lot of people over here who
don't know no English at all," Ed went on. "Not so

much in Germany, but in France, hell, them dumb
Frogs just stare at you as if you was talkin Gook
Poverty and iggorance. That's what my uncle told me
we'd find, and he's right. Poverty and iggorance. He
was over here for the War, and that's all he saw was
poverty and iggorance.''

I stole a glance at the waiter. He was taking down
our order. From the expression on his face you'd have
said he was cleaning up after a diarrhetic dog.

"Take this town, for instance. Nice idea, having
water instead of streets and everything, but every
thing's so old and damp it's falling apart. Why don'
they fix it up? I was thinking they could do the houses
with fiberglass, the way they do boats. But they don'
got the money, and they don't got the knowhow.
Poverty and iggorance.''

I was sorry Virgil was missing this, but he was
calling upon his vast reserves of expressive ability to
convince our waiter, who was slowly but determinedly
shaking his head.

"Remember to call the Ambassador, Eddie," said
Millie Kay.

"The Ambassador?" I asked.

"Yes, we got a complaint about what happened in
Verona," said Millie Kay.

"Damn Wops," said Big Ed. "Don't mean you or
the Doc, of course. We got talked into going to an
opera in Verona. In this great big, old run-down arena
must be hunnerds of years old."

"About two thousand. The Romans built it."

"Well, whatever. Anyway it was at night, see? Great
big show, with horses and elephants—somethin' about
Egypt."

"*Aida.*"

"That was the name, I think. Anyway, there they

was, singin' at the top of their lungs, marching around, so I thought I'd take a few pictures just to show my drivers that Sinatra isn't the only dago that can put on a show, and all hell breaks loose. 'No flash, no flash!' his guy kept saying. I gave him a bunch of that play money to shut him up, and he went away, and I took a few more, and he come back with two guys in uniform, some kind of police, and they made us leave! Threw us right out! Now you know they can't do that to us! We're Americans, they've got no jurisdiction! But I got the guy's name. We'll see who's boss around here. I'll get the Ambassador to kick that guy's ass in, and if he don't I'll raise hell back home against the Ambassador."

I didn't want to miss it. "No need to call the Ambassador, Ed! Let's go to the American Consul here in Venice this afternoon! Verona must be in his territory!"

"There is no American Consulate in Venice." It was Virgil, who had just turned back to join us, his job done. There was fatigue in his voice.

"Virgil, that's impossible. There are consulates in all major cities. Hundreds of thousands of Americans come to Venice every year. There must be a consulate."

Virgil smiled, motioned to a passing waiter—a different one—and asked for a phone book. When it was brought, I looked under *consolati*. There were dozens of them: all the major countries, and Liberia, Monaco, Lebanon, Bolivia, Finland, the Ivory Coast—but no "Stati Uniti." I closed the book slowly. "Evidently we can't afford it," I said. "And they've closed the consulate in Trieste as well. The closest one's in Milan," said Virgil.

"That's okay, I'll call the Ambassador. I don't want no flunky anyway. Go right to the top, I always say," said Big Ed.

The food began to arrive. Virgil had done wonders, reconciling the Neanderthal desires of Ed and Millie Kay Dohler with all but the most intransigent laws of *alta cucina*. Dainty little earthenware pots of Dijon mustard, English catsup, and a sort of tartar sauce were duly provided, but the spaghetti and the fettuccine were *al dente*, because the chef, according to the waiter, had threatened to quit rather than make them "soft." Virgil had only a dish of red salmon caviar, which he nursed through the whole meal.

"Go ahead and eat somethin' else, Doc, it's on me, and it's all tax deductible."

"That's extremely generous of you, Mr. Dohler, but I seldom get hungry—on warm summer days. And you and your charming wife must do me the honor of being my guests. After all, this is my country, and it is a question of elementary hospitality."

"It's hard to say no to words like that, Doc, but I'll find a way to get even, you can bet your fish eggs on it. Hey, Freddie, is your stuff good, whatever it is?"

"Capitone. A kind of fish. Very good. Mild and tender."

"Millie Kay eats fish. Go on, Millie Kay, try a bite of Fred's stuff; if it turns out to be good, you can learn to order it."

"Don't look like no fish I ever ate," grumbled Millie Kay as she took a big chunk off my plate without asking. She suspiciously chewed on a small corner of it, then happily put the whole piece in her mouth. "Hey, pretty good!" she exclaimed with her mouth full. "What kinda fish is it?"

Virgil looked at me sternly, but I didn't give a damn. It was a mixture of sadism, anger at her for her Stone Age manners—and perhaps embarrassment in wondering just how much difference there was between me and the Dohlers. Whatever it was, the devil was in me, so I told her the truth with her mouth still full.

"It's eel."

To her credit, she did get her napkin up to her mouth before loudly expelling the eel. Then she lurched up and bolted for the powder room. I only had time for a moment's interior glee before Virgil cut me down with four quick Italian words: *"Sei peggiore di loro."*

That was the difference between me and the Dohlers: I was worse. "I'm sorry, Ed, I didn't think—I mean, I should've known better."

Big Ed was staring at my plate. "You know, I read somewhere that even in the States now there are places where you can buy them things. Don't look so bad like that. Hell, if a guy's hungry enough—my uncle says during the war people over here was eating cats."

"Still do, in some places. It's a specialty in Vicenza." Big Ed now began staring sadly at his huge steak. "But never in restaurants," I hastily added. "That's prime beef you've got there. And I would never eat a cat."

"Mr. Dohler, I should like to hear more about your work—about your fleet of lorries," said Virgil to change the subject.

"My what?"

"Your trucks, Ed."

"Oh, yeah. Well, it's not such a big fleet—eighteen trucks. But specialized, see? Climatized compartments. Cost a goddam fortune, but we can set the exact temperature for anything—mushrooms, baby chicks, fancy paintings, orchids—even your friggin' eels. We'll keep 'em in water at whatever temperature you tell us."

"How clever. And frozen products as well, I presume?"

"Yeah, sure. That's easy. No real precision involved.

Now with some things we've only got a couple degrees tolerance—certain pharmaceuticals like vaccines and stuff. That's when it gets hairy, but we're just about the best around. I started as a trucker, see, just like anybody else, but I saw that a lot of customers were ticked off about the conditions a lot of stuff was gettin' there in, you know, and other guys were using planes 'cause they didn't trust the trucks with certain stuff, so I drove like hell and saved my money and went way in hock and bought my own truck and had it fixed up like I wanted it, you know, climatized, and started hauling on my own. All day and all night, to prove I could do it. Drove like hell till it caught on, till I got a name. Still have kidney trouble from drivin'. You ain't a kidney doctor, by any chance?"

"I'm afraid not. I'm a—a neurologist."

"Oh, yeah. Well, that's great, Doc. And Fred, what are you doin' now? Teachin', maybe."

"No. I'm a writer." I said this too softly, and had to repeat it.

"That's great, Fred. God, I could never do that stuff you guys do. Readin' and writin' and readin' and writin' and thinkin' all the damn day. But the world needs truckers, too."

Virgil leaned closer. "Mr. Dohler, the world needs men like you far more than it needs most writers." I didn't look up, but I felt Virgil's eyes.

Millie Kay came back, but wouldn't sit down. "Not so long as he's got that—that slimy thing on his plate!"

Virgil peremptorily summoned the waiter to have my plate removed. I had only eaten about half of my eel, but I had to smile and say I had had quite enough.

"Dear Mrs. Dohler," began Virgil, "I beg of you to forget this unhappy incident and join us again."

"I'm sorry, Millie Kay," I said.

"C'mon, Sweetie, the coast is clear," said Big Ed.

She sat down, but refused to touch her salmon again. "Probably shark, or something," she said. I could have said something about shark meat, but provoking Virgil again seemed unwise.

Big Ed decided to cheer us all up. "Wanna know how Fred here got the name "Fartin' Fred?"

"Nothing would delight me more," said Virgil with a vengeance.

"Ed, ol' buddy, you're the only one who ever called me that."

"There we was in this Freshman U.S. History course, a real mob scene, about two hundred guys in there, and the prof is a tough old broad named Carmaker, or something . . ."

"Carmeyer," I corrected; "Estelle Carmeyer. Politically to the right of Genghis Khan. She taught that American government has been in the hands of leftist radicals ever since Burr shot Hamilton."

"Yeah, well, one day she's rantin' away about some damn thing and ol' Fred in front of me is getting madder n'hell. At one point she turns around to write some big word on the blackboard . . ."

"Two words. 'Strict construction.' "

"Yeah, okay, so when she finishes writing she bangs the chalk on the board and the chalk falls and she yells 'strict construction!' and bends over to pick up the chalk and ol' Fred, perfect timing and everything, he blows one of the finest hand-farts I've ever heard. You know, like this:"

He put his hands to his mouth, and I really thought he was going to do it. I believe he meant to, but he glanced at Virgil before cutting loose, and the pain on the old Roman's face was eloquent enough; Big Ed put his hands down with a laugh:

"Hah hah! I wouldn't never do it in a poshy spot like this, Doc. I'll give you a sample when we get outside. Hey, how about you guys coming with us this afternoon! We're goin' to that island where they blow glass—instead of farts. Hah hah!"

"If you're interested in buying the best Venetian glass, I might suggest that the island of Murano probably isn't the best place to go. The most reputable firms are close by: Pauly, at the Ponte dei Consorzi, or Salviati . . ."

"My cousin Billie Mae was over here once," said Millie Kay, "and she said we gotta go to Morono. She wants some more of those little horses they made right before her very eyes. They's all broke now. Her damn cat. We gotta go to Morono."

Evidently that settled it. "Okay, Sweetie, but I want you to pay attention to the Doc here when it comes to buyin' your junk cause he'll tell you what's good and what isn't."

"I gotta get those horses for Billie Mae."

"I mean besides the horses. For yourself. A chandelier or somethin'."

"Got no place for a chandelier. 'Cept maybe the guest bedroom."

"We'll get a nice big 'un, Sweetie, and have 'em ship it over. But you mind the Doc here."

"Ed, I'm afraid that the doctor and I will be busy this afternoon."

"Aw, c'mon, Fred. You were ready to come to the Consulate with me—and besides, Eyetalians has always got time for their friends, ain't that so?"

"Quite so," answered Virgil. "Our business can be attended to later this afternoon." I wasn't sure whether he was just being polite, or was still teaching me a lesson, or was in some way fascinated by the Dohlers.

"Well, as long as we don't take too long . . ." I mumbled.

"Hell, no!" roared big Ed. "With the Doc to point out the good junk for us we'll be in and out in no time. And I'll have a speedboat to take us there and back to wherever you're goin'!"

XVI

━━━

And so it was that the four of us found ourselves bouncing from wave to wave on our way to Murano. Big Ed had given the boat driver twice as much as he had asked for and had told him to set a new record. I was glad I hadn't been allowed to finish my eel. Virgil was a picture of exhilaration.

"I say!" he shouted to me over the motor, "I'm definitely going to buy one of these! It's more exhilarating than the Ferrari!" I smiled weakly. Big Ed saw my distress and decided to take my mind off the boat. " 'Beer, beer for old Notre Dame!' " he started to roar. He tried to stand up, but Millie Kay was hanging on to him for dear life and wouldn't let him. He continued our song anyway: " 'You take the Notre, I'll take the Dame!' " I had to join in:

> "Send the Freshmen out for gin,
> Don't let the sober sophomores in!"

My heart warmed to the hallowed lines, and by the end I was roaring as loud as Big Ed:

*　　*　　*

*"While the loyal faculty
Lies drunk on the barroom floor!"*

Virgil looked puzzled but happy. Then Big Ed sang a very raunchy version that I pretended not to know. When we reached Murano, Virgil asked Big Ed to sing him "the original lyrics." Big Ed didn't think he could do it. I promised Virgil I'd sing them for him later.

Murano is a good-sized little island around behind Venice proper; Virgil informed us that there were many buildings of interest, particularly the Church of St. Peter the Martyr, with paintings by Bellini; but of course we headed straight for the glass factory. Naturally, it was full of tourists. Big Ed pulled out a huge wad of lire, and soon we had a young glassblower all to ourselves. First he made seven little horses for Millie Kay's cousin Billie Mae. The last two were a matched pair, on Big Ed's insistence: a stallion humping a mare.

Virgil spent this time attempting to instruct the Dohlers on the history of glassblowing.

"It was first used by the Syrians during my lifetime—I mean, during the first century B.C., but Rome quickly became the center of this art. It was practically lost, of course, during the Dark Ages, until the Venetians revived it. The glass factories were all moved from the main island here to Murano in 1291 to remove the risk of fire, and also to make it harder for the glassblowers to escape and divulge their secrets to other cities. If they did so, reprisals were inflicted on their families—but many managed to escape in any case, and the art spread throughout Europe."

"That's great, Doc," said Big Ed without taking his eyes off the molten blob of glass. "Sure is somethin', all the shapes they can make!"

"And what, do you suppose, is the most difficult shape to give to glass?" asked Virgil.

"Gee, you got me, Doc. A spider web, maybe?"

"Child's play. We . . . I mean the Romans could do that. No, my dear sir, what the Romans, the Venetians, and in fact no one could do until the nineteenth century was to make a decent window pane. Flat, colorless, optically undistorted glass only came with the Industrial Revolution."

"Well, I'll be a horse's ass!" Big Ed's comment was not inspired by the object currently being made, inasmuch as the blower had begun making a series of simple flower vases.

"You know, it really don't look so hard," said Big Ed. I'll bet I could blow some sort of a vase."

"Mr. Dohler, it requires a long apprenticeship to . . ." Too late. Big Ed walked around the workbench so that his back was to the glass furnace about ten feet behind it, and motioned to the glassblower that he wanted to try. The young man laughed and shook his head vigorously. Big Ed got out his wad. The young man smiled and kept shaking his head. Big Ed started peeling off hundred-thousand lire notes. The Italian stared, still smiling. When Big Ed got to five he stopped smiling, but kept shaking his head. When he got to ten he started looking all around the factory. With his head facing the other way, he stuck his hand out toward Ed, who gave him the ten bills.

"Ed, that's about six hundred dollars," I said. "This guy's risking his job."

"That means there ain't too many Americans can say they've done this, is there?"

"Mr. Dohler, you're dealing with about 1600 degrees Fahrenheit, and . . ."

"I sure as hell ain't goin' to touch it, Doc, I'm just goin' to blow into it."

"*Tenga; faccia presto,*" said the glassblower, thrusting the blowing end of the seven-foot tube into Big Ed's hand. Big Ed blew. The golden glob at the other end didn't seem to change at all. The young Italian moved to retrieve the tube.

"Not yet," said Ed. "Here comes a six hundred dollar blow."

He lifted the tube out of its notch. We all stepped back instinctively. Big Ed saw us and he, too, stepped back, to frighten us less, or perhaps to escape the glassblower who was reaching for the tube, a disgusted look on his face. Big Ed stepped back farther, and at the same time blew like Gabriel calling forth the dead. In fact his "horn" lurched forward and his butt lurched backward. Right up against the small open door of the furnace. Ed was off-balance from stepping back, and for a good three seconds his rear was wedged half inside the furnace.

A heartrending bellow filled the factory. Ed finally thrust himself forward, threw the tube away and began a high-stepping run, each step cadenced by a mournful cry. The tube landed on the floor—but not completely. The end with the molten glass landed on my left foot, and stuck to my light summer shoe. I don't think my foot stayed in the shoe for more than two seconds, but it was enough; I was badly burned and started to scream. A bucket of water was produced and I plunged my foot into it. Virgil held me up until a chair was found that I could sit on. Millie Kay had run after Big Ed. I was later told he had run out of the factory and jumped into the water.

To keep from raving from the pain I tried to concentrate on what was going on around me. All sorts of people were milling around, soon joined by *carabinieri*. The young glassblower was wildly accusing all four of us of having immobilized him and commandeered his tube. *"Che monata! Che stronzata!"* he kept yelling. Next to him Virgil was attempting to explain things calmly, but the *carabinieri*, in brief, told them both to tell it to the judge. As they were being led away, Virgil shouted to me:

"Alessandro Poerio! Alessandro Poerio! November 3, 1848! Remember for tonight!"

The pain was excruciating. I told myself that was a good sign, because it meant the burn couldn't be too deep, otherwise the nerves would all be dead. I don't know how true that is, but half my brain grabbed onto this idea with all its feverish might. The other half, to keep from screaming, kept repeating what Virgil had shouted to me. The ambulance speedboat finally came. The stretcher-bearers took my foot out of the bucket and the pain increased. I would have sworn my foot was actually burning, sizzling away down there. I screamed bloody murder, and they put the foot back in the bucket. I wouldn't let them take me until they agreed to leave it there. I dangled my leg off the side of the stretcher and a volunteer walked along beside us carrying the bucket. The doctor on the boat, however, wouldn't let me keep the bucket because he wanted to examine my foot. No choice but to take it like a man, which isn't easy with a pain threshold as low as mine. Mercifully, I don't remember much of my trip to the hospital or of the treatment I received; the doctor must have given me some kind of sedative or anesthetic. I do recall that people kept trying to get information out of me:

"Nazionalita'?" someone would ask.

"Statunitense."

"Nome e cognome?"

"Alessandro Poerio."

"Data di nascita'?"

"Tre novembre 1848."

That slowed them up, but in the end they decided I meant 1948 as the year of my birth. When I finally came to my senses I was in a long, old hospital room with the beds all lined up on one side and two large windows on the other.

"Signor Poerio! Signor Poerio!" A doctor and a nurse were standing on the left side of my bed. The doctor was white-haired and friendly looking; the nurse was young, brown-haired, strongly built—and she was wearing dark glasses. I stared at her. She was holding some small old book.

"Mr. Poerio!" the doctor continued until I focused on him. "I wanted to tell you, Mr. Poerio, that your foot will be all right. A second-degree burn. Very painful, I'm sure, but in three weeks it will be fine."

Now I felt the pain again, but not half so bad. A hot throbbing. "I'd like to sit up," I said.

"Just push the button." It was the nurse, who came around to the right side and showed me a button that bent the bed so that I was sitting up. I could see my foot now, all white and fat with gauze.

"How is my friend Mr. Dohler?" I asked the doctor.

"He's in another room. His wife insisted on a private room. He'll be all right. We'll have him walking soon enough, but not sitting. Not for a while. If you prefer, we can put you into a private room, Mr. Poerio; we hardly ever use this room anymore, but our nurse here suggested . . . it really is a striking coincidence, you know. I understand that you are an American, but your Italian parents must have told you who your namesake was. Do you know something about the poet, Alessandro Poerio?"

"Unfortunately not. I think I should explain that . . ."

"Well! I won't say it was lucky of you to burn your foot, but this is surely something you ought to know. He was a fine poet, but an even finer patriot. He fought and died to free Venice from the Austrians!"

"Think of it, Mr. Poerio!" said the nurse. "He died in this very room! Look on the wall there!"

Between the two windows I could now see that there was an old marble placque. It was hard to read because of the light from the windows in my eyes, but I slowly worked it out with the nurse's help. Roughly, it went like this:

> *On the night of November 3rd, 1848,*
> *in this room illuminated*
> *by the bombs of a merciless enemy*
> *and by the lustre of his pure spirit,*
> *ALESSANDRO POERIO,*
> *who had sung so sweetly*
> *and fought so bravely,*
> *succumbed to the gravity of his wounds.*

"The nurse thought you should be put in here, at least to see the placque. But we can easily change . . ."

"Oh, no, no, no, this will be fine! I . . . I'm touched by your thoughtfulness, I really am. But . . ."

"And think of the coincidence of the dates! You were born exactly one hundred years to the day after he died! Remarkable! But of course, that's quite probably why your father gave you your name. Could it be that you are somehow descended from the great Poerio family of Naples?"

"I doubt that very much. You see . . ."

"I thought you might like to learn something more about your namesake," said the nurse, "so I brought this book along from our library." She handed it to me. It was published in 1919, and the title was *Una Famiglia di Patrioti.*

"By Benedetto Croce!" I exclaimed.

"Yes, indeed!" said the doctor, obviously pleased that the name meant something to me. "One of our greatest philosophers took the time to write this book about the Poerio family. You will discover, for example, that Alessandro's brother, Carlo, was a minister in the first government of the Risorgimento, for which he then spent eight years in irons! And their father— but it's all in the book, which I am sure you will want to read."

"Certainly. You're very kind, both of you. And can you give me any information about the other friend who was with me—Dr. Maro?"

"I'm sorry," said the doctor, "I've been told nothing. Nurse, have you heard anything?"

She smiled slightly. "There's a policeman downstairs whose job it is to see to it that Mr. Dohler and you remain here in the hospital. But he told me that the glassblower has begun contradicting himself. Unfortunately, Dr. Maro can't be released until tomorrow morning, because the questore is in Rome, the vice-questore is ill, the comissario is on holiday and the vice-comissario died of a heart attack last week."

"What happens tomorrow morning?"

"The vice-questore has given assurances that he will be well." She turned to the doctor. "La Signora Cardini in 226 has asked to see you, Doctor. Very insistently."

"As always. Very well, then. Be sure to ring if there's anything you need, Mr. Poerio. I'll be by in the morning."

Just before she left the room behind the doctor, the nurse turned, smiled, and shook her head. I shrugged my shoulders.

So I was on my own this time. Well, Virgil would probably turn up alongside me back in 1848. I looked up and down the room. There were eleven beds, all empty except mine, the middle one. Pretty grim. No way you could get me to stay here except for the Poerio business. The stones that groan—better check that out.

I put my right hand over my head behind me until it touched the wall, then I closed my eyes and emptied my mind. People in pain, real pain—a lot of them. Someone softly crying, *"Mio Dio, Mio Dio!"* I opened my eyes and looked around me again; the beds were as empty as before.

I looked at my watch—seven o'clock already. Better start boning up on my "namesake." Wished I could remember more about 1848. The great year of revolution in Europe, I remembered that all right, but what about Italy? I thought the Risorgimento came later.

I started reading the book, and found out that it didn't, that the movement to unite Italy and free her from foreign domination actually began around 1820 and only ended in 1870 when Papal Rome finally fell. In 1848, when all hell was breaking loose everywhere, Venice took advantage of the general confusion to throw out the Austrians and proclaim the rebirth of the Venetian Republic, which had been snuffed out by Napoleon fifty years earlier. It didn't last long, only about seventeen months; on August 30, 1849, old Marshal Radetzky marched back into Venice, and that was it until 1866. But evidently those were seventeen glorious months for Venice—she gave it a real good try. Of all the Italian cities that temporarily broke free in 1848—Milan, Brescia, Palermo, even Rome—Venice held out the longest. Well, it made sense, I thought. Venice is relatively easy to defend. That's how Venice got started.

And Alessandro Poerio? Ten guys like him could have chased Radetzky right back to Vienna. He kept volunteering for the most dangerous missions until he finally got his leg so badly broken they had to take it off. I was looking forward to meeting him. Croce's erudite, demanding Italian, together with the continuing effects of whatever sedative they had given me, soon made it clear that the meeting would take place before I finished the book. It was probably about 10:00 p.m. when I dropped off, with the light still on and the book in my hand.

XVII

I reopened my eyes. I was in the same room. It was still dark outside. My foot was still bandaged and hurt. I closed my eyes again, thinking I evidently had to sleep a little harder if I wanted to get back to 1848. Then the other sensations came. It was chilly in the room. I was under a heavy blanket—and the bed wasn't the same. Then I heard other voices: low voices, suffering voices. I sat up in bed. In the orange light of a few oil lamps I could see that all the beds were full, and there were more than eleven of them now; there were fifteen, shorter and narrower than the one I had fallen asleep in. Then I noticed that the darkness behind the two windows was a different kind of darkness, blacker in general, but often tormented by the flickering light of passing torches, or fires burning in the distance. Only then did I realize that I still had the book in my hand.

"What's that you're reading, friend?" It was the man in the bed on my right who had spoken, a man with shining eyes who was too young to be Poerio, who was forty-six when he died.

"Oh, a book," I answered cleverly; "a history book. My name is Alderini—Federico Alderini. What's yours?"

"Giorgio Schinella. I was in the left column. And you?"

I knew what he was talking about: the three-pronged attack on Mestre, the successful action against the Austrians of a few days ago in which Poerio had been wounded.

"I was in the right column," I said.

"You took the brunt of it, they say. But Poerio was telling me that the center column saw the most action."

"Poerio? Where is he?"

"Hah hah hah!" the man laughed gaily. "An hour ago he was where you are, in that very bed. He's in a bad way, you know. They didn't amputate enough, so they're giving it another try. But the poison is in his blood. The gangrene. I'm afraid we've lost him. When they come for me, I'm going to tell them to take the whole damn leg off. The doctor's been trying to save it, but it hurts so bad I'm on laudanum all day and all night. Want to see it?"

And without waiting for an answer he flipped off his blanket and showed me a tightly bandaged leg that was red in many places where the blood was seeping through. The foot was bare and purple. He smiled brightly as if displaying a trophy.

"It was an Austrian officer with a sword," he said. "He was slashing away on all sides—killed two of us and then split my leg open from here to here." He traced a line from mid-thigh to mid-calf. "But I got the bastard. Had my little flintlock all loaded." He leaned so close I thought he'd fall out of bed, and whispered with glee, "I blew his fuckin' head off. No kidding, brains all over. He got my leg, but it cost him dearly." He winced, and fell back onto his bed. "Hurts like hell, hurts like hell." He began to weep. "A wife and four children and twenty acres to farm on one leg.

But I got the bastard." He reached down beside him and brought out a brown bottle. He shook it, opened it, and took a swallow. When he had put it away, he said, "This stuff kills the pain well enough, but you can't sleep. You have crazy dreams, terrible dreams, and you wake up. What happened to your foot?"

My foot was so big with bandages that even under the blanket it was obvious that was where I was injured. "Oh, nothing serious, really. Burned it."

"If you're in this room, it's pretty serious. They call this the meat locker. Probable amputations. Next stop is the butcher's block, in most cases."

"No, no, no, no, I won't be here long—actually I'm only here because I've got to talk to Poerio."

"Normally that would be easy enough, because he's a fine man to talk to. We've gone on for hours. But when he comes back here—if he makes it back—he won't be able to say much of anything. Not so much the drugs but the exhaustion. But normally he goes on and on."

"About what?"

"About Cavour and Mazzini and his friend Tommaseo and the destiny of Italy and even about the pope. Did you know that the pope used the word 'Italia' in a blessing?"

"That's good. That's very good."

"Poerio says it means that Pius the Ninth has implicitly recognized the existence of Italy. The pope admits that the Italian nation exists, he says. Then he taught me a poem of his:

"Bevve la terra italica
del vostro sangue l'onda
e piova piu' feconda
giammai non penetro' . . ."

*   *   *

I started to wonder what was keeping Virgil. He would have had something intelligent to say. What I said when the soldier finished was, "That's very patriotic. I'm anxious to meet him."

There came a ghastly sound from the bed on my left. The man there had seemed to be sleeping before, but now his eyes and mouth were wide open.

"That was the death rattle," said Schinella, crossing himself. "Michele has left us. Just as well. He didn't want to live after his legs were blown off. All three of them."

"Even in the middle. . . ?"

"That's the one you hate to lose. Mine's in fine shape. Look, I'll show you . . ."

"Schinella! Giorgio Schinella!" Three men had entered the room. My friend froze with his thing in his hand.

"Over here!" he said in a strangely high-pitched voice.

"Put it back!" I whispered, and he did.

"Let's see the leg, Schinella," said the eldest of the three men. He wore very tight brown pants and a blousy shirt that was speckled with fine little drops of blood. He had a black case which he set down on the floor.

"I think Donati's dead, Doctor," said Giorgio: "Michele Donati, over there." The doctor walked around my bed to the open-mouthed man, held his wrist and put his ear to the open mouth for a few seconds, then sighed and said "Take him away, lads." We need this bed for Poerio." Then he looked at me. "Who are you, sir, if I may ask?"

"Uh . . . my name is Alderini. Federico Alderini."

"I see. Well, I'll have a look at your foot in a moment."

"How is Poerio, if I may ask, Doctor?"

The doctor sighed again, and shook his head. "A matter of time. He'll be here soon. Now, Schinella . . ." And with that he began unwrapping my friend's leg—if you could still call it that. I stopped looking before he got to the knee. The smell was awful.

A minute later I heard the doctor say, "It's all infected, Schinella. We'll have to take it off. I'm sorry."

"You did your best, Doctor."

There was some confusion at the door. The same two men who had carried out the dead man were now wheeling someone in on a table. They stopped alongside me and lifted a man off the table and onto the empty bed—an awkward job, because the man had lost a leg at the hip. The bandaged stump seemed a solid clot of blood. The man's head was turned toward me, and his eyes were open but glazed. He had a high forehead, short, curly black hair, and a little moustache. He was sweating profusely and breathing irregularly. While the two assistants were still covering the man up and trying to make him comfortable, the doctor started unwrapping my foot.

"Where on earth—I should say who on earth wrapped this foot? Too loose, too much—a burn, is it? A nasty one, at that . . . not infected yet, but almost certainly will be. No ointment of any kind! What is this white powder—looks like bread flour! Never heard of that. Sir, if you lose this foot, it will be because you entrusted it to some quack instead of a real doctor."

He reached down, brought up his black case, put it on my bed, opened it and took out a bottle and a small brush. He started shaking the bottle. "This is an emulsion of my own devising," he said. "Olive oil, pollen—and several secret ingredients. It might help. It's certainly better than nothing."

No sense in putting up a fight—I would wake up with my foot free of the good doctor's olive oil, I was sure. He poured some on, which didn't hurt, but when he started brushing it around, I had to grab the sides of the bed and bite my lip. Someone laughed feebly. It was the man on the left—Poerio.

"Lad, you have a great deal to learn about pain," he said softly. "My leg—my leg is on fire, it's devouring me—and as you can see, it isn't there!"

"Sir, in your weakened condition you should refrain from speaking," said the doctor who was now tightly rewrapping my poor foot, which much preferred its previous treatment. When he had finished, he put away his things and said, "In a few days I'll take another look, Signor Alderini. Livio, in ten minutes' time come and get Signor Schinella and bring him into surgery. Courage, gentlemen." And with that all three of them strode out.

"Good riddance!" Giorgio started to shout. "Good riddance to this smelly thing. Call this a leg? Putrid meat, I call it!" And he got out his bottle again, shook it up, and drank it all down.

"Alderini. Your name is Alderini," said Poerio with great difficulty, but he obviously wanted to talk—to forget the missing leg that hurt so terribly. "Where are you from, Alderini?"

"Winnetka," I blurted out. "A little town near . . . near Milan. And you? And where are you from?"

"You must have come with Sirtori, then. Colonel Sirtori, a brave leader—as his men, too, are brave. All brave men. Is it not marvelous, Alderini, how brave men from all over Italy have come to defend Saint Mark's Republic! And it is said that even the General will come; Manin pretends that we don't need Garibaldi, but in his heart he must realize that the simple presence of the Hero of Two Worlds is worth five regiments! The General will come, Venice will break the siege—and all Italy will someday be free, Alderini, as surely as God loves His Virgin Mother."

I reached out my hand to him. What is so beautiful as the fire of an ideal burning in a man's words? His hand clasped mine. "I can swear—I can promise you that it will be so; Italy will be united and free," I said. Poerio looked at me hard, and believed me. He smiled, and relaxed.

Time to get back down to business. "And where are you from, then?"

"From Naples, from Naples. A land still under the Bourbon tyranny. But we, too, shall have our glorious day—as you have assured me with your patriot's vision, Alderini."

"Uh . . . I'll bet that Naples is beautiful, isn't it?"

"There is no real beauty without liberty. Right now Venice is beautiful, your Milan is beautiful, far more than my poor Naples."

Here was a fine kettle of fish. Poerio wasn't Apollo! I rolled back onto my pillow and stared at the high, dirty white ceiling. Where the hell was Virgil? Well, Apollo had to be around here somewhere, like the time in ancient Rome with the cart-driver. Sat there the whole time with us . . . I turned to my friend Giorgio. He, too, was staring at the ceiling, with his eyes and mouth wide open, but definitely not dead because his eyes kept darting all around as if he were watching a ten-ring circus. He was, in short, completely spaced out with his laudanum, which I remembered was a mixture of opium and alcohol.

"Giorgio, where are you from?"

He answered immediately. "A beautiful, beautiful, beautiful land! The ground is spongy, the trees keep growing and growing! But no birds—no birds—no birds!"

I leaned close to him: "What is your name?"

"No birds! There are no birds!"

"What is your name? Your name, Giorgio!"

He turned and stared wildly at me. "Alderini! Find the birds! I'll die without the birds!"

"Okay, but I have to know your name."

"My name? Isn't my name . . . Alderini?"

"No, I'm Alderini!"

"What's my name, then?"

"You're Schinella. You are Giorgio Schinella. Say it!"

"You are Giorgio Schinella."

. . . And to think I only had to get him to say it once, because inadvertently I had already asked him his name when introducing myself. Once more would do it, because the third was practically automatic.

"Say it right, Giorgio! Say 'I am Giorgio Schinella.' "

"Look!" He was pointing violently at the ceiling. 'Fish! The fish are flying through the trees! All red and yellow—but no birds. Schinella, find the birds for me!"

"You are Schinella! Say it!"

"Alderini, don't torment the boy! What do you mean by asking him his name again and again?" It was Poerio, and the effort to speak was costing him dearly.

"I can't explain, except to say that it's terribly important—and I've practically finished."

"The fish! Growing fish! Oh, God, the fish, keep them off!"

And in came the two assistants to take him away. I had a problem, but they had one, too.

"Fight the fish! Fight the fish!" he screamed, and started bucking and bouncing high off the bed. The assistants had an awful time of it, and in fact Giorgio fell to the floor twice before they finally managed to strap him to the table. Then he seemed to calm down.

"Wait!" I said. "Before you take him away . . ." I got as close as I could to my heavily breathing friend.

"What's your name, for the love of God?"

He turned and looked at me sadly. "I'm in the belly of a fish," he sighed. Then he closed his eyes, and was wheeled away.

I lay quietly for a while, looking at the ceiling absentmindedly keeping an eye out for Giorgio's birds. Well, the gods do leave it up to chance. I might easily have asked Giorgio right off where he was from, even without having the idea that he could be my man. I mean I was free to do so. At least I thought I was free and that's the same thing, really. In practice.

"Were you successful in what you were trying to do?" asked Poerio in the thinnest possible voice.

"What? Oh, no . . . no. I wasn't."

"Perhaps when they bring him back . . ."

"Perhaps. But I'm afraid they won't bring him back. He won't survive the operation." I turned toward him. I felt free to say what I pleased—to be unpredictable. I hoped some god was starting to squirm. "And the moment he dies, *caro* Poerio, I will disappear, Poof, like that. I'll return to my own age—to the future— one hundred forty years from now."

He smiled. "That's why I don't take laudanum, Alderini. I only need one dream in my life—a dream that will come true."

I smiled back. "Of course, you have no reason to believe any of what I'm saying. But keep your eyes on this bed . . . please. When I disappear—if I disappear—it would be the proof of what I'm saying, wouldn't it?"

"I suppose it would be the proof of something or another."

"Then let me tell you that someday on that wall, between those two windows, there will be a marble placque dedicated to you by a grateful nation—a united Italy."

He stared at the space I had indicated. He thought for a full minute before speaking. "And will this Italy take her rightful place among the powers of Europe?"

"Oh, she'll have her place, all right. But in my age the European nations will no longer be the great powers of the world. The essential struggle will be between the United States and the Soviet Union."

"The United States! The young American republic—but a land of slavery!"

"No, no, that will soon be eliminated. Abolished."

"And the other power, the Union of some sort—where is that?"

"I'm sorry, I should have said Russia."

"Russia! But there is no tyranny like the rule of the czars!"

"The czars will be gone. There will be a great revolution. Russia will be communist. Marxist. Ever heard of Karl Marx?" This was a shot in the dark, but not completely. I remembered from my book (safely tucked under my pillow) that Poerio had traveled and studied extensively throughout Europe, particularly in Germany.

"Marx, Marx. A young Prussian philosopher. My friends in Brussels wrote me something about him and a man named Engels. They've just published a pamphlet called the *Communist Manifesto*. A crude affair, I'm told, but not without a certain appeal to machine workers. They should all unite, or something. Pity we

have so few such workers in Italy. They should try
England."

"They will, they will. But their ideas won't catch on
there. They'll catch on in Russia and China, in the
next century."

"In China!" Poerio laughed weakly. "Well, my dear
Alderini, if you do disappear, you'll certainly leave me
with something to think about."

"Here's something else to think about." I had decided to show him the book. He looked at it without
taking it.

"I'm afraid I'm not up to reading anything, my
strange friend; I'm quite exhausted. But you may read
to me, if it gives you pleasure."

I started thumbing rapidly through the book, looking for something that might startle him. Then I came
across some lines of his poetry—from his Hymn to
Sleep. I began:

> ". . . *Salve, O Divino,*
> *O pietoso a lenir gli affanni nostri . . .*"

"How kind, how very kind!" said Poerio, and closed
his eyes. I continued softly:

> "*Infin che quella di che rendi imago*
> *Ultimamente a medicarli accorra.*"

Then I felt the jolt, the momentary blackout. I was
still in bed with the book in my hand, but I knew poor
Schinella had died, and one hundred forty years had
passed. I didn't even bother to look around. I just lay
back and waited for morning.

XVIII

Virgil came by at ten. The glassblower had completely broken down, and my trusty guide had been released with the apologies of the vice-questore. He hadn't changed his clothes. He had a tightly-rolled-up newspaper sticking out of his back pocket.

"The point is, where were you last night?"

"In a jail cell, of course."

"I mean, why weren't you with me in 1848?"

"Have you ever tried to sleep in a jail cell?"

"Virgil, for Chrissake, the world depends on us, you know!"

"Jail is hard to take at my age."

"Do you know what happened to me back there? In 1848?"

"And how should I know that?"

"I didn't get through to Apollo."

"That much I assumed."

"Mainly because Apollo wasn't your friend Poerio."

"Oh, dear."

Well, I told the story as best I could, and Virgil was very sympathetic. "You certainly did your best. I don't think I could have helped much."

"I'll bet you would have pretended to be a doctor.

You would have gone with Schinella, and at least have kept him alive."

"I'd have been unconvincing as a surgeon. I detest the sight of blood."

"You did all right when Conradin's friends were getting the ax."

"I was otherwise employed. I could never have wielded the ax."

"Oh, well, *acqua passata*, as we say here in Italy. But now we're in a bit of a bind, aren't we, with this foot of mine."

"Have you tried to walk on it?"

"Yes, when I went to the bathroom this morning. I saw stars for ten minutes. No way. Maybe you'll be on your own tonight, the way I was alone last night."

"No, no. Your dream is essential. You'll be with me, no question about that."

"Maybe with crutches . . ."

"It's no place for crutches. You'll need to be ready for anything. Italy's darkest hour, my boy. We will need each other. I so hoped it wouldn't be necessary."

"Good morning, Mr. Poerio!" It was the nurse with the dark glasses. I hadn't seen her since she gave me the book.

"Good morning, nurse. This is my friend, Dr. Maro."

"Glad to see you are out of jail, Doctor," she said with a smile as they shook hands. Virgil looked at her very hard.

"I see that I had no reason to worry about my young friend's welfare," he said.

"Oh, no, we're doing our best for him. How does your foot feel today, Mr. Poerio?"

"Actually my name isn't Poerio, you know. I'm Alderini. Fred Alderini. Or Del, if you like."

She smiled. "I think you should use the name that most suits you."

"But I want to thank you for the book . . . I was very curious about Poerio."

"A fine man, wasn't he?"

"He certainly was. So was another patriot who died here, Giorgio Schinella."

"Yes. If there were a book about him, I'd have given it to you," she said simply. Then again, brightly: "How is your foot this morning?"

"I suppose it's coming along, but I find I'm unable to put any weight on it—unable to walk."

"Don't be silly."

By this time I was pretty sure about who was behind those dark glasses, so I swung my legs over the side of the bed and let my feet touch the floor. I remember thinking about the cripples that Jesus told to rise up and walk. I felt a tingle in my burned foot that quickly spread through my body. I was ready. I jumped to my feet.

"Aaaaiiiiaaaahh!" I pitched over onto the next bed, my foot throbbing angrily with searing pain.

"Whatever were you thinking of?" said the nurse. I peered out at her over my clenched teeth. She was definitely amused. Virgil was not, but remained at a distance, in silence.

"I suppose," I said sufferingly, "that I was hoping for some sort of miracle." I looked at her. "Stupid of me, wasn't it?" I said accusingly.

"You can walk out of here whenever you want to," she said curtly. "The power to do so is in your own mind. Your clothes, and a new pair of sandals, are in that locker in the corner. Good day, gentlemen." And she walked to the door. Before leaving, she turned back and said, "The mind has great power. Determination and confidence, gentlemen, in everything you do. Never believe in the limits, gentlemen." And with that, she closed the door.

I sat for a moment in communion with my foot. It was telling me that if I tried another stunt like jumping to my feet I'd be a cripple for life.

"She stuck to playing the nurse right to the end," I said. "I wonder why."

"By now she expects us to recognize her even in disguise—and to trust her."

"Listen, Virgil, I did trust her, more than I've ever trusted anyone, when I tried to stand up . . ."

"Evidently that wasn't the way to do it."

"I know. The power is in my own mind. Listen, I've tried all the experiments, the party games with ESP and kinesis and everything. I can't even make a candle flame flutter. Damn near burst a blood vessel trying once."

"Oh, I don't think it's a question of effort. It's more likely to be a question of necessity. Your foot will have to listen to Reason."

"My foot has reasons which Reason cannot know."

"All right, but let's get down to business in some way, unless you plan on lying here nursing your foot while the world ends. Radiation burns are much worse, you know. I'll get your clothes. You can start unwrapping your foot."

"But . . ."

Virgil brought my things. I stared at the new sandals in terror while I unwrapped my foot.

"Leave that last bit of gauze on. The sandal will go on over it. Now put on your sock."

I did. In fact I got completely dressed, without standing up. The left sandal went on very nicely, I must admit, but even the touch of the leather strap not fastened but simply laid across my instep, provoked angry messages and doubts about my sanity from my foot. I buckled it with great delicacy and a thousand apologies.

"Okay, let's see the newspaper," I said to Virgil. The headline was "Pope Still Critical." I quickly scanned the article. The best surgeons in the world were on the scene, but they had only agreed on one thing: the pope couldn't be moved. The Russians were cooperating in every way. There were still reports of rioting here and there in Lithuania: in Klaipeda a government building had been burned. Nothing a couple of tank divisions couldn't handle.

"One would say that the situation is practically under control," said Virgil.

"Would one? And yet the world is due to end tomorrow. Have you read the rest of the news?"

"No, I haven't. I can't bring myself to give great importance to this guessing game."

I looked up at him. "Virgil, a week ago I was a fairly normal person. I am still having a lot of trouble with all this. Anything that connects what we're doing every night to the world I used to belong to is a big help to me."

"Yes, you've said that before. And it would be comforting to you to find some indication that the world will end tomorrow."

"Yes. Yes, it would."

"Read on, then," he sighed. I read the "News Index" out loud.

"Italian government resigns over wording of telegram to Kremlin.

"Grounded submarine on scientific mission; Sweden accepts Russian apologies.

"New Zealand declares neutrality.

"Phaeton missile launching set for noon tomorrow."

"Stop," said Virgil. "There it is."

"There's what?"

"The end of the world. That Phaeton missile."

"Are you kidding? That's a European missile that's going to put a new communications satellite in orbit. We heard about it yesterday."

"I remember. But yesterday I didn't hear the name of the missile. It used to be the 'Arianna.' "

"This is a new one. What's the problem?"

"Do you know who Phaeton was, Del?"

"Can't say as how I do."

"He was the son of Apollo and the nymph Clymene. As a sign of his father's affection, he insisted on being allowed to drive the Sun Chariot alone for one day. Of course, he was unable to control it. The great chariot dived down too low, much too low—and created the Libyan desert. Libya, Del. Phaeton destroyed Libya."

"Okay, very good. Qaddafi is in Libya, and the bombs he has planted go off all over if he's killed, and this provokes a nuclear war. Armageddon. I can see the poetry of it all. Tomorrow, Apollo will not be in control of the sun and the energy it represents, so the world will be destroyed by nuclear explosions. Very fitting, I suppose, to have that come about because of a missile named Phaeton, which represents another time that Apollo lost control. But . . ."

"The *only* other time. But what is most appropriate is the reason: excessive affection. Apollo loved his son too much, and he loves men too much. He was wrong to give them his power."

"Lovely, lovely. I'm sure Jupiter or whoever thought this up is already taking bows. My problem is, I don't see how a dinky missile with a satellite aboard is going to bother Qaddafi. I mean, it would have to come down right on his . . ."

Virgil began nodding his head slowly.

"You don't think . . . ?"

"I don't care how unlikely it sounds. That is part of the beauty—the whimsy of it. Phaeton is going to go completely out of control tomorrow and is going to part the hair on the Colonel's head."

His certainty took hold of me. It was going to happen. All set up, unless the two of us could spoil the party. We hurried out of the hospital without being stopped by anyone—a last service rendered by my "nurse," I suppose. I was fifty yards from the hospital before I remembered my foot. It was no longer sending me messages. It had gotten the message from me somehow.

XIX

"Where exactly is this terrible place we're going to?" I asked as we threaded our way through the morning crowds. "I remember you said Friuli-Venezia Giulia, but that's a big area . . ."

"Trieste. We must go to Trieste. Only about one hundred sixty kilometers."

"That's a break. And who's our man tonight?"

"I have no idea. I just know he'll be there. We'll have to do some looking around."

"Are we heading back to get our things now?"

"No. We need costumes for tonight—uniforms. Venice is one of the best places in the world to buy costumes in."

"Because of the Carnevale."

"Exactly. Last February I participated in the festivities. We're going to the place where I bought my costume."

"What were you dressed as?"

"As a Roman poet. Virgil."

"Imaginative. How come you had to buy a costume? Couldn't you have just got out an old toga of yours. . . ?

"They make them better today. They don't itch."

The costume shop was inconspicuous on the outside, with a very conspicuous crowd on the inside: astronaut mannequins leering at Marie Antoinette, cardinals blessing cavemen. Virgil went straight to the counter.

"Signor Asquini, I again need your services."

"Virgil! I remember you as Virgil, sir, because you wore that costume so splendidly!" said Signor Asquini, who was a fat, red-faced old fellow who didn't at all look like a tailor. He wasn't, Virgil told me later. His wife did all the work.

"My friend and I need Italian Army uniforms, ready to take away. World War II."

"Regular army?"

"Yes. Milizia Difensa Territoriale."

"Dress or daily?"

"Daily."

"What rank?"

"Captain would be fine. Two captains."

"I only have one captain ready. It should fit you, sir."

"And what can you do for my friend?"

The man sized me up critically. "A bit tall—either a major or a corporal."

"Major will be fine," I said.

"No, Del, a major is an *ufficiale superiore*. He wouldn't go where we're going. You would attract too much attention—too many questions."

"Listen, can't you degrade the major's uniform a bit?" I asked Signor Asquini. "I mean knock off a star or a stripe or something?"

"No, no, the differences between a captain and a major were somewhat more serious. Something could be done, but—unfortunately my wife isn't here at this moment, and you gentlemen seem to be in a hurry."

"You'll have to settle for being my corporal, Del."

It wasn't a long way back to Do Veci where we picked up our bags. Virgil did his best to try to pay for the rooms we hadn't stayed in, but the manager very graciously refused when he heard our sad story; I think he enjoyed the part about Big Ed's butt.

It *was* a long way back to Piazzale Roma and our car, but we couldn't find a free taxiboat and the *vaporetti* were down to the gunwhales, so we had to elbow our way with our packages and suitcases down the *calli* and over the *rii* for forty minutes before falling into the sensuous arms of our Testarossa. For the first time I was glad that she had air-conditioning. It may be, as Italians say, a sign of decadence and alienation, bad for the health of both car and passengers, but after the Venice crowds I was happy to have the sense of peace and isolation it gives.

"Okay, Virgil, I want to hear all about your plan for tonight."

"Of course."

"I mean, this is our last chance. Whatever happens, it won't be because we didn't do our best."

"Quite."

"We've got to work it all out. I mean, the other times maybe you knew what you were doing, but I was just ad-libbing. The world is going to go boom tomorrow; no more screwing around."

"Del, Diana must have had a reason for selecting you, an American, for this mission. I think it's because as an American you bring a fresh, spontaneous attitude to Italy and her past . . ."

"By that you mean I know little or nothing about it."

"Well, I think that may be a part of it. You don't go barging around as certain self-styled experts most surely would. You don't have a great many preconceptions, and I think that Diana is counting on your fundamental . . . your basic American innocence to counter my rather excessive experience."

"You've been reading Henry James."

"Splendid fellow. Here in Venice, Once, he . . ."

"There you go again. No more screwing around, Virgil. My American Innocence has not exactly done the trick as of yet, has it? This time were're going back there like gangbusters, we're gonna grab Apollo by the throat and throttle away until he spits out his name three times."

I looked at Virgil. He was slowly shaking his head.

"Well, maybe not. But we're going to have a decent plan. No more diddly."

"Diddly?"

I sighed, and stared ahead for a few minutes. We had already left the causeway and were wheeling through Mestre to pick up the autostrada for Trieste.

"To get back to my plan for tonight, Del . . ."

"Don't call me Del. Call me Fred. My name's Fred."

Virgil took a moment before answering. "It's just that Diana has always given importance to names, to the D.A. business, you know, and . . ."

"That nurse in Venice was Diana, wasn't she?"

"I think there's very little room for doubt."

"So do I. And at one point she said, 'You should use the name that suits you,' or something to that effect."

"Yes. Yes, I believe she did."

"Fred is the name that suits me okay?"

"Very well, then. We can consider this dispensation to be another sign of Diana's favor . . . Fred."

"Thank you."

"Furthermore, 'Fred' sounds more American, and I'm convinced that your being American . . ."

"And here we go, back to Henry James."

"Whatever could you possibly have against Henry James?"

"Nothing. I even went through a James phase once. But it was a phase I got over, like my Trollope phase and my Faulkner phase."

"And what phase are you in now?"

"In between phases, but I'll never have another if we don't do the job right tonight."

"And tomorrow night we'll all be reading Henry James."

"Not if I can help it."

"That's the spirit!"

"Listen, you said we're going to the most tragic scene in Italy's history, and I know we're going back to World War II, so I would have thought you meant the reprisal in the Ardeatine caves. I read a book about that. There were three hundred thirty five people, lots of them just taken off the streets, shot in the back of the head. How terrible can you get? I mean, that's the most famous atrocity of the war, as far as Italians are concerned."

"Perhaps, but not the worst. The worst single Nazi atrocity here in Italy was probably Marzabotto, which may not be so well-known, particularly abroad, but every Italian knows about it—one thousand eight hundred thirty people massacred, men, women, and children. Another 'reprisal.' "

"But that's not where we're going."

"No, we're going to Trieste—to an old rice-hulling building called the Risiera di San Sabba."

"Never heard of it."

"Nor have many Italians. It isn't famous like the Ardeatine Caves or even Marzabotto. It isn't something anyone likes to remember. It isn't something *I* like to remember."

We drove on in silence for about two minutes. Then:

"You see, Hitler had decided that the whole area now known as Friuli-Venezia Giulia, with parts of Slovenia and Croatia, should eventually be incorporated into the German Reich. Partly to punish Italy for its betrayal, partly because, as an Austrian, he believed that whatever was once Austro-Hungarian should naturally become German—*Anschluss* on a grand scale. And partly, of course, to give the Third Reich direct access to the Adriatic. In fact, the Nazis called the area the *Adriatisches Kusterland*—Germany's Adriatic coast."

"And so?"

"And so the area was destined to be treated like Poland: a gradual Germanization, confiscation of all wealth, and thorough political and racial purification."

There was another minute of silence. But I had already got the picture. At least I thought so.

"I understand. The Nazis built one of their concentration camps in Trieste. In this rice building."

"Not a concentration camp. An extermination camp. The SS chose the rice-hulling building because of the tall smokestack—forty meters. All they had to do was convert the drying-stove into a crematory oven."

"I looked at Virgil, and there were tears in his eyes.

"Virgil, I admit this is pretty terrible, but the whole Holocaust was a terrible thing. I mean, the Nazis, at least Himmler and his SS, everybody knows how . . ."

"You still don't understand, do you? Of course not. You don't want to understand. Deep down, you're still Italian. Well, the fact is, my dear Signor Alderini, that a good number of the SS on guard duty at the Risiera di San Sabba were Italians. And what is even worse, most of the poor devils who went there were turned over to the SS by Italians."

The old "It can't happen here" syndrome. I confess I found it hard to believe that Italians could do things I had no trouble believing the Germans capable of.

"Italians in the SS?" I said.

"Yes, indeed. Volunteers, many of them."

"Tyrolese Italians, I'll bet, with German names, like the skiers."

"Hardly. Their leader at San Sabba was SS Hauptsturmfuhrer Ernesto Sazano, from Naples."

"And these Italians actually executed . . ."

"It would seem not. They were guards, primarily. The actual functioning of the camp was in the hands of the Germans. Except perhaps in emergency situations, when there were a great many people to be disposed of in a short time."

"How was it done?"

"Most of them were gassed. There was a small gas chamber, and several trucks were also modified for this use. But many were shot, and others were clubbed to death."

"And then the bodies were burned. . . ?"

"Yes. At night, usually. In the morning two Germans with a horse and cart took the remains in big cement bags down to the sea and emptied them into the water."

"How many?"

"No, not many. Nothing like the huge death camps in Germany and Poland. San Sabba operated for only about a year, the last year of the war. The oven had a capacity of about fifty to seventy bodies a day, but it ran at full capacity only in the last few months. Conservative estimates put the figure at about five thousand cremated. But that's not counting the Jews."

"What's that supposed to mean?"

"The Jews were not killed at San Sabba, in general. They were simply gathered there, until there was a trainload of them. All told, about twenty thousand Jews were sent north from San Sabba. To Auschwitz at first, then to Dachau and Buchenwald. About fifteen hundred returned."

We drove on in silence. My father was born in Buffalo, and had never had any real ties with the old country: his father, who had made the crossing in 1913, died when my father was only four. During the war my father was a marine, and fought in the Pacific. For all that, I didn't like the idea of Italians in the SS. And I thought about the newsreels and photographs of what the Allies had found when they broke into the "lagers."

"Virgil," I finally said, "think hard. Maybe there's a way we can avoid this."

"Dante said something very similar to me at the Gates of Hell."

"Seriously, I mean, how about World War I? I'm willing to bet you anything that Apollo got killed in that one, too."

"Unquestionably. But I have no idea as to where. I get this feeling, you know—obviously Diana is involved. We can't take chances, Fred, and I know we'll find Apollo at San Sabba. The feeling is terribly strong."

"Shit."

"Quite."

We crossed the Tagliamento River at Latisana and entered Friuli, Italy's bulwark against Mitteleuropa. Not much of a bulwark, actually, considering the number of times it's been overrun. Virgil started doing his thing, giving me the whole history. I didn't object, but I didn't pay much attention. It wasn't going to be my fault if the world ended tomorrow.

Virgil was only up to the Turks when I decided to

break in. "What good are these dumb uniforms?"

"Do you want to turn up in Bermuda shorts?"

"It might be better. In the first place, you bought Italian army uniforms, but the Italians in San Sabba were SS, right?"

"Correct. I thought we could pretend to be there on orders from Generale Esposito, the Italian commander for the area."

"What orders?"

"Well, to look for someone who had information the General needed."

"In the late movies on TV the Germans are stupid enough to fall for those tricks, but in reality I think we'll get shoveled right into that oven of theirs if we try it."

"I'm rather counting on Diana to have us materialize, or whatever it is we do, right in the prisoners' cell block . . . thus avoiding unpleasantries with the SS."

"You're setting us up to get shafted again, Virgil. We find Apollo, get him to say his name once or twice, then blitzkrieg! in bust the SS, they have a fit, Apollo croaks and I wind up with my ass in a sling as usual. I can hear Jupiter and his friends up there gloating already."

"How can we possibly keep the SS from breaking in?"

"We can't. But we can make our work with Apollo faster and easier—and we can keep the SS from having a fit if and when they break in. Maybe they'll even go away."

"And how might all this be?"

"Elementary, my dear Virgil. We have to turn up in San Sabba dressed as prisoners. The other prisoners, Apollo included, will open up much more readily to us, and if the SS break in, we won't stick out like the sore thumbs we would be in these uniforms of yours."

"Perhaps you're right. Something similar had occurred to me, but . . . I don't think I can manage it. I don't think I can cope. The humiliation . . . No, I don't mean that. The dehumanizing . . . the reduction. You become something very squalid. No Roman nobleman could suffer such a loss of self-esteem. He would fall on his sword, he would slit his wrists, he would search for death with a lover's ardor. . . ."

"Hold on a minute. After all I've been through, you can stiffen your upper lip and gut it out for once. If we just keep our minds on getting to Apollo, we'll be all right."

"Perhaps if we went as SS officers . . . if we could find the uniforms . . ."

"And you consider that less repugnant than being a prisoner?"

Virgil was silent.

"Forget all the uniforms, Virgil; we could never fool the real SS. And what's more, it's against Diana's will."

"And how do you know that, if I may ask?"

"A feeling, backed with logic. The first thing Diana wants us to do is ask Apollo where he's from, and he's supposed to answer 'a beautiful land.' There we are in uniform, SS, worst of all: can you imagine some guy so scared he's wetting his pants, answering us with 'I come from a beautiful land.'? I mean, even if he's president of the Chamber of Commerce all he's going to say is 'Trieste, Sir,' or whatever. Anything else would be completely unnatural. Diana did not have it in mind. If we're to have any chance at all, Virgil, we have to do it her way."

We drove on, past Lignano and then Palmanova. Virgil was visibly disturbed. After a deep sigh, he said:

"Listen, Fred, we'll go dressed as prisoners, not

because you've convinced me it's the best way, but
simply in deference to the predilection Diana has shown
in your regard, which makes you . . . your feelings as
to her wishes worthy of respect. But I'm afraid I shan't
be much help."

That was good enough for now. The best thing
would be to get his mind off San Sabba for a while,
and his being the best guide in history made that easy.

"What's that big white thing up on the ridge, there,
to the left?"

"Oh, that's a famous military cemetery. This was
one of the important fronts in the First World War, you
know. Very moving, really. The tombs are mass graves
arranged in a solid terraced block, twenty-two rows all
the way up the side of the hill, as if standing at
attention. The tombs of their commanders are at the
bottom, facing their men as if calling the roll. In fact,
on each tomb is a list of the men buried there, about
two hundred fifty per tomb, and on top of each list
there is only one word, writ very large: PRESENTE!
It's written four hundred times. There are one hundred thousand men at attention up there, all present
and accounted for, as one says, I believe."

"Very nice. Very moving, I'm sure. How to ennoble
the stupidest, dirtiest, cruelest thing that men do."

"Fred, I told you back in medieval Naples what I
think should be done with warlords, with those who
start wars. But those men . . . those boys buried up
there were doing a job that had to be done."

"What about the Austrian boys buried somewhere
on the other side of the hill? Did their job have to be
done, too?"

"Well, yes. At that level, yes, I think so. The cruelty, the stupidity you talk about must be attributed to

the proud old men with dead hearts who use armies to correct their dipomatic and economic blunders."

"So I suppose the SS we'll be seeing tonight were all good kids doing a tough job."

"No, no, of course not. A man is always a man, and must take responsibility for what he does, orders or no orders."

"Virgil, old friend, I think you still haven't lived long enough. We've got to evolve to the point where the cruel old men can rant and rave and call for war as much as they like, but the people, I mean all the people on all sides, will just refuse to answer the call. The Italians should build another monument right next to that beautiful cemetery of yours. Put the tombs of the commanders at the bottom, just like yours, and then all the way up the side have pictures of kids playing and people working and dancing and talking and making love, and one word, writ large four hundred times: ASSENTE! All absent and accounted for, Commander, you'll have to stick the war in your ear."

"One would need such monuments on both sides of the hill, however."

"On all sides."

"By any chance, you weren't one of the Flower Children, were you? Your age would be about right— and so would this dream of yours. Learn to think about men as they are, not as you would wish them to be."

"Is that what you did in the *Aeneid*?"

That shut him up for a while—all the way to the beautiful Coast Road that gently leads down into Trieste. When we passed Miramare Castle, he started telling me the story of Maximilian, the Hapsburg prince who lived there before he became Emperor of Mexico. Before Virgil finished the story, we were already down in the center of the city.

"Are we heading straight for San Sabba?"

"I don't know . . . it's on the other side of the city, on the way to Jugoslavia. Are you hungry?"

"A little, I suppose."

"San Sabba won't do much for your appetite. I suggest we stop for something now, here in the center. I know a little place where we can get an excellent bowl of Jota. Nothing pretentious—or would you rather I got out Padovani's book?"

"Jota?"

"Yes, it's a Triestine speciality. We can park here and walk to it."

"Here" meant right down at the water's edge, practically the center's only parking area. Then we walked diagonally across Piazza Unita' d'Italia, one of the stateliest squares I had ever seen. Virgil was getting moody again, so I spoke up:

"Imperial, there's no doubt about it. You can tell this was the first port of the Austro-Hungarian Empire. The Empress Maria Theresa made this town, didn't she?"

"Hardly."

"Okay, who did?"

"My friend Octavian. It was called 'Tergeste' then, and it wasn't much, at first. I remember the day he showed me the maps and the plans. He built the harbor, the walls, the towers—a great fleet was based here. Tergeste became an important port for a far greater empire than the Austrians ever put together."

"No offense meant."

"And none taken. I was just reflecting on the growth and spreading of civilizations."

"Oh."

"Empires, my boy! Great advances in culture and

civilization have always been the fruit of empire. And
do you know how empires are built, Fred?"

"Here we go."

"Not by people playing and dancing and answering
'*assente!*' when the roll is called, I can tell you!"

He went on and on as we weaved through the back
streets of central Trieste, going from empire to empire
to point out the great cultural leaps that each one
represented. He was up to the Moguls and the Taj
Mahal when we stopped in front of a very unassuming
little trattoria.

"Best Jota in Trieste," he said.

"I hope the history lesson is over."

"I think I've made my point."

"Hogwater. It's commerce, not armies, that brings
civilization. In the old days the armies built the roads and
garrisons that were then used by commerce, I'll admit.
But that hasn't been necessary in a long, long time. The
Venetians proved that. Now, what the hell is Jota?"

"It's . . . it's a soup with beans, sauerkraut, potatoes and pork rind," he said dully.

"Sounds like soul food! Lead on, brother!" I slapped
him on the back, and in we went.

It was a hot day, so I only had one bowl of the stuff,
but it was very good. Virgil had a child's portion. He
also had me try a side order of *chevapchichi*, the little
Serbian sausages that are so popular in Trieste. All
washed down with some chilled Pinot from Gorizia.

"Now I'm ready for anything," I announced.

"Anything? Then let me say that the Venetians
didn't stop the Turks at Lepanto with trading ships but
with warships! They . . ."

"I meant anything but that! Let's go to your lager."

"First let's check into a hotel. I suggest the Duchi
d'Aosta, in that big square you like so much."

When we got back out onto the street, I said, "Really very good stuff! I think I'll open up a little Jota-to-go place back in Chicago when this is over. The ingredients cost about seven cents a bowl. Think of the profit margin!"

"When this is over," said Virgil as we started to walk, "I'll take you to a splendid place to eat, a bit outside Trieste. Overlooking the gulf. Suban's, it's called. The first Suban was one of Maximilian's tailors. A delightful fellow. My carriage had hit a stone, lost a wheel, and thrown me into the thorn bushes, tearing up my clothes in the worst way. This was in 1863, I recall. I was a guest at Miramare at the time, and this Suban, Giovanni was his name, worked day and night to make me a marvelous new suit of clothes. He wouldn't hear of being paid, because he was simply 'at the service of the Archduke's guests.' But we often talked, and I discovered that he was a tailor by family tradition, but by secret vocation he was a cook! And I thought, if he's half the cook that he is a tailor, he must be given a chance."

"So you gave him some Roman jewels, or something."

"No, no, I told you he would accept nothing of the sort. I gave him some numbers."

"Numbers?"

"To play at 'Lotto.' You know . . ."

"The Numbers game. It's illegal in the States."

"It's a part of our culture here. Anyway, I had this feeling . . ."

"And your numbers hit."

"All five of them. A *cinquina secca*. The tailor quit his job and bought the place where we'll go tomorrow noon. If . . ."

"I know, I know."

XX

We checked into the hotel, took showers, and then went to the car.

"There's another thing that bothers me," I said as we were getting in. "The fact that we have no name to go on. That means we have no date, either."

"I can't help it. I personally don't know the names of any individuals who died there. I suppose we are expected to leave it up to Diana to put us back there at the right time. Then, all in all, it shouldn't be too difficult to search our man out. There are only seventeen cells in the block reserved to those marked for extermination. Perhaps about seventy people, but we can safely skip the women and very small children."

"Still believe Apollo won't be a woman, huh?"

"It would be in such poor taste."

"Okay, my turn to defer to you. Still, with that number of candidates, I think we should make some sort of effort . . ."

"Too much effort is worse than too little."

I decided to concentrate on digesting my Jota and *chevapchichi*. I noticed that Virgil was simply following the signs that said "Jugoslavia" and "Confine di

Stato." Then I noticed a yellow one that said "Risiera di San Sabba."

"Well, at least they're not trying to keep it a secret," I said.

"No, no, it was made a national monument in 1965. The ex-partisan groups, in particular, don't want the Risiera forgotten. But no one sends postcards home from this place. We're getting close."

"I know."

"You know?"

"I can already feel it. I can sense the anguish without touching the stones."

"It's at the end of a street called Rio Primario . . . help me look for it . . . here it is!"

Above the name of the street was another sign saying "Strada Senza Uscita"—Dead End. For five thousand people. I could hear them all, at a great distance.

The Risiera is really a complex of big old brick buildings, from four to six stories high. To get into the inner courtyard you must now walk between two free standing blank concrete walls, four stories high, at least a hundred feet long, and only nine or ten feet apart. No signs, no comments. The effect is what the architect must have intended: a time tunnel, drawing you back to something unspeakable. This effect was multiplied in me, and by the time we emerged into the inner courtyard I wouldn't have been at all surprised to see Germans goose-stepping in all directions. Instead there was no one. We were alone—not even a custodian. Virgil broke the spell, for which I was grateful.

"It's all quite different now, of course. On the night of April 18, 1945, the Nazis blew up the oven and the smokestack. This whole courtyard was full of rubble when Tito's men broke in here the next day. But when the Italians cleaned up a few months later, they found three bags of bones and ashes that the Germans hadn't had time to dump. Anyway, the oven was up against that wall, and you can still see its outline."

"What's that at the base?"

"That's where they buried those three bags of ashes."

We walked over. A simple slab said *"Ceneri delle Vittime,"* ashes of the victims, and then, Virgil assured me, the same thing in three other languages: Slovene, Serbo-Croatian, and Hebrew. I backed away.

"Now, we have to go over there," said Virgil quietly. "The cell block for the condemned. They've left it just as it was."

We entered a long dark room, like a stable. On one side and at the far end there were doors, all open, each with a little hole. Seventeen doors. My mind was swirling with strange, terrible echoes, but now I was not repelled, or afraid. I felt compassion, even kinship. I walked to the first door and looked in. The cell was about eight feet high by seven feet long by five feet wide. On one side there was a double bunk bed—no mattresses, just wooden planks.

"How many did you say they put in a cell?"

"From two to six. But no one had to put up with it for more than a few weeks. Usually just a few days."

"Strange that everything's open like this, and unattended."

I walked inside. The walls were covered with writing. Unfortunately in Italy the walls of most monuments are covered with writing, thanks to a mindless compulsion to etch one's ephemeral name onto something permanent. But I immediately saw that these were the desperate last messages of the condemned: names, dates of capture, relatives to notify, final blessings for children. No one, not one tourist so coarse as to scratch his frivolous name on such walls. I understood why they could leave everything unattended, in this particular monument.

I gently put my fingers on the wall, which I knew would feel alive with sorrow; but for the first time since I had begun touching stones with Virgil, I felt that it was my sorrow, too. I let my fingers touch each name. Each one sent me a different sensation, a different note of suffering.

"I think that's sufficient, Fred. I think we can leave, now."

"No. I'm doing something important. I'm supposed to do this. I think I can find our man this way. Let me touch all the names."

And so it went. I went from cell to cell, passing my fingers lightly over all the writing I could see in the dim light. I discovered that the sensations were even more distinct when I wasn't simultaneously trying to read the names, so I learned to look away, and even to close my eyes. When I did, I could smell the people who had been stuffed into these wretched holes—the pungent, unmistakable odor of bodies sweating with fear. I wanted to embrace each one, carry each one out through the time tunnel to the light of a different day.

As soon as I walked into cell number six, I knew my search was over. His presence was almost oppressive—I could hear his breathing. There were many names here. I saw what appeared to be a long list on the back wall. I put my hand up at the top of the list and turned to look at Virgil, standing in the doorway.

"He's in here, Virgil," I said quietly, and let my fingers start down the wall. They got as far as shoulder level.

"Here he is," I said. The attraction I felt drew my whole hand flush against the wall. Excruciating sadness, my sadness, indistinguishable from the sadness pressing in on me. My hand wasn't covering the date: April 7, 1945. I took my hand away. The name was faded, but carefully written: Alderini.

I don't remember much about how I got back out to the car. I don't think I ran, but I didn't just walk out; more like stumbling, I suppose, with Virgil helping me.

I sat there breathing heavily. Virgil turned on the motor to get the air-conditioning going.

"There are several possible explanations," he began. "It could simply be someone else named Alderini."

"Wrong. Try again."

"Perhaps tonight you yourself will have some good reason for writing your name there."

"Wrong. Not my writing."

"Well, it's quite likely we'll be asked our names. Then when we leave, one way or another, the prisoners left behind will assume we've been taken away to be executed."

"Why isn't your name there?"

"Fred, I don't know. Perhaps it is in another cell. We'll just have to wait and see."

"I'm going to get killed back there. Exterminated. I am one of those five thousand dead."

"It's possible, I suppose. But remember, your real body will be lying in bed in a hotel, regardless of what they do to you."

"Virgil, as you explained to me once, the shock is quite likely to kill the me that's lying in bed, too."

"Just keep telling yourself to stay calm."

"Stay calm!"

"What choice is there? Can you refuse at this point?"

I looked out the car window. A family with two little children was walking into the monument. The children were skipping. "No, no, of course not. But suppose this means we'll fail again tonight."

"Why should it mean that? It may well mean success. If Apollo doesn't die, because he discovers who he is, I mean to say, if he chooses to live on in that particular body, then dying may be the way chosen for us to leave 1945 and return to the present. Diana never entered into these details. But Apollo is back there in 1945 waiting for us; there's no question about that, and no choice but to search for him, trusting Diana that it can be done. There is a way. Every night there's been a chance, and there'll be a chance tonight. You know, it's very doubtful that Apollo's name should be among the relatively few that are preserved on those walls . . ."

"Virgil, it would do no good for me to continue touching names, assuming I could. The only tragedy can sense now is my own."

"I heartily concur; furthermore, it may be just as well that we have no idea which of the prisoners might be Apollo. No prejudices, you see. No wasting time on the wrong man, as happened with Poerio and Vercingetorix. You can start at one end of that horrible place, and I'll start at the other: 'Where are you from? Where are you from?' just as fast as we can and . . ."

"What if we're locked in those cells? Cell 6, for example?"

"I believe the prisoners were locked up only at night. I don't know, I don't know. Diana won't drop us into an impossible situation."

"Well, for what it's worth, we know the date now, April 7, 1945. Imagine that. The Third Reich was a few weeks from collapse and those fanatics were still busy gassing and burning people."

"Busier than ever. The last two months were the worst. Evidently some of them believed, right down to the end, that the Fuhrer had secret weapons that would save the day."

"Good thing Apollo didn't give the knowledge of nuclear power to the Germans."

"Oh, but he did, didn't he? Einstein! $E = mc^2$, you know. Relativity! How lovely it all is! Of course motion and time are relative—it's the basis of divine whimsy. Unfortunately, Einstein had trouble with the probability factor in Quantum theory. . . ."

"The victory at Lepanto served no real purpose, you know. The Venetians had to give Cyprus to the Turks anyway."

We smiled at each other, drove back into the city center and parked the car in the same spot as before, right on the edge of the dock.

We had no place to go. We had no desire to go anyplace. We got out of the car and walked fifty feet to a bench that faced the sea, and sat down.

"What about our clothes tonight?" I recalled.

"Not really a problem; there were no prison uniforms, because no one stayed long enough. They just kept wearing the clothes they were captured in. We can buy cheap dark suits and white shirts, and then dirty them in some manner. In those days the men always had suits on, you know."

"Whatever you say."

"I shan't pretend to be a doctor this time, because I would instantly be asked to tend the sick and wounded. This time I'll simply be a—a professor of Ancient History."

"And why were you arrested, Professor Maro?"

"For hiding a Jew in my home. And what about you, Signor Alderini?"

"I'm an unemployed English teacher. And I'm in prison for having a radio transmitter in my home."

"That won't do. You'd have been tortured at SS headquarters downtown for information about your contacts. You'd be in a pitiable state."

"I am, with this foot."

"True, but not refined enough. Fingernails pulled out, genitals burned—that's the sort of thing you would need. Think of some other crime."

"Okay, I was overheard in a bar to say that Hitler sucks."

"To say what?"

"That Hitler is a deranged criminal, and the only ones more deranged are those that believe him."

"That will be fine."

"Sorry about the uniforms."

"I'm sure Signor Asquini will take them back. I'm a good client. I'll order something very elaborate for next year's Carnevale."

"Maybe I'll fly back and go to the Carnevale with you. I'll use the fat advance they'll have given me for the book I'll be writing about all this."

"That would be great sport. I have an idea. I'll order a Dante costume which you shall wear, and I can use last year's costume!"

"Virgil and Dante in Hell. You don't like to step much out of character, do you?"

"Not necessarily in Hell. There's Paradise as well."

"We would need a Beatrice."

"Bring one with you from Chicago."

"No. I could ask Concetta to come up from Naples."

"A charming young lady. But aren't there any charming young ladies in Chicago?"

"Too many. Too many charming young ladies who remind me of my wife. I killed her, you see. Playing a stupid game. So absurd. Your life loses all its proportions. Anyway, Italian girls have this great advantage with me, they don't remind me of her. Don't you ever meet women who remind you of Delia, old friend?"

"Yes; with a smile, or a certain tone of voice. I, too, tend to avoid such women. There was one in Siena in the eighteenth century who bore an astonishing resemblance to Delia. I stayed away from the city for forty years."

"The pain of nostalgia."

"The pain of shame, I'm afraid. Delia needed so much more from me than I was able to give. Our relationship had very little . . . physical consistency, Fred, regardless of what I may have let you believe. But I always remember one evening when we were walking through the woods, those same woods where I met you, and she put her arm around my waist."

"Yes?"

"Well—I put my arm around hers."

"Very good."

"It seemed like the thing to do."

"Quite. And then?"

"Then we stopped. We turned toward each other. Practically speaking, we were embracing."

"Beautiful."

"Yes. For a moment, it certainly was. I am a man of few regrets, but I would give a great, great deal to return to that moment, and do something . . . and say something different."

"What did you actually say?"

"I said it was getting late and chilly."

We sat looking at the harbor, and out farther to th
sea where a tanker was almost imperceptibly sneakin
across the horizon. Then four very sleazy young me
came ambling along, and stopped to look at Virgil'
car. They walked over to inspect it more closely. The
may have thought they were keeping their voices down
but we could hear every word they said.

"*Cazzo! Che macchina!*" said the first.

"*Cazzo!*"

"*Cazzo!*"

"*Cazzo!*"—said the others in agreement. Amon
young Italian males this reference to their sex organ i
roughly equivalent to "gee whiz!"

"*Cazzo!*" the first proceeded. "Let's take it for
ride!"

"No way, *cazzo*," said the second. "If you open th
door, *cazzo*, there'll be sirens and fireworks."

"*Cazzo.*"

"*Cazzo.*"

Ain't right somebody has a car like this."

"Probably some pimp, *cazzo*."

"Girls all day and all night, *cazzo*."

"All the ass he wants, *cazzo*."

"Hey let's dump the damn thing in the water!"

"*CAZZO!*" the others replied.

Virgil and I looked at each other. We smiled and sa
back. On their last afternoon, let these born loser
work off a little frustration. And work they did. Th
side of the car was no more than four feet from th
edge, but a Testarossa weighs over a ton and a half
and these four pasty-faced, smoked-out kids were hav
ing a hell of a time trying to flip her over. I wa
tempted to pitch in, but thought better of it. A sma
group of people had stopped to watch.

"They must be crazy," said one of them. "Hey, are you guys crazy? Leave that car alone!"

"Hush, Dino," said his wife. "Don't get involved."

"Maybe it's a movie."

"What's the world coming to?"

Virgil laughed at that one, and the man who said it turned around. "You think it's funny?" he said. "What if that was your car?"

SPLASH! In it went, finally. The four boys ran away, yelling their *cazzos* as often as breath would allow them. The group of people, joined by many others, walked to the edge and stared at the slowly sinking car.

"Let's go look for those clothes," I said.

"I know a good place. There's an open air clothes market not far from here."

We got there in ten minutes. It took us another ten minutes to find what we wanted. We got everything two sizes too big. One size, because clothes were worn baggy in those days, and one more, because just about everybody was losing weight then—the good guys, anyway. I insisted on paying, for a change. I even argued the lady down about ten percent.

"If you had dropped the clothes on the counter and walked away, she would have taken off ten percent more," said Virgil as we walked away.

"That's not always true. At the Flea Market in Rome I tried that once, and I had to come crawling back. Something I badly wanted. Very embarrassing."

"Nothing like the crawling we'll do tonight."

"Don't think about that part of it. The real you will be in bed in a hotel, remember? That's what I'm supposed to keep thinking while I'm being massacred."

"Young men have flexible minds. After two thousand years . . ."

"Listen, let's think about the best way to get these clothes dirty. It has to be done right, you know. We don't want to overdo it. We need dust, not dirt. Discreet dust. Hard to find where everything is paved."

"Come along, then. There is some very discreet dust not far from here."

"In fact, we turned a couple of corners and found ourselves in front of the ruins of a Roman theater, with its stone seats sloping down a hillside and narrowing in on the stage.

"You see," said Virgil, "the 'orchestra' in front of the stage isn't paved. We can go down through the *aditus maximus*. Watch your step."

When we got down into the dusty semicircle, we took our clothes out of the bags and spread them out on the ground for a moment on both sides. Then we rolled them up and stuffed them back in the bags.

"That'll be fine," I said. "Let's go."

"Can't we sit down a moment? That's a steep climb for an old man."

We sat on the bottom row of seats. Virgil wasn't a bit tired, he was just thinking about the old days.

"Ever here for a play?"

Virgil laughed sadly. "My dear Fred, the theater is not one of Rome's gifts to the world. Except for the works of Plautus and Terence and a few others—my friend Various Rufus perhaps—the only intelligent things we staged were Greek. And after the Republic, Rome very rarely staged anything intelligent. This particular theater was built by Trajan. Hah! A provincial, all his life! As a man of culture, he was a very good soldier. Most of the entertainment provided in this theater would have made that film we saw in Ferrara look like *King Lear*. Keep the people happy, you see."

"Is that the name of the game, Virgil?"

A few minutes later he answered. "Ask me when t's over." Then he stood up and started away.

Back at the hotel we had a bite to eat, watched the news on television in the lounge, then headed for our rooms. I put on my dusty shirt and suit, took a look at myself in the closet-door mirror, and took them back off again. I got into bed wondering how long it would take me to get to sleep. I'm usually pretty good at finding the right thoughts, but this time nothing worked for over an hour until I tried something new and stuck with it: Diana's eyes.

XXI

The smell. I was ready for everything but that smell.
Burnt flesh. The hair especially—the smell of burnt
hair predominated. I started to gag.

"Who are you?"

I looked up into the face of a man about my age,
dressed very much the way I was. He was thinnish but
not sickly, and had a stubby beard. I glanced quickly
around. I was sitting against one of the two wooden
columns that held up the ceiling of the long room with
the seventeen cells. The doors were all open, just as I
had seen them many years from now. About fifty
people were sitting or standing all up and down the
room. I turned my face back to my inquisitor.

"I . . . my name is Alderini. How can you stand this
smell?"

"What sm . . . Oh, you will get used to it in a few
hours. Don't think about it. When did you get here?
During the last lockup, I suppose."

"That's right. Say, where are you from, anyway?"

"From Monfalcone. What's the news from outside?
How close is Tito? How close are the Allies?"

"I . . . they're coming. They're coming. Be here in
about three weeks. Now . . ."

"Three weeks! Three weeks! No one lasts three weeks!" And the man moved slowly away. I looked around for Virgil. He was sitting under the other column, talking earnestly with a man and a woman. I quickly made my way over to him.

". . . although my real interest lies with the Late Republic. A fascinating period, when you consider . . ."

"But Professor, do your colleagues know you're here? Your family? What are they doing for you? What hope is there?"

"Virgil looked around, perhaps for an answer to that last question. He saw me, and I answered it for him.

"None. None at all, Virgil, unless we find our man."

"But . . . but I've already begun. These good people are from Pola."

"Get up off your duff, Professor, and start at the far end. And forget the Late Republic for a while."

The woman Virgil had been talking to looked bewildered. "Who are you looking for, in this place?"

"No one," I said, "A man from . . . from my town. I can't explain." And I hurried away. Virgil moved toward his end of the room, shuffling slowly just like the other prisoners.

"Where are you from?"

"From Muggia."

"From here. Trieste."

"From Cervignano."

"From Gabrovizza."

"Why are you here?"

"Why am I here?"

"What hope is there?"

"Three weeks. Maybe—maybe less. Maybe a matter

of days. Yes, maybe even tomorrow. They're very close."

All these people, and many others yet to arrive, would be ashes before the three long weeks ended. I have always believed that by telling a man the truth you show respect for his basic human dignity. It was I who told my uncle Bill he was dying of cancer, and he thanked me for it. But my uncle hadn't implored me to give him the gift of hope, as these people were doing with their red-rimmed eyes.

"Where are you *from?*"

"What does it matter?" A little old man answered me. He had been following me around for some minutes. "It's where we're all going that matters—up the smokestack. As you know damn well."

"It does matter, believe me. Where are you from?"

"I'll prove I don't believe you. I'll tell you something I never would if there were any chance you or I might survive—might leave this place." He leaned forward. His breath was a dead man's. "I sent at least ten people here myself." He grinned excitedly. "The first three or four were bastards who deserved it. Communists, Jew-lovers . . . I had plenty of proof. The Nazis paid me, promised me more . . . I got rid of all my enemies! The worst ones, anyway. It was easy to invent situations, plant radios and leaflets—I showed them what power was! But then . . . but then the Germans found out what I was doing—but I don't care. I showed them. I showed them." And he started moving away. Then he looked back and said, "Ask the boy in 4 where he's from. He hasn't talked to anyone else."

I was surprised to learn that anyone would remain of his own will in one of those holes when the doors were open. I walked over to cell number 4. A blond

young man, perhaps twenty years old, was squatting
on the top bunk in the far corner. He had to keep his
head bowed to avoid the ceiling. He stared at me in
terror.

"Hello. Where are you from?"

His head jerked up and cracked against the ceiling.
He winced, and slowly opened his mouth. He spoke as
if it were the last thing in the world he wished to do.

"I . . . I am from a beautiful land. From Carnia. A
beautiful land." Then his mouth clamped audibly shut.

"Virgil!" I shouted out the cell door. A white-haired
prisoner turned around in the gloomy light and came
my way.

"Have you found him, Fred?" he asked.

Before I could answer, the heavy oaken door at the
end of the room swung open and six German soldiers
marched in, with automatic rifles pointed and ready.

"In your cells, vermin!" barked their leader. The
prisoners needed no prodding. The cells were havens
of life. Two women and a man rushed into cell 4. They
were dismayed to see Virgil and me; it meant a turn-
over in occupancy.

"No, don't worry, we weren't assigned to this cell,"
I said.

"We'll be leaving soon," added Virgil.

One of the women broke into a mixture of sobs and
laughter that only ended when one of the Germans
slammed and bolted our door. We could hear all the
doors being closed this way. Then we could hear—
music. Loud martial music blaring from a loudspeaker.
The man saw my surprise.

"To cover the screaming," he said. "If it's not enough,
they'll get all the dogs to bark."

"Virgil," I said, "I don't think we have much time."

We turned our attention to the young man, who was still sitting in the same position, staring at the door.

"What is your name?" I asked him. I knew it wouldn't work. He was no longer aware of me.

"The poor boy speaks to no one," said the man. "It happens, you know. State of shock."

"Virgil, your gods have loaded the dice. This guy's catatonic."

"What's your name, young man?" he asked.

"Maria Radich!" said one of the Germans outside. A woman wailed, loud enough to be heard between the notes of the music.

"They go from cell to cell," said the man with us. "Soon they'll be here."

"My name!" said the young man suddenly. "My name is *not* Maria Radich!"

"That's right! But what *is* your name?"

"My name! It's a secret! They can't take me without it!"

"Amazing," said one of the women. "He's never spoken before this!"

"Loaded dice, indeed," said Virgil.

"Your secret will be safe with us!" I said. We want to help you, but we must know your name!"

Again the German voice was heard above the music: "Tone Jerman!"

"No!" said the young man. "Ha ha! That's not my name!"

"You've forgotten it!" I said.

"No, I haven't!"

"That's too bad. A man who forgets his name is lost!"

"I know my name!"

"A man with no name has no friends."

He looked at me wildly, pathetically, his eyes glittering with a watery light of their own. "Come here! Come here and I'll give you my name."

I moved close and he bent his head still further down.

"But you must take care of it!"

"The best. The best possible care."

"My name . . . my name is . . ."

Ka-chunk! The cell door was unbolted and opened. "Emma Vidali!" said the German who stood in the opening with his gun pointed at us. A swarthy sort, not very Aryan at all. "Giovanni Vidali!" The man and one of the women embraced in silence. The German reached in, grabbed the man by the collar and pulled them both out of the cell. Then he looked at his list again! "Rodolfo Tonelli!" he said with a smile. A high-pitched wail was heard, so all-pervading it was hard at first to determine where it was coming from. The young man on the upper bunk had thrown his head back and was crying his despair to the ceiling, only inches away. I almost laughed when I realized what I had to do.

"I am Rodolfo Tonelli," I said. The boy stopped his strange crying. Virgil grabbed my arm without a word. The German was amused. I don't think he believed me for an instant. But he put his hand on my shoulder, not on my collar, and said, "Come, then!" firmly— but with respect. All the while he kept his eyes fixed on the real Tonelli, who was gaping at us all.

"Go for it, Virgil!" I said sternly.

"What? Yes, of course, rest assured, I . . . Farewell, my friend!" He released my arm and I left the cell.

"Go stand in line!" said the German. A double file of prisoners was forming in front of the oaken door. One of the guards came to shove me along, but the leader, my friend with the list, said, "Leave him alone!" and I took my place in line unmolested.

When there were about twenty of us, we were marched out of the cell block and across the inner courtyard I had first seen so many years later. This time, however, the tall smokestack and the big brick crematory were very much intact, and loomed before us. Only a wisp of smoke emerged from the smokestack into the moonlight. A quiet scene, I thought, in contrast with the music crashing off the walls as if trying to break out. We were herded through a large opening in the wall about forty feet beyond the crematory. There was a guard on one side of this opening. The prisoner in front of me had something to say to him:

"*Italiano di merda.*"

"*A li mortacci tua!*" the guard answered in thick Roman.

We found ourselves in a garage big enough for about four trucks, but only one was there. No lights were on, but the moon—Diana's moon—was bright. I remembered what she had said about seeing the secrets of the night.

A man emerged from the shadows—a great, hoglike creature with huge arms, wearing a filthy butcher's apron. It was immediately clear that he was very, very drunk. In his left hand he held a bottle, and in his right he wielded a vicious little club made of an almost-rigid length of iron cable with a handle fastened on one end and a metal knob at the other. The German soldiers laughed.

"Ready to go, Saskia?"

"How many head?" growled the Ukrainian.

"Twenty-two."

"Twenty-two head, twenty-two cracks."

"A pack of cigarettes says you can't do it."

"No. Bottle of Slivovitz."

"Okay, for a bottle of Slivovitz. Prisoners!" The swarthy German turned to us. "Strip! Everything off! Everything! Move!"

We started to undress. A few people whimpered softly, but a general daze had settled over us all. I felt as if this wasn't really happening to me, and in a sense I was right, but I think I would have felt the same way in any case. I'm sure that's how the other prisoners felt. How else can I explain why no one bolted, no one attacked a guard, no one attempted some final gesture of revolt? It would have meant this unspeakable thing was real, and no one could admit that. The Ukrainian drank and the Germans joked and we all undressed, all actors in a grotesque play.

"You. Rodolfo Tonelli. Leave your underwear on."

So I was going to be allowed to keep this vestige of dignity, to die in my underwear, and not naked like an animal.

"Come with me, Rodolfo Tonelli."

I followed the swarthy German through a door, and there it was: the oven, with its door open, glowing red inside.

"Now stoke the fire, Rodolfo Tonelli. Take the wood from the pile in the corner and throw it in, until the flames leap out at you. Do this, and you will die like a man. Not at the hands of that beast. Hurry, now."

And he walked back into the garage, leaving me alone. While I was wondering what to do, I found myself throwing wood into the oven. Did it really make any difference who threw the wood into the oven? Soon the flames roared high and bright and so hot it was hard to get close enough to throw in more fuel. Then the swarthy German came back alone.

"The other prisoners are . . . ready now. And so is the furnace, I see. Very good, Rodolfo Tonelli. I give you a choice. You can remain alive, for perhaps thirty more minutes, by helping us—with the other prisoners. Some of them look heavy. Or you can die now. Choose. You are a man, you will die when you choose."

I chose to live. The reason was obvious: more time for Virgil to try to get through to that basket case. He could stick around only as long as my dream lasted, and my death would certainly end that. But I didn't need any reason. I'm afraid I wanted to stay alive, even if it meant living the most shameful half-hour a man can imagine.

I will not write about that half-hour. At the end my German took out his luger. "And now you must die, Rodolfo Tonelli. Standing, like a man. I salute you." And with that, he fired a bullet straight into my heart.

XXII

I died. It wasn't such a terrible experience. A moment of convulsive pain in my heart, then coldness and numbness—I only barely felt the floor when I fell. The sounds in my ears became the sweet rush of ocean water. Each corner of my mind was lit for one last instant before being disconnected—lit with a soft glow of acceptance and peace. When the last light went out, I was a newborn baby again, and then I was nothing.

When Virgil started beating on my chest, I remember a general feeling of irritation at being brought back, which became very specific when I realized he was also attempting to give me mouth-to-mouth respiration.

"Fred! Fred, thank goodness! Fred, can you hear me?"

"Yes. Where are we?"

"In the hotel. We're back, Fred. How brave you were! What a fine thing it was!"

"Did it do any good?"

"I beg your pardon?"

"Virgil, did you get through to Apollo?"

"No. No, I'm afraid not."

"Shit."

247

"The poor fellow was quite beside himself."

"Shit on the whole business."

"He kept saying 'I have no name! I have no name! He took it!'—meaning you, of course."

"A great big crock of shit, Virgil."

"Finally I went along with him. I told him he was safe without a name, but when they let him go he would need his name back, and the way to get it back was to let his mirror image ask him his name three times. So to demonstrate, I pretended to be a mirror and began with 'What is your name?' After many misgivings he finally said 'Rodolfo Tonelli.' That poor woman who was left in the cell with us was convinced that I was dafter than the boy! At any rate, I had asked him for the second time and he was still contemplating his answer when I found myself back in my hotel room. I realized what must have happened and hurried over here to help you, of course."

"Virgil, I didn't know what 'low' really meant until I got involved with these gods of yours."

"I must admit that . . ."

"The word 'cheap' has a whole new dimension."

"I'm sorry I wasn't able . . ."

"Virgil, you did just fine. Nobody could expect more. Either from you or from me. Those immortal twits you call the gods have been using us for kicks. And anybody who can chuckle over the same gag six straight times is pretty hard up. It was a strictly no-win situation."

Virgil walked to the window and looked out at the new day dawning—the last day. After a few moments he looked up and said slowly,

> *"As flies to wanton boys are we to the Gods;*
> *They kill us for their sport."*

* * *

King Lear. It came to my mind yesterday in Trajan's theater. But I find it so hard to believe. It's so unlike them. So lacking in style, so . . ."

"So sadistic. Your divine whimsy is getting a little hard-core."

Virgil sighed. "I was sure that your heroic gesture would have proved decisive. What more could we possibly have done? What could we have overlooked?"

"One thing, maybe." I sat up in bed. I was coming around nicely for someone who had been dead. "Apollo is alive today somewhere, remember? And he's going to die tragically, like the rest of us, in a few hours."

"That thought had occurred to me. But I have no desire to run about in the streets asking people where they're from."

"Bravo, Virgil."

"If Diana and her friends wish to save the world, it's up to them at this point. We have done quite enough, and I for one intend to live my last few hours in dignity."

"Right on!"

"And if we should absolutely trip over someone who insists on telling us he's from a beautiful land, I for one would be quite tempted to send him on his way without further adieu, because it would all just be too, too shabby.

"Ever read *Cat's Cradle*?"

"I'm afraid not."

"It's a book by Vonnegut where the world ends— everything freezes. And this guy decides to get frozen up on a hill or something, flat on his back, thumbing his nose up at God forever." I demonstrated.

"Heavens. Going a bit far, perhaps."

"I'm ready to go farther. This is Italy, where the

symbols are different so when we see the fireballs or mushroom clouds or whatever, I'm going to show your gods where Grandpa carried his umbrella."

"Where Grandpa carried. . . ?"

I grabbed the spot in the crook of my arm where Grandpa carried his umbrella.

"Oh, dear."

"With a little luck I might get fused into this position. I saw pictures of Hiroshima . . ."

"That will do. I'd really rather not go into it."

"Dying isn't so bad, Virgil. You'll see."

"The dying doesn't frighten me. I've done that once before. It's afterward that could be unpleasant this time."

We showered, got dressed, and had breakfast. I found I could only stand up or walk for short spells without getting dizzy. We stepped outside, but it was muggy hot. We decided to wait for the end of the world in the air-conditioned hotel lounge.

"Nice not to have anyplace to dash off to," I said, looking into my glass of chilled Verduzzo. I never drink before noon, but an exception seemed to be justified.

"Indeed it is," said Virgil to me through his glass. "Not that we could do much dashing without the car."

"That was a great car, Virgil."

"It was. But it's time for a change. I think I'll get a Bentley. Or a Rolls. I'm feeling older."

There was a long silence, the first of many. We sat sipping wine all morning long. Virgil would murmur things like "Paradise Lost, Paradise Regained, Paradise Lost Again. Hah! Milton, you stubborn old fool, there's no way to 'justify the ways of God to men,' because they have no justification."

And I would murmur things like "Shit. A great big crock of shit."

At a quarter to twelve we were the only people in the lounge, and the bartender asked us if we would mind if he turned on the television. They were going to televise the launching of the new European missile, the Phaeton. I giggled a bit, then said, "On one condition—that you tell us where you're from."

"I'm from Duino. Why?"

"Oh nothing, nothing. Go ahead and turn it on."

"Why did you ask him that?" said Virgil, with one eye considerably wider than the other.

"I hoped he would say 'from a beautiful land.' Then I would have said, 'That's nice. I'm from Winnetka. Bring us some more wine.'"

"Quite right."

"You know, I'm sort of surprised Diana hasn't dropped by disguised as a bellhop or something, to give us hell."

"I shouldn't mind having a word or two with her."

"In ninety seconds," said the television announcer, *"The Phaeton missile will lift off into the heavens for its first mission. Phaeton is the first of a new generation . . ."*

"Phaeton, Phaeton," I said. "What's in a name? Your gods sure like to play with names. This whole asinine business has been a story of names: D.A., get Apollo to say his name . . ."

"True, true. The gods do indeed care about names. But they're not alone in this, Delbert Frederick."

"Hmm. I looked them up once. Know what Delbert means? It's Old English. Means 'day-bright.'"

"How very nice."

"My wife had a beautiful name. Daphne."

"Twenty-five seconds to lift-off!"

"Your wife's name was Daphne?"

"Beautiful, isn't it? Means 'laurel tree.' Daphne was a nymph of some sort, in Greek mythology—as I'm sure you know."

"Dieci, nove, otto, sette . . ."

"She was Apollo's first love," said Virgil, who was looking at me very hard with his winey eyes.

"Ignition. We have lift-off!"

I turned to watch the long, thin missile start so gracefully on its terrible mission. Virgil didn't take his eyes off me.

"Where did you say you were from, Fred?"

I was still intently watching the missile. "Frederick is from Old German," I said without turning back. "It means 'ruler who brings peace.' "

"What I asked you was where you're from."

"Winnetka. Chicago. Told you a million times."

"Chicago. Ugly-sounding word in Italian, you know."

I turned back around. "Hah. I know. '*Ci cago*.' Means 'I crap here.' "

"Unfortunate coincidence. What do you suppose 'Chicago' really means?"

"It's an Indian word. Not really clear. The City Council doesn't like it, but the experts believe it means 'Land of the Skunk,' or 'Land of the Big Stink.' "

"My. my. And 'Winnetka'?"

"Another Indian word, but no doubts about it. It means . . . It means . . ."

"It means 'Beautiful Land,' doesn't it . . . Fred?"

"We now have a report that Phaeton is off course and out of control!"

"Forget it, Virgil. Apollo I'm not." I felt very cold.

"Day-bright! The day-bright ruler who brings peace! The Sun God himself! Today!"

Now I felt hot. "Nobody is less a god than I am, believe me."

"The missile has not attained orbit, and will therefore fall back to earth!"

"It makes everything fall into place, Fred!"

"Don't push me over the brink. I don't want to be a god!"

"All efforts to deviate or destroy the missile have failed. It will crash in North Africa in six minutes."

"What is your name, Fred?"

"My name . . . my name is Delbert Frederick Alderini. This is madness, you know."

"Divine madness. All the gods are mad. What is your name, Fred?"

I closed my eyes and threw myself back into the leather armchair. "Stop it, stop it please. I'm losing my mind."

"The missile will crash in Libya, in the Tripoli area! The Libyan authorities are being notified . . ."

"My name is Delbert Frederick Alderini."

"And now, for the third time: What is your name?"

I began to laugh. I laughed and laughed, as only a god can laugh. I took full possession of life again. It was mine to play with, my consciousness had broken free. For a moment, an earthly moment, my spirit rushed like a great wind through the enormous, dusty rooms of the divine nature that had slept so long in me. Then I remembered the game—to give my true name, when asked the third time. I stopped laughing, and directed the waves of my voice so that only the mortal in front of me could hear:

"I am Phoebus Apollo, son of Jupiter, son of Latona, and God of the Sun! And you shall ride with me in my chariot this day, old man!"

"Not unless you stop that missile, Great One."

I laughed again. "That was taken care of the instant I pronounced my name! Old friend, I want you to continue calling me Fred. It is a privilege you have richly earned. And I have no intention of abandoning poor Fred so soon. He, too, has richly earned his right to live."

"The missile has changed its course! It appeared to be heading straight for Tripoli, but for reasons yet unknown Phaeton has veered away, toward the open desert. Impact is expected in less than two minutes. Everyone here is breathing deep signs of relief."

Virgil breathed one, too, then said "Wonderful! All quite wonderful. I'm so ashamed of the things I said and thought about the gods. I hope Diana . . ."

"I'm with her now, Virgil! I'm with my father and sister and all my friends, and they have been greatly amused. No one is angry with you—you have done your job well, and will be rewarded."

"What greater reward than the friendship of the Sun God?"

"Tonight you will make one more trip into the past, old man. Without your friend Fred. You will find Delia in your arms again. You will be allowed to change that night of your life—unless you want to tell her again that it's getting late and chilly."

I choose to end my story here. I live and write as Fred Alderini, and he is happy enough. He lives in isolation, in the hills, but at night I often let him return to his Daphne, as I sometimes return to mine. I live in him, but I can live in all places, great and small. The Universe is my playground, and as even men have learned, the play's the thing. Even men, in their own dimensions, can laugh and play with life, which is why I love them. I know, better than all the other gods, about the strange bravery their laughter requires. I know now what it is to be a man; unfortunately, men cannot know what it is to be a god. It is not the pleasure, it is not the power; it is the wonder.

I cannot share the wonder with my mortal friends, but I can share the pleasure and the power. Right now I am climbing into the heavens in the Sun Chariot, and dear old Virgil is at my side as he frequently is; it is unusual even among the gods to find someone who understands and appreciates my fine horses as he does. He would like me to let him take the reins, but I have had enough of his driving.